Honeymoon For One

Honeymoon For One

Beth Orsoff

amazonpublishing

Published by Amazon Publishing
P.O. Box 400818
Las Vegas, NV 89140

ISBN-13: 9781612184876
ISBN-10: 1612184871

For Steve

CHAPTER 1

"How exactly is an emery board supposed to help me break out of jail?"

"I don't know," Jane said. "It's what they always smuggle in to prisoners in the movies."

At that moment, I wanted to throttle Jane, but since I was on the inside of a jail cell and Jane was on the outside, it was unlikely to happen. "A metal file," I hissed. "Not a paper one!"

"Where was I supposed to get a metal nail file in the middle of the night? You know they don't let you carry that stuff on the plane anymore. Terrorists could use it as a weapon."

And I could use it to kill you. But then I'd really never get out of this mess. While I was only being falsely accused of murder, there was still hope.

I moved from the louvered window, with its layers of chicken wire marring what otherwise would've been a beautiful view of the Caribbean, and sat back down on my makeshift bed—a beach chair covered with a towel. The only other accoutrements in my cell, which until a few days ago had been the police station's storage room, were two metal file cabinets, a ceramic bowl filled with semiclean water, a half-used bar of soap, and a bucket for after-hours emergencies. During the day, the police officers were kind enough to accompany me to the bathroom. It wasn't much cleaner than my bucket, but it had the benefit of indoor plumbing. Welcome to the Camus Caye police station and temporary women's prison.

Jane and I froze. We'd both heard it. Something that sounded like metal scraping against rock. Jane, who was standing on an overturned garbage can so she could reach the window of my cell, pushed her face as close as she could to the chicken wire without actually touching it. Despite her revulsion at my accommodations, she looked like she wanted to join me on the inside.

I moved back to the window so we were face-to-face through the mesh.

"What was that?" Jane whispered.

Before I could answer, the scraping switched to a rustling from the edge of the clump of bushes separating the police station from the café next door.

"Oh my God," Jane said. "What if it's a murderer or a rapist?"

"Lurking *outside* the police station? It's probably an animal looking for food." Hopefully, a very small, vegetarian animal.

"That doesn't look like an animal to me," she said, staring at the tall, shadowed figure moving toward us.

The figure stopped just outside the pool of light emanating from Jane's keychain flashlight and tossed his weapon onto the ground.

"Lizzie," Jane whispered, as if the figure standing five feet away couldn't hear her, "he's got a machete. He's going to slit our throats."

Before I could point out that if he really intended to slit our throats, he'd probably still be holding the machete, the figure spoke.

"You ladies need some help?"

CHAPTER 2

Let's back up. No, I didn't kill anyone. Yes, I'm in jail. And no, the dark figure with the machete didn't slit our throats. But this would all make a lot more sense to you if I backed up further.

Believe it or not, a mere ten days ago my biggest problem in life was that I had to go on my honeymoon alone. That and the fact that I'd been ditched at the altar. Although technically speaking, it wasn't actually at the altar. My ex-fiancé told me the night before the wedding that he wasn't really the marrying type after all.

You would think that after five years of dating, the last two living together, he could've come up with a better excuse than that. But that's all he said, over and over again, as I first laughed (I really thought he was punking me), then screamed so loudly I was surprised the neighbors didn't call the cops ("fucking son of a bitch" seems to stand out in my mind), and ultimately cried. That's when he grabbed his suitcase, which the SOB had packed that afternoon while I was out buying edible underwear, and left.

Obviously, the wedding was off, but I refused to cancel the honeymoon. I'd spent months reading travel magazines, debating the pros and cons of every tropical destination, until Steven— Mr. I Don't Care As Long As You'll Be Wearing A Bikini—and I settled on Belize. Once we'd chosen the country, I bought three guidebooks and read each of them from cover to cover (even all that boring stuff about the history of the place that no one ever reads) to determine where to stay for maximum luxury, privacy, and range of activities. After narrowing it down to five potential regions, I spent weeks online reading reviews of every hotel, restaurant, and tour operator in the area. This was supposed to be the best vacation of my life, damn it. I was not letting all of that time, money, and energy go to waste just because Steven decided he wasn't the marrying type after all.

But that didn't mean I was looking forward to it. Besides my depression over losing my friend and lover, my humiliation at having been dumped practically at the altar, and the massive blow to my ego, the Blue Bay Beach Resort only hosted a maximum of eighteen couples per week. While all of that individual attention was a selling point when I thought I'd be vacationing with my new husband, it now meant further humiliation. Besides eating every meal alone and taking every tour alone, I'd be spending my days explaining to the hotel's thirty-four other guests and two-to-one ratio staff members why I was staying in the bridal suite alone. Assuming anyone would even talk to the only single girl at the couples-only resort.

I was dreading it. But not enough to cancel the trip. Besides, thinking about the warm Belizean sun tanning my shoulders while I waded into the gentle aquamarine waters of the Caribbean Sea was the only time I'd stopped crying the last three days. And yes, I did memorize that line from the hotel's brochure. But even Jane thought I was better off reading the Belize guidebook over and over again than Steven's wedding vows, which in his haste to leave me he'd left sitting on top of our dresser. Of course, I already knew what they said—I'm the one who wrote them. What can I say, Steven begged me to. He's an accountant who can barely scribble a grocery list.

"Do you think that should've been a clue?" I asked Jane, my best friend and almost maid of honor.

Jane grabbed the drink from my hand and set it down on the empty table next to us. I didn't care. I was sucking on ice anyway. I motioned for the waitress to bring me another vodka mojito. Since Jane and I were two of only three patrons in the bar conveniently located just outside the airline terminal's security gate, the service was exceptionally good.

"Lizzie, you need to stop drinking."

"Why?"

"Because you're going to a foreign country. You have to keep your wits about you."

I glanced down at my watch. It was almost midnight. "I'm not going to be there for another ten hours. The vodka will have worn off by then."

I was prepared for Jane to launch into her lecture on the perils of foreign travel, one I'd heard many times before, but instead she leaned in and whispered, "Don't turn around, but the drug dealer at the bar is heading this way."

Naturally, I turned around anyway. I'd noticed him when Jane and I had walked in, but only because he was the only other customer.

I turned back to Jane. "Why do you think he's a drug dealer?"

"Did you miss the gold chain?"

I looked back again as the man tried to balance a beer bottle and a cocktail in one hand and his jacket and carry-on bag in the other. He was on the short side, with a caramel complexion, a full head of dark gelled hair and, based on the tufts sticking out from the top of his black polo shirt, a hairy chest too.

"I could be wrong, but I don't think wearing a gold cross automatically qualifies someone as a drug dealer. And you're supposed to leave the racial profiling to Homeland Security."

"Being vigilant is not racial profiling. Look how nervous he is. He's checked his watch ten times in the last ten minutes."

"Maybe that's because he doesn't want to miss his flight."

"Hi," the drug dealer said, now standing next to our table. "I'm Michael." He extended his hand, which held both his beer and my cocktail.

"Thanks, Michael, I'm—" and before I could grab the drinks from him, the glass tipped over, spilling my mojito all over the table, and his beer down the leg of his khaki pants.

"Shit!" he said, then, "Excuse me."

The waitress was there in an instant with napkins and a wet rag. "I'll just bring you a fresh one," she said and smiled at me as she wiped up the spill.

I didn't want company. All I wanted was another drink. But I didn't want to be rude either, so I asked Michael to join us. When he turned around to pull over a chair from the next table, Jane gave me a death stare.

"What?" I mouthed.

She shook her head. I swear, sometimes Jane was worse than my mother. She found disaster lurking around every corner.

CHAPTER 3

The waitress brought me another drink, which Michael insisted on paying for, then said, "Let me try this again. Hi, I'm Michael Garcia."

"I'm Elizabeth Mancini," I replied, shaking his outstretched hand, "but everyone calls me Lizzie. And this is Jane Chandler."

Jane offered Michael a half smile and a limp handshake, and he graciously accepted both.

"So where are you going, Michael? I assume you're not just here for the drinks," I added before taking a sip.

"Belize," he replied.

"What a coincidence! So am I." OK, maybe I shouldn't have ordered that third cocktail.

"I know," he said and smiled, showing off his very white teeth. "I saw your guidebook."

Jane kicked me under the table, but I ignored her. There was nothing nefarious about him knowing my destination. My *Lonely Planet Belize* was peeking out from the front pocket of my beach bag, which was doubling as my one carry-on item. It would've been surprising if he hadn't seen it.

"Are you staying on the mainland or one of the cayes?" I asked.

"Camus Caye," he said.

"You're kidding! Me too."

Jane gave me a meaningful look complete with arched eyebrows. "What a coincidence," she said in a tone that might

7

have sounded friendly to the untrained ear, but definitely wasn't.

"Not really," I replied, looking directly at Jane. "As you know, Camus Caye is Belize's most tourist-friendly island." Jane should know. She was the one who highlighted the passage in my "Best of the Caribbean" issue of *Travel* magazine.

Michael looked from Jane to me, then took another swig of beer.

"Which hotel?" I asked. I knew them all.

"Tortuga Inn."

I hadn't heard of that one. It must be a budget hotel. But I knew tortuga. "That means turtle! You're staying at the Turtle Inn."

Jane pulled the half-empty glass from my hand and replaced it with her bottle of water. "Drink it," she commanded.

"*Habla Español*?" Michael asked.

Jane snorted.

"Not really," I said, ignoring her. "I just know a few words."

"I'd be happy to show you around the island if you like. Both of you," he added, smiling at Jane.

"I'm not going," Jane said, at the same time I said, "But I thought they spoke English in Belize." I was sure I'd read that somewhere.

"They do," he said, "officially. It's just not the same English we speak here. But if you stick to the tourist areas you'll be fine."

I was going to ask how many kinds of English there were, but Jane beat me with, "Do you travel to Belize often?"

I could see her switching into interrogation mode. I always told her that she should've been a prosecutor instead of a professional organizer. Not that she had to "be" anything, since she lived off her trust fund anyway.

"No," Michael said, "but I spent a year there working on an archeological dig."

"You're an archaeologist?" He didn't look anything like Indiana Jones, and he wasn't carrying a bullwhip, but I suppose in real life they never do.

He shook his head. "Anthropologist."

Jane and I nodded as if we understood the distinction—we didn't, or at least I didn't.

Before Jane could follow up, we heard the boarding announcement for flight number 607 to Dallas with continuing service to Belize City, and the three of us stood up to leave. Michael swung his knapsack over his shoulder and reached down for my beach bag.

"That's OK," I said. "It's not that heavy."

"Please," he said, "it would be my pleasure."

Jane rolled her eyes and I tried not to swoon. It's not that I was attracted to Michael; I wasn't. Between a slick Latin lover and a clean-cut all-American, I'll always choose the all-American. Maybe it was because of my own dark coloring— I'd inherited my features from my dad's side of the family. He used to tell me I looked like a young Sophia Loren. Hah! Sophia Loren minus the big boobs, the smoldering eyes, and the long, shapely legs. Basically, that leaves me with dark hair, olive skin, and hips but no bust (unless I'm wearing my push-up bra). So even though I wasn't attracted to him, I still appreciated Michael's attention.

Jane grabbed my beach bag from Michael's hand and blindly reached inside. "I just need to get something, a personal item." He looked bewildered, so Jane added, "A *feminine* personal item."

"Oh," Michael said and took a step back as if he could've caught a disease merely by being in the presence of such a product.

"Lizzie, why don't you come with me to the ladies' room."

"But they're already boarding."

Jane pulled my ticket out of my hand. "You're in row eight. You've got plenty of time." This from the woman who would fake a limp so she could board the plane with the first-class passengers.

I turned to Michael. "It was very nice meeting you, and thank you again for the drink."

"It's not goodbye," he said, holding up his own ticket. "I'm in row nine."

"Then goodbye from me," Jane said, grabbing my arm. "And I hope you have a lovely trip." Then she marched me across the hall into the women's restroom before Michael could respond.

"What was that about?" I yelled as soon as we'd rounded the barrier wall. "I don't have your tampons."

"I had to say something. He was holding your bag."

"And that's a problem?"

"For one thing, you're not supposed to let strangers have access to your luggage. That is specifically against airline regulations. And second, you have no idea what he could slip into your bag when you're not looking. For all you know, he could be a dope smuggler and he wants to use you as his mule."

Those words would have been ridiculous coming out of anyone's mouth, but when being delivered by a five-foot-two blonde wearing pearl earrings and a sweater set, they were laughable. For the sake of our friendship, I tried not to. "You think he's smuggling drugs into Belize? I'm no expert, but I'm pretty sure the drug trade flows in the opposite direction."

"It could happen. You don't know."

"He's an anthropologist."

"And criminals never lie."

I was about to tell her to stop being so paranoid when the final boarding call for Flight 607 blared over the PA. Instead, I grabbed my beach bag and hugged her. "I've got to go, but I promise I'll be careful."

"I'm serious, Lizzie," she said, hugging me back. "You're traveling alone in a foreign country. You need to keep your guard up."

"If I don't leave now, I won't be traveling anywhere," I said, releasing myself from her grip. "But I promise."

"And no drinking," I heard her shout after me as I rushed through security.

Fat chance of that happening. I was on my honeymoon.

CHAPTER 4

I reached row eight, still panting from my sprint to the gate, and found Michael seated next to the window. As soon as he saw me, he jumped up and reached for my bag. "Let me help you with that."

What was with this guy and my luggage? "I can manage," I said, shoving the bag underneath the seat in front of me, even though there was plenty of room in the overhead bin. I didn't think Michael was a criminal, but no sense tempting fate.

"I thought you were in row nine?" I asked, buckling myself into 8C.

"This seat was empty, so I switched. I hope you don't mind."

"Of course not." Actually, I'd been hoping for an empty row so I could lie down and sleep.

We both read the in-flight magazine through the safety lecture and takeoff. Michael waited until the beverage service began before resuming our preflight conversation.

"You never told me where you're staying."

I knew if Jane were here she'd tell me to lie, but I couldn't think of a good reason to. "At the Blue Bay Beach Resort."

Michael raised his eyebrows, but didn't respond.

"What? Have you heard bad things about it?" All the reviews I'd read were raves. The only negative comment I could find was a complaint about the mosquitoes, but that was during the rainy season, which was still a month away.

"Are you meeting someone there?" he finally asked.

"No, why?"

He shrugged. "I've always heard that hotel was popular with honeymooners."

He must've read the guidebooks too. "Yes, I know."

Michael waited for me to elaborate. When I didn't, he pulled his paperback out from the seat pocket in front of him.

I searched my beach bag until I found the book I'd packed for the plane. It was a Pulitzer Prize–winning novel, but I gave up after five pages. "It was supposed to be my honeymoon."

Michael looked over at me, a confused expression on his face.

"That's why I'm staying at the Blue Bay. This trip was supposed to be my honeymoon."

Michael folded down the corner of the page he was reading and closed his book. "Did he die?"

"Did who die?"

"Your fiancé?"

"No, why would you think that?" My white jeans and hot-pink T-shirt didn't exactly scream "I'm in mourning."

"That's the only reason I could think of not to go on a honeymoon with you."

Talk about cheesy. "Does that line usually work for you?"

Michael laughed. "It's my first time. I heard it in a movie once and always wanted to try it out myself."

I was glad I'd missed that flick. "Did it work in the movie?"

"Yup."

Figures.

"What happened?" he asked. "Did you catch him cheating and give him the boot?"

By the time we landed in Dallas, Michael knew the complete rise and fall of my relationship with Steven, and I learned that he had a serious ex-girlfriend whom I suspected he was still in love with. Michael waited until we were sipping coffee in the Dallas–Ft. Worth Airport Starbucks before he offered to marry me.

CHAPTER 5

"You want to what?"

"Keep your voice down," Michael said. "Most people are still sleeping at this hour."

"Sorry, but did you just offer to be my husband for eight days?"

"No, I offered to *play* your husband."

Even my pretend husband didn't want to marry me. What was I doing wrong? "You're out of your mind."

"Just think about it," he said. "You don't want to spend the whole week having to explain to everyone why you're there alone and tagging along with honeymooners on all your excursions, do you?"

"No." I was dreading all that.

"So I'm offering to play your husband for the week. You can even call me Steven if you want."

That's the last name I wanted to hear. "And how exactly would this work?"

"I'll pay my own way if that's what you're asking."

Good to know, but, "No, I meant where would you, um, sleep?"

I could feel my cheeks heating up. Thankfully, Michael had the good manners to focus on prying the plastic lid off of his coffee cup. "I assumed I would sleep at the Tortuga Inn and join you in the daytime, but if you have other ideas—"

"No, the Tortuga Inn works for me."

"Then we're set?" Michael asked.

"I didn't say that." Jane would kill me if she knew I was even considering it. Of course, she'd never have to know. But I did promise to keep my guard up... "Michael, please don't take this the wrong way, but what's in it for you?"

"Besides the obvious—getting to spend the week with a beautiful woman?"

Aah, the Latin charm. "Yes, besides that."

"That's it."

I stared at him.

"Honestly," he said. "I'd like the company."

I continued staring him down. There had to be more to the story.

"Remember when I mentioned that I broke up with someone recently too?"

"Yes."

"She was supposed to come on this trip. I couldn't cancel because I have business in Belize, but I really don't want to spend the week alone either."

"What kind of business?"

"Mayan antiquities."

"Mayan what?"

"Antiquities. Jewelry mostly, but some pottery too."

"I thought you were an anthropologist."

"I am," he said. "I'm an associate professor at Cal State. But the pay's not great and I do a little antiquities dealing on the side. I've made more money in three trips to Belize than working the entire year at the university."

"Then why bother teaching? Why not just deal, or whatever you call it?"

"Because I love it."

I understood. I loved what I did too. Not every minute of every day, of course. And I've definitely questioned my career choice on more than one occasion (when researching the mating habits of migrating geese, for example). The pay—let's not even talk about that! But overall, I loved being a freelance journalist. I not only got to spend most days working from home in my underwear, I also spent much of my time learning all sorts of new things. (Besides that geese mate for life, did you know that Teri Hatcher's father was a nuclear physicist?) Then I got to share that information with millions of other people (or at least the handful that actually read my articles). I can't think of a more rewarding career than that. OK, maybe heart surgeon. But since I barely passed high school biology, that one probably isn't going to happen.

"So do we have a deal?" Michael asked.

I was saved by the bell, or rather the announcement that Flight 309 to Belize City was boarding at Gate 82.

CHAPTER 6

Luckily this flight was packed and Michael was stuck sitting ten rows behind me. It gave me time alone to think. Could I really spend a week with a stranger pretending to be my husband? I'm a big one for lists, so I pulled a pad and pen from my purse and started writing down the pros and cons.

Pros:
- *Don't have to spend the week explaining about Steven*
- *Someone to go sightseeing with*
- *Someone to eat meals with (Note: Find out Michael's schedule—if working, how much free time?)*

Cons:
- *Can never tell Jane*

Three to one in favor, I had to say yes.

The humidity smacked me in the face the minute I stepped off the airplane. I could practically feel my curly hair frizzing up. There was no point in fighting it, so I pulled my long mane into a ponytail and stuffed the stragglers up inside my straw hat. Between the hat, the bag, and the outfit, no one was going to mistake me for anything but a tourist.

I met up with Michael in baggage claim and he immediately embraced the role of attentive new husband. He dragged my huge suitcase off the conveyor belt and lugged it with his small one into the customs area. Then he unzipped both of our bags for the agent, who barely searched them before waving us through.

"Maya Air or Tropic?" Michael asked as I followed him into the main terminal of the Belize International Airport.

I pulled out my packet of travel vouchers from Honeymoons Express. "Maya Air."

Michael rolled our luggage over to the ticket counter and checked us onto the next interisland flight to Camus Caye.

"That's our plane?" I asked as we walked out onto the runway. I'd flown commuters before, but this one couldn't have had more than ten seats.

"Twelve," Michael corrected, "if you count the pilot and the flight attendant."

Good thing Jane hadn't come. She's a nervous flyer even on jets.

Twenty minutes later, we landed at the Camus Caye Municipal Airport. Michael retrieved our bags while I searched for our transportation. The travel agent assured me that a driver would be waiting for us at the airport. He wasn't difficult to spot, since he was the only one holding up a sign with "Mancini/Schwartzfarb" scrawled across it.

"Your fiancé's name was Schwartzfarb?" Michael asked, although it sounded more like an accusation.

I nodded sympathetically. "Better get used to it. You're Mr. Schwartzfarb for the next eight days."

The driver tossed our bags into the back of the van and suggested we sit in the air-conditioned interior while we waited for the second couple to arrive.

"Do you think it looks odd that we're not wearing wedding rings?" Michael asked after the driver slid the door closed behind us.

I hadn't thought of that. "I don't know. I'd always planned on leaving my rings at home. Jane says traveling with expensive jewelry can make you a target." And I knew that wasn't just her paranoia, because all the guidebooks said so too.

"Wedding bands aren't expensive."

"How do you know?" He hadn't mentioned that he was divorced.

"I think I'll go into town this afternoon and buy us some. Do you prefer fake silver or fake gold?"

"Neither. I'll tell people my wedding band's diamond and I left it at home." Which would've been true if I'd married Steven.

"OK, Mrs. Schwartzfarb, have it your way."

Michael certainly seemed to be taking his new role to heart. I hoped he realized the charade stopped at the bedroom door.

Ten minutes later John and Cheryl Kelley, newlyweds from Chicago who were also staying at the Blue Bay Beach Resort, joined us. John immediately started talking sports with Michael, and Cheryl insisted on telling me about their fabulous wedding on a rented yacht on Lake Michigan. Besides depressing the hell out of me, I realized pulling off this fake marriage for a week wasn't going to be as easy as I'd thought. Michael and I would have to come up with a story and stick to it. We could explain away why we didn't know each other's favorite flavor of ice cream, but not a discrepancy over where and when we'd gotten hitched.

CHAPTER 7

The hotel looked exactly like the picture online. A long wooden dock really did stretch across clear, calm, turquoise water, disappearing into a pearly white beach. Blue lounge chairs dotted the sand, and behind them, a row of thatched-roof bungalows formed a crescent moon.

"May I have the name of the reservation?" the desk clerk asked in heavily accented English. Her name tag identified her as Maria S.

"Mancini," I said. "Elizabeth Mancini."

Maria S. typed away at her computer. "Ah Ms. Mancini, congratulations! You and your husband are staying in the Papaya Bridal Suite. Is he here with you?"

I scanned the lobby, pretending to search for Michael. We'd decided on the walk to the lobby that it would be better if I checked in myself. I knew the reservation was under my name, but I didn't know if the hotel had Steven's information too. "I'm sure he's around here somewhere. Probably looking for the bar."

Maria S. smiled. "I'll need both your passports to check you in."

Damn! I gave my purse a cursory glance before I said, "My husband must still have them," and went outside to look for Michael. I found him parked in a lounge chair, eyes closed, shaded by a palm tree. "I need your passport, and if you could change your

19

last name to Schwartzfarb in the next ten seconds, that would be really helpful too."

Michael pulled his passport out of his knapsack, but instead of handing it to me, he grabbed mine. "I'll take care of this."

"What are you gonna do?"

"Relax, Mrs. Schwartzfarb. You're about to become Mrs. Garcia."

Michael handed Maria S. both passports and gave her his best smile. After a few seconds of typing, Maria S. stopped.

"Is there a problem?" Michael asked.

"I'm not sure," she said. "Your wife's information is correct, but yours is all wrong."

"Let me guess. You've got me listed as Steven Schwartzfarb?"

"*Sí*," Maria S. answered. "How did you know?"

Michael laughed and shook his head, then started talking to her in Spanish with the occasional English "travel agent" thrown in. At first Maria S. seemed confused, but soon she was chatting Michael up in Spanish, typing away. When she finished, she handed Michael both of our passports and told us, in English, to have a seat. "Ramon will be back shortly to show you to your room."

"What did you say to her?" I asked when we were side by side on the sofa.

"I told her my bride was a very modern woman who insisted on making all the reservations in her maiden name. But somehow, instead of my name being listed as the second person, your travel agent, Steven Schwartzfarb, ended up with that honor."

"And she believed you?"

"I told her I thought Mr. Schwartzfarb secretly had a crush on you and that maybe he did it on purpose to make me jealous."

He certainly was fast on his feet. "Are you sure you've never done anything like this before?"

"Positive."

"Well you're a pretty good liar for an anthropology professor."

"Thanks. You'd be surprised at the excuses my students give me."

Obviously, he was learning from them too.

They called it a suite, but it was really just one large room. The sitting area, which was populated by orange-cushioned rattan furniture and nubby purple rugs, was separated from the bedroom area, which held a king-size four-poster bed and two nightstands by a cherrywood dresser. It didn't have the luxury of a Four Seasons, but with its interesting mix of color and décor, it definitely had character.

"You want some champagne?" Michael asked when we were alone in the bridal suite.

I looked at my watch. It was still morning in Los Angeles, but it was afternoon on Camus Caye. "Sure," I said and flopped down on the rattan chair, immediately overcome by exhaustion. I never did get my nap on the plane.

Michael lifted the sweaty complimentary bottle from the ice bucket, which was leaking a ring of water onto the coffee table, and popped the cork. "A toast," he said, handing me a glass. "To new beginnings."

"And relaxing vacations," I added, clinking my champagne flute against his. It tasted like bubbly grape juice, and not the expensive kind, but it was cold and I was hot.

"What do you want to do first?" Michael asked, topping off both of our glasses.

"Sleep." I knew I shouldn't, that if I slept now it would take me days longer to recover from the jet lag, but my eyes were literally closing on me.

The last thing I remember was standing up to walk to the bed, but thinking the couch was so much closer. I woke up three hours later, shivering, alone, and incredibly groggy. The air-conditioning had finally kicked in, but Michael and my suitcase were gone.

CHAPTER 8

After a few minutes of frantic searching, I finally found my suitcase. Someone, presumably Michael, had moved it to the top of
the closet. As soon as I lifted if off the shelf, I knew it was empty.
But I didn't panic. I could see my sundresses hanging in the corner
and figured the rest of my stuff must be in the room somewhere. I
checked the dresser next and sure enough, Michael had unpacked
my clothes. I didn't know whether I should be grateful to him for
saving me the trouble or outraged at the invasion of my privacy.
What sort of person, especially a guy, did something like that?

My passport, money, and credit cards were all still in my
purse, so clearly Michael wasn't a thief. But he'd disappeared
without a word, or even a note, knowing I had no way to reach
him. I noticed that his luggage was gone too, so it was at least possible that he left to check into his own hotel and planned to return
later. I decided to call the Tortuga Inn to confirm my theory, but
after two minutes of fruitless searching, I remembered that the
Blue Bay's guest rooms had no phones. Part of the "getting away
from it all" experience. It had seemed like a good idea when both
my landline and cell phone were ringing simultaneously.

I knew what Jane's answer to "What sort of a guy does something like that?" would be, so I checked the bras and panties next.
They didn't look like they'd been fondled, but since I actually
remembered to pack the travel-size bottle of Woolite Jane insisted
I bring, I figured I might as well use it.

After I'd wrung the suds from my underwear and still no Michael, I decided to hell with him. I changed into my bathing suit, locked the door behind me, and headed to the pool. I was surprised to find it practically empty. Despite the perfect weather, only two couples were sunbathing. The first, who looked like they were barely out of college, were pressed up against the wall of the deep end, sucking face. Definitely young newlywed behavior. The second couple, who I guessed were midthirties, were reading books and tanning themselves on side-by-side lounge chairs.

I dumped my beach bag on a lounge two chairs over from the thirtysomething woman and went in search of a towel. The hut next to the deep end looked promising. I could see a stack of blue towels folded on the rear shelf, but there was no one at the desk. I waited a few seconds before I tried the door, but it was locked. I could either wait around hoping the towel person showed up this century, or I could hop up on the counter and grab the towel myself.

I gripped the counter in the most ladylike way I knew (butt in, face out) and jumped. After several failed attempts, I abandoned ladylike and tried facing in. My hip bones were clinging to the edge and I was just swinging my left leg over the top when I heard, "May I help you?"

I managed to turn my head around while swinging my right leg up too, leaving me stomach down, face out, staring at a perfectly sculpted bronze chest. It was a nice view to have while I caught my breath, and it got even nicer when the chest lowered itself down to reveal muscled shoulders, followed by a firm jawline, a bright-pink sunburned nose, and two blue-gray eyes peeking out from under a thatch of wavy blond hair.

"Are you OK?" he asked.

"I'm fine," I said, attempting to roll over onto my back without falling off the edge. "I just need a towel."

The chest walked around to the side of the hut, unlocked the door, and handed me two.

"Thanks," I said, pulling myself upright on the counter. I hesitated for a moment, trying to figure out if there was any way I could lower myself back down gently, before accepting that there wasn't and leaping off. The landing wasn't quite as smooth as I'd hoped. I'm not what you'd call a natural athlete.

"Are you hurt?" the chest asked, running around front to join me.

Only my pride, I determined as I involuntarily inhaled his scent—Coppertone mixed with something I couldn't quite place. Something briny and masculine. The opposite of Steven's fifty-dollar-a-bottle Armani aftershave.

"I could've sworn we had a first aid kit," he said, scanning the shelves of the towel hut.

"No need," I said, brushing the pebbles from my skinned knee. "It's hardly even bleeding anymore."

"Are you sure? It's no trouble. I have to go back to the boat for the rest of the gear anyway."

"What boat?"

I followed his finger until I spotted the skiff tied to the end of the dock. "I'm the scuba instructor," the chest announced.

For the first time in my life, I had an overwhelming urge to dive down to the bottom of the ocean wearing giant flippers and a fifty-pound air tank strapped to my back.

CHAPTER 9

"My name's Jack," he said, extending his hand.

It was calloused but very warm. "Lizzie," I replied. "Lizzie Mancini."

We both stood there, smiling awkwardly and nodding our heads, until he finally said, "I should get back to the boat," and turned to leave.

"Wait!"

He turned back.

"What if I want to take scuba lessons? Do I talk to you about that?"

"Sure," he said, taking a step toward me before reaching over my head to grab a brochure from the rack above the counter. He had to be over six feet tall. "This has all the information you need. The new session starts tomorrow. We meet here at ten a.m. Are you sure you don't want that Band-Aid?"

"No," I said, ignoring the trickle of blood running down my leg. "I'm fine."

"Then I hope to see you tomorrow, Lizzie."

I watched him walk past the thirtysomethings still reading and the twenty-year-olds who had moved from the pool to a single lounge chair where the husband was massaging his wife's thighs with sunscreen, before I lost sight of him behind a clump of trees. I knew I should've packed that vibrator I'd gotten as a joke gift at my bridal shower—at least I thought it was a joke. It looked like it was going to be a hot and lonely week.

If only I'd been that lucky.

CHAPTER 10

I was contorting my upper body in ways that would surely require a chiropractor visit when I returned home in an attempt to spread suntan lotion on my own back, when I heard a familiar voice.

"You need some help, honey?"

I flipped over and watched Michael, now in khaki shorts and a Hawaiian shirt, stride toward me. "Did you have a nice nap?" he asked.

"Where the hell have you been?"

"Buying you a present." He winked as he sat down on the edge of my lounge chair. "The rings," he whispered and held up his left hand, which was now sporting a plain gold (colored, at least) wedding band. "Yours is in the room. And what happened to your underwear? They're all over the bathroom."

"How did you get into the room?"

"With the key, of course," he said, producing it from his pocket. The bellhop must've given him two. "We really need to talk."

Michael groaned. "Nothing good ever comes after that statement."

My anger immediately turned to depression. Steven used to say the exact same thing.

Michael followed me back to "our" room where we spent the next hour and a half working out the ground rules of our pretend marriage:

1. No kissing.
2. No hugging.
3. Definitely no sex.
4. Hands off personal items.
5. If you're going out, leave a note.
6. Everything else is negotiable.

Michael said he could live with that. He'd already checked into his hotel in town and planned on sleeping there (at least that's what he told me). He'd also rented a golf cart, the predominant form of transportation on the island, to drive himself back and forth.

"Anything else?" he asked.

"Your schedule. I know you're working this week, so does that mean you'll just be around in the evenings?"

"Lizzie, I'm meeting with antiquities dealers. It's not a nine-to-five kind of job."

"So you won't be joining me for dinner?" I thought that was the whole point of this charade, at least for me.

"We'll just have to take it day by day."

Winging it wasn't a concept I normally embraced. But this vacation was anything but normal. "OK, just let me know in the morning if I'll be seeing you that day."

"Why? If I'm not available are you going to set up a hot date?"

Of course Jack was the first thought that popped into my head. And before you start judging me, just remember it was Steven who dumped me. If I were a guy, you'd be telling me to get back in the saddle and screw every woman in sight. While I had no intention of sleeping with every man I met, a one-night stand (or a few nights if the sex was really good) with a hot scuba instructor I'd never have to see again might be just what I needed.

"Lizzie, it was a joke." Michael interrupted my reverie. "Are you hungry? Because I'm starving."

I looked at my watch. "It's only six o'clock."

"That's dinnertime in Belize. Most restaurants won't seat you past seven."

"But we haven't even figured out how we met yet."

"C'mon," he said, standing up. "I can be much more creative on a full stomach. Do you like conch stew?"

"I don't know. I've never had it."

"Good, then you can cross this off your vacation to-do list: tried traditional Belizean dish."

His sarcasm actually made him more attractive.

Over dinner at a tiny restaurant that wasn't listed in any of the guidebooks, Michael and I concocted the story of our whirlwind courtship. The whirlwind part was Michael's idea. He concluded that if people thought we'd known each other for only a few weeks, it wouldn't seem odd that we were missing a few details. At the time, it made perfect sense.

CHAPTER 11

After dinner, Michael drove us back to the Blue Bay, where we wandered over to the hotel's bar. Since neither of us wanted to watch *Seinfeld* reruns on the satellite TV, we headed to the billiards room. John and Cheryl Kelley, the couple we'd met on the ride from the airport to the hotel, were playing on the only table. We said we'd wait, but they insisted we join them for a game, which turned into four games, three of which we lost. Michael swore it was the piña coladas hindering his aim.

"You'd make a great pool shark," I said to Cheryl. With her chubby cheeks and innocent blue eyes, she could really clean up.

"My dad owns a bar in Chicago," she said, sipping her ginger ale. "It's second nature to me."

The three of us and Cheryl (it turns out the blushing bride was actually two months pregnant) staggered back to the bungalows together. It was my unlucky night. John and Cheryl's hut was right next door, which meant that Michael had to wait in my room until we saw their lights go out. It's not that I found his company objectionable, but the room was swaying (or maybe it was me who was swaying) and I was ready for bed.

"Are you sure you don't want me to stay?" Michael asked, before he followed with, "I'm teasing," and kissed me on the cheek.

The fact that I'm not attracted to short Latin men probably saved my life.

The next morning I found Michael in the lobby sipping coffee and watching CNN. He accompanied me to the hotel's restaurant where the hostess seated us at a table on the shady side of the patio. I recognized the two couples from the pool yesterday, but I didn't see John and Cheryl.

"You're not wearing your ring," Michael said while we waited for our coffee.

"I forgot." Even though the cheap wedding band Michael had purchased looked nothing like the heirloom platinum engagement ring Steven had given me (and promptly taken back), wearing any ring right now was too painful. Besides, after breakfast I was heading over to my scuba diving lesson with Jack. Which reminded me that I still needed to find an excuse to ditch Michael, at least from 10:00 a.m. to noon.

"So what's on your agenda for today?" I asked.

"I have some business to take care of this morning and a meeting this afternoon. Would it be OK if I picked you up here around six? We could go to dinner and then out dancing if you're up for it."

"Perfect." I didn't even need to lie to Michael to get rid of him. Obviously, my fling with Jack was meant to be.

I arrived at the pool at five minutes to ten. Except for the woman working at the towel hut, it was empty. "This is where we meet for the scuba class, right?" I asked while I signed for two towels.

"Yes," she said, glancing up at the clock on the wall. "Jack's always a few minutes late."

I carried my towels to a lounge chair and lathered up with sunscreen while I watched the other couples arrive. First came the twenty-year-old newlyweds I'd noticed at breakfast and the pool the day before. They must've recognized me too because they said hello as they walked by. The second couple looked like new arrivals. They were both tall, blond, and milky white. They sat down next to me and immediately started applying SPF 50 to every uncovered inch of their bodies.

Jack arrived ten minutes later carrying two mesh bags—one filled with masks and snorkels, and the other with foot fins.

"Are you all here for the Discover Scuba class?" he asked as he dropped the bags by the side of the pool.

We nodded our assent.

"Excellent. My name's Jack Taylor, and I'll be your instructor for the next two days."

I stopped listening after that. Jack had peeled off his faded T-shirt, and all I could focus on was the narrow band of blond hair that started just below his chest, continued down the center of his very taut abs, and disappeared into the top of his low-slung shorts. God it was hot out here.

Watching him walk across the pool deck, I was in full fantasy mode when the woman next to me said, "Do you think he'd let us pay at the end of the class?"

"Huh?"

"For the class. He said we had to sign up now, but do you think that means we have to pay too?"

I'd forgotten about the paying part. I'd locked my wallet in the room safe before breakfast this morning. I told her I'd go ask and followed Jack's path across the pool deck, catching up with him in the towel hut. The girl working at the counter greeted him with a grin much wider than the one she'd given me.

"Excuse me, Jack."

He turned and smiled, and when he said, "Hey, Lizzie, I'm glad you made it," I nearly melted.

When I recovered the power of speech I said, "Thanks, Jack. I really want to learn to dive, but I left my purse back in—"

"No problem," he said. "You can bill it to your room." Then he bent down in front of the safe.

"Do you need some help with that?" the towel girl asked, bending over so he was eye level with her cleavage.

Could she be any more obvious?

"Thanks, Carmen, I've got it covered," he said, but not before licking his lips as he caught sight of her boobs. I couldn't really blame him. They were spectacular.

Jack grabbed a stack of forms from the safe and slammed it shut. "Just fill out the top section and sign underneath," he said as he handed the first one to me.

I wrote "end of the row facing the beach" on the blank line next to room because I couldn't remember the number and I certainly wasn't going to write down Papaya Bridal Suite. I assumed I was the only Lizzie Mancini staying at the resort this week so they'd figure it out.

"Ah, the bridal suite," Jack said when I handed him back the form.

Damn!

"Doesn't your husband want to learn to dive too? Most couples take this together."

The exact conversation I was hoping to avoid.

CHAPTER 12

I pretended I hadn't heard the question and followed Jack back to the shallow end of the pool where the rest of the couples were waiting. After we filled out our medical questionnaires, Jack collected the forms and returned them to the towel hut while the rest of us waded into the water.

We spent the next two hours learning how to use buoyancy compensators and regulators, clear our masks, stabilize our ear pressure, and stay buoyant, but not too buoyant, in the water.

"You all did great today," Jack said when he ended the session fifteen minutes late. "Tomorrow we're going directly to the dive site, so we'll meet at the dock. Ten a.m. and don't forget to bring your towels. We won't have any extras on the boat."

I made sure I was the last to return my equipment so we could have a moment alone.

"Do you really not have any extra towels on the boat or were you just trying to scare us?" I asked as I struggled with the clips on my BC, the scuba diving equivalent of a high-tech life vest.

"Why?" Jack said, unhooking the last clasp for me. His shoulders looked even broader now that they were only six inches away. "Are you planning on forgetting your towel?"

"No," I said, slipping out of the vest and handing it to him. "Just wondering."

He placed the vest on top of the pile and gathered up the remaining fins. "I always have a few, but I prefer people bring their own."

"Why? Are you afraid we'll steal them?"

He smiled, revealing a deep dimple in one cheek. "You wouldn't ask that if you saw them. Mine I have to wash. Yours go back to the hotel laundry."

"Don't you work for the hotel?" I assumed he did.

"No, I work for Belize Divers."

I could've come up with more questions—How long had he worked there? Did he like it? How did someone who sounded like an American end up working for a dive shop in Belize?—but Jack had finished packing up the equipment. He called out to someone in Spanish, and two hotel workers sauntered over and began carrying the equipment out to the dock.

"I'll see you tomorrow, Lizzie," Jack said as he picked up his mesh bags and followed the men out.

Clearly, he wasn't interested in flirting with a married woman. If I were looking for a relationship, I'd consider that a positive attribute. But since all I wanted was one night of great rebound sex (or maybe a few nights if it was really good), I found it quite frustrating. Yes, I realized that it might be that he just wasn't attracted to me. But my ego had taken enough of a beating lately, so I decided to believe it was my marital state that he found objectionable rather than just me.

After class, I ordered lunch poolside, which was much less uncomfortable than eating alone in the hotel's dining room, then headed out to the concierge desk. Maria R. (there really were two of them) walked me through the activities book. Since none of the tours I was interested in—visiting a Mayan ruin, cave-tubing, and a shark and stingray snorkeling excursion—were available that afternoon, I left with brochures for each and told Maria R. I'd be back.

I was still planning my week from the beach chair in front of my bungalow when I heard, "Don't waste your money on the snorkel trip."

I looked up from the brochures to find Jack in shadow, backlit by the sun.

"I'm surprised to see you. I would've thought you'd be sick of us tourists by now."

"You tourists pay my salary. I try to remember that. Besides, we're all tourists sometime."

Mr. Easygoing. Definitely the opposite of Steven, who used to fly into a tizzy if his *Wall Street Journal* didn't arrive on time. I grabbed my beach bag from the empty chair next to mine. "Here, sit down."

"I can't," he said, glancing at his watch. "I have to get the boat back by four to prep it for a night dive. I just stopped by to pick up my check."

"I thought you don't work for the hotel."

"I don't," he said. "You pay the hotel, they take their commission, then cut a check to Belize Divers for the rest."

"And if you forget to deliver the check to your boss you don't get paid?"

"No, my dad would probably pay me anyway, but I'd have to listen to him complain about it for the next week, or until I screwed something else up."

He worked for his father and was constantly disappointing him. So much to explore. "Are you sure you don't want to sit down?"

Before he could answer, we both heard someone call "Lizzie" and searched for the source. Michael was waving to me from fifty yards down the beach. I had no choice but to wave back.

"I should probably go," Jack said.

"You don't need to leave." I'd get rid of Michael somehow. But he picked up his pace and arrived thirty seconds later, sweat trickling down his forehead and out of breath. Despite the constant heat and humidity since we'd arrived, this was the first time I'd seen him perspire.

"What are you doing here?"

"Nice to see you too," he said, and kissed the top of my head before offering his hand to Jack. "Hi, I'm Michael, Lizzie's husband."

Was that really necessary?

"Jack Taylor," he said, shaking Michael's hand. "I'm the scuba instructor."

Michael sat down in the empty chair I'd offered to Jack. "So how's my girl doing?"

"Good," Jack answered before I could. "They're all doing great. And I really do need to be heading out. Nice meeting you, Michael, and Lizzie, I'll see you tomorrow."

"Ten a.m. at the dock, right?"

"Right," he said.

"And don't forget your towel," we both said in unison, and then laughed.

At least Michael waited until Jack was a few feet away before he said, "What was that about?" in a rather accusatory tone for someone who was only *playing* my husband.

I watched Jack stroll down the beach a few more seconds before I turned back to Michael. "We *so* need to talk."

He groaned, just like a real husband. "Can it wait until later? All I really want now is a cold beer and your room key."

"My key? Wait, what are you doing back here this early? I thought we weren't meeting until six."

"We're not, but I lost my room key. I asked for another at the front desk, but they told me they'd have to charge us seventy-five dollars to replace it."

"That's outrageous!"

"I agree," he said. "That's why I need your key. I'm going to take it into town and have a copy made for two bucks."

I pulled the room key out of the zippered pocket in my beach bag. It was a metal key, not a computerized card, but it stated Do Not Copy at the top of it. "How are you going to get around that?"

"Don't worry," Michael said and tucked it into his shorts pocket. "I know a guy. See you at six." He took off down the beach before I thought to ask him how he lost his key in the first place.

I spent the rest of the afternoon weighing the pros and cons of continuing this charade with Michael. This time I didn't need to make a list.

CHAPTER 13

It wasn't that I didn't enjoy Michael's company and didn't appreciate what he'd been doing for me, but he was getting a little too comfortable playing my husband. And despite his acknowledgement that our relationship was platonic, I could tell he wanted more. Not that he wanted to marry me. He just would've preferred spending the week as my real lover rather than my fake husband.

And yes, I admit, my motives weren't altruistic. Having Michael around was ruining any shot I might have with Jack. Now I just had to figure out how to get rid of Michael, in a nice way, and have Jack find out about it so I looked like the injured party instead of the shrew. Too bad Jack thought we were already married. I could have had Michael dump me at the altar. I was getting good at that.

I showered, dressed, blew dry my hair, and applied makeup, but I still hadn't devised a plan to ditch Michael. I paced the room until six fifteen, and when Michael still hadn't showed, I walked over to the lobby.

He wasn't there either. I didn't know what else to do, so I ordered a drink at the bar and waited some more. I was wandering around the lobby with my piña colada when John and Cheryl spotted me. I couldn't have missed them since both their faces were bright pink and Cheryl was wrapped in a floor-length sunflower-yellow sarong.

"There you are," she said. "We just stopped by your room, but you weren't in."

I didn't think Michael would've made plans with them and not told me, but I'd only known him two days. "I'm waiting for Michael. You haven't seen him, have you?"

"No," John said. "We wanted to invite you to a rematch pool tournament tonight. You game?" He laughed and said, "Get it? Game?"

"Got it," I said and gave him a fake smile. He was a lot funnier when he was drunk, or at least when I was drunk. And with his yellow polo shirt tucked into his khakis, he was also committing the unpardonable sin of dressing the same as his wife. "I think we're going to have to take a rain check on that one. Michael wants to go dancing tonight."

"Ooo dancing," Cheryl said. "Honey, let's go dancing with them instead."

"Are you sure you're up for it?" John asked, patting her belly.

"I'm pregnant, honey, not an invalid."

I liked Cheryl better when she let her inner bitch shine through.

John ordered a beer for himself and a ginger ale for Cheryl and the two of them sat with me until Michael breezed through the lobby twenty minutes later wearing black trousers, a white linen shirt, and his ubiquitous gold chain. Whatever tension he'd been carrying earlier had disappeared.

"I thought we were meeting in the room," Michael asked, when he spotted me on the sofa.

"So did I, but when you didn't show up—"

"Cut me some slack, babe," he said, checking his watch. "I'm barely five minutes late."

Babe? "Michael, it's six thirty-five. You're thirty-five minutes late."

Cheryl stood up and tugged at John's arm until he stood up too. "We should be going."

"You don't need to go," I said out of politeness, as opposed to actually wanting them to stay.

"We do," she said. "If I don't keep eating, the nausea takes over and I'll spend the rest of the night with my head in the toilet."

"Rain check on the dancing though," John added.

"Were you two coming dancing with us?" Michael asked.

"Another time," John said as Cheryl pulled him away.

Michael waved them off, then turned back to me. "Nice save, huh?"

"What save?"

"The way I got rid of them with the fake fight."

"So you did know you were half an hour late?"

"I'm really sorry about that. I got hung up with a colleague, and then I still had to copy the key. Here," he said, handing me mine, "before I forget."

"You have colleagues on Camus Caye?" I thought his colleagues were all back in LA.

"I don't want to talk about work. C'mon," he said, taking my hand after I slipped the key into my purse. "If we don't get to the restaurant by seven they won't seat us."

"Where are we going?"

"A place you'll like. They have tablecloths."

That was fancy by Camus Caye standards. Good thing I'd worn a sundress.

It was obvious this place was a tourists-only restaurant the minute we stepped inside. Not only did it have linen tablecloths, but everyone eating there was either American or Canadian. I didn't hear one word of Spanish or Belizean Creole the entire meal.

"What's good here?" I asked as I perused the menu.

"I don't know," Michael said. "I've never been here before."

"Then why'd you pick it?"

"Because I thought you might like it."

He slid his hand across the table but I managed to grab my water glass before it reached me. "Michael, we need to talk."

"At least let me order the wine first."

I waited until after the waiter had poured us both a glass of pinot noir before I said, "I don't think this is going to work."

"Why not? We've already gotten past the hard part. It's all downhill from here."

"I'm just not comfortable with all this lying to everyone." I thought that was nicer than "I'm just not that into you," and more original than "I'm not ready for a relationship right now."

"You mean John and Cheryl?"

"I mean everyone."

"I see." He leaned back in his chair and swallowed half his glass in one gulp. "There's someone else, isn't there?"

"Don't be silly." I took a long sip of my wine so I didn't have to meet his gaze.

"It must be someone from the hotel since the only times you've left the resort were with me."

"Michael, stop."

"Since the rest of the guests are probably spoken for, it has to be someone who works there."

Michael refilled his wineglass and topped mine off too. "I can't really see you with a maintenance man," he continued. "A chef maybe. Or a bartender. Or maybe the hotel manager."

"This is exactly why this was all a bad idea. You're jealous and we're not even dating."

"It's that scuba guy, isn't it?"

I looked out the window, which was really just an opening in the wall, and admired the sunset. The sky was pink, the palms were swaying in the evening breeze, and the waves were lapping at the shore. Perfect. Then I looked back at Michael's angry face. This was ridiculous. I barely knew the guy. I didn't owe him anything.

"Isn't it?" he said again, his voice rising.

"Michael, enough!"

Was it my imagination or did the restaurant din just drop a few octaves? I looked around and the couple at the next table were definitely staring at us, but when they caught my eye, they looked away.

I turned back to Michael and lowered my voice. "This was supposed to be harmless platonic fun."

"And it has been," he said, "so why can't we continue?"

"Because I don't think that's what you really want."

When he started to protest, I cut him off. "And you're right. There's someone else, potentially."

"The scuba guy?"

I nodded.

"I knew it."

Michael finished the rest of the wine and ordered a second bottle. I would've been concerned except instead of making him angrier, it seemed to soften him up.

"So how are you going to explain my sudden absence?" Michael asked at the end of our mostly silent meal.

"I don't know. I guess you could leave on a business trip?"

"Leave my *honeymoon* for a business trip?"

"You got a better idea?"

He swished the last of his wine around in his glass, and then gulped it down. "We could have a fight."

"And you get mad and walk out on me?" This was starting to become a theme.

He smiled widely. "I'll leave you in a jealous rage."

I considered it. "But how would people know? Or were you thinking of making it a public breakup?"

"Sure," he said. "But you have to promise to do something for me first."

Always a catch. "What?"

"Pretend to be my girlfriend when we get back to LA."

"Michael, I—"

He held up his hands to stop me. "Just until we clear customs. My ex is a baggage screener at LAX and—"

"Your ex-girlfriend's a baggage screener?"

"Yeah, what's wrong with that?"

I couldn't help thinking about Jane's drug dealer theory. I still didn't believe Michael was a violent criminal, but it was an odd coincidence. "Michael, you're free to date whoever you want."

"Good," he said. "Because I want you to help me make her jealous."

"And how am I supposed to do that?"

"Just act like we're together and I'll take care of the rest."

It wasn't much to ask. Not really. And I felt like I owed him one. "OK, Michael. But how do you know we're even on the same flight?"

"Don't worry. I already changed my ticket."

CHAPTER 14

I asked Michael to drop me off at the lobby to avoid any uncomfortable goodnight scenes at the door. Since we were breaking up the next day anyway, I was no longer concerned with appearances. But it was only nine o'clock and I wasn't even tired yet. I wandered around the hotel looking for something to do, but the gift shop was closed, and no one was playing pool. There were a few people at the bar, but I didn't want any more to drink. Then I remembered that the resort offered free Internet service.

I asked at the front desk and the clerk directed me to a room the size of a closet containing a small desk with an old PC on top. I sat down and typed in my server address, and in under a minute I logged into my e-mail.

I had a few messages from editors, a bill from my wedding florist, and a bunch of junk mail. No messages from Steven begging me to take him back, but I had one from his parents apologizing for how things had turned out and wishing me well. I skimmed through the headlines on a few days worth of online newspapers, deleted a whole bunch of spam stock tips and offers for cheap Viagra, and then found the message from Jane:

I knew you couldn't go a week without checking your e-mail! I hope you're having fun and staying safe. Remember, bottled water only and SPF 30 or higher every day. And only take the group tours offered through the hotel. Don't be taken in by those local scammers.

See you next week!
Jane

I loved Jane. She was the only person I knew who worried more than my mother. Of course, my mother didn't have Jane's array of phobias to rely on. Did you know the same person could be afraid of both heights and enclosed spaces? I didn't until I met Jane. Our friendship worked because Jane could count on me to do things she never would and I could count on her to make me feel adventurous. At least that was her shrink's theory.

I started typing:

Greetings from Camus Caye. You'll never guess what I've been up to. Remember Michael from the bar? He's now Mr. Schwartzfarb. Or I'm Mrs. Garcia. Not officially, of course. The explanation's too long for an e-mail but suffice to say the "marriage" is over. I met someone else here who's much more my type, so I'm getting rid of Michael tomorrow. If all goes well, I'll be newly single by Thursday, leaving me 4 full days to pursue Rebound Man. Did I mention he's HOT! It's OK to fool around with someone you just met so long as you're on vacation and you'll never see him again, right? I'm pretty sure that's the rule. And DON'T WORRY, I'll use protection.
See you soon,
Lizzie

I hit send before I remembered to tell her about the e-mail from Steven's parents. Jane always said I loved them more than I loved Steven. Apparently, the feeling was mutual.

The next morning I overslept, but I still made it to the dock at precisely 10:00 a.m., where Nick and Janet and Bill and Stacy, the two couples from my Discover Scuba class, were already waiting. Jack, of course, was ten minutes late.

I'd watched the Discovery Channel and seen those Jacques Cousteau specials when I was a kid, but actually breathing underwater and swimming side by side with fish was a whole new experience for me. Jack led us down to a coral reef and then through the remains of an underwater shipwreck. We all scoured it for buried treasure (pillaged long before we arrived), but I did come face-to-face with a moray eel. I couldn't believe it when our forty minutes were up and Jack gave us the signal to surface.

When we were all safely aboard the boat, Jack helped us with our equipment while Manuel, our gold-toothed Belizean boat captain, piloted us back out to sea. Next stop—Shark Ray Alley. At least for those of us who were willing to swim with sharks. Jack told us whoever didn't want to could stay on the boat and watch the action from above.

"You're gonna go, right?" Jack said, sitting down next to me.

It had seemed like fun when I was reading about it on dry land. Now I wasn't so sure.

"It's perfectly safe," he added.

"How can swimming with sharks be perfectly safe? They do eat people, don't they?"

Jack shook his head. "Shark attacks are incredibly rare. *Jaws* is the worst thing that ever happened to sharks."

"What about Shark Week on TV?" Steven and I used to watch it every summer.

"They're at least more evenhanded."

"What are you, some kind of shark activist?" I'd never heard anyone defend sharks before.

"Marine biologist, although my specialty is sea turtles."

Wow, didn't see that one coming. I'd assumed he was a diving instructor/beach bum. I didn't even know they had a university in Belize. I wanted to find out more, but Manuel cut the engine and Jack jumped up to anchor the boat.

CHAPTER 15

Manuel slipped the boat in between six others, but ours was definitely the smallest group. The water was filled with over a hundred snorkelers. I decided if a six-year-old boy was brave enough to swim with sharks, then I should be too.

Jack jumped in the water first, followed by me, Stacy, and Bill. Nick and Janet opted to remain on the boat with Manuel, who had pulled out a deck of cards and was setting up a poker game. I suppose when you see sharks every day, they're no longer a thrill.

We swam out to the deeper water and watched as another tour operator fed the sharks bits of chum. He didn't actually stick his hands inside their mouths, but even throwing food to them while they circled and chomped down on floating bits of raw meat with their rows of tiny razor-sharp teeth was more than I'd have been willing to do.

After a few minutes with the sharks, Jack led us back to the shallow water where the stingrays congregated. Jack called out to Manuel, who set down his cards long enough to throw him a plastic bag filled with tiny pieces of fish.

Jack grabbed a handful and held it just below the surface. Instantly he was swarmed by what looked like three-foot-wide gray sand dollars stuck on the ends of sharp sticks.

"You can pet them," Jack said. "Just stay away from the tail."

They felt like velvet. Slimy wet velvet. But they were gorgeous and graceful, and they liked to play. We were all very disappointed when Jack told us it was time to leave.

When we arrived back at the resort, the five of us thanked Jack and Manuel for a great trip as they helped us off the boat. When the couples began walking toward the beach, I stayed behind.

"Aren't you coming?" I asked Jack, who was hauling a hose out onto the dock. I don't know why I automatically assumed he'd be coming back to the resort with us, but I did.

"No, I have to rinse off the gear. I'm taking another group out this afternoon."

"From our hotel?" Maybe I could tag along. I just had to get to the pool long enough for my big fight with Michael. He promised to meet me at twelve thirty and it was already twelve fifteen.

"No, from the Tradewinds. It's on the other side of the island. But I'll be back here tomorrow morning if you want to take the class again. A lot of people repeat it."

"Um, maybe." I wasn't opposed to the idea, but I'd signed up for cave tubing tomorrow morning.

"OK, Lizzie, I'll see you around."

Could he be less interested? Of course, he still thought I was married. I started to walk down the dock when I had an idea. A lame idea, I admit, but my only idea. "Jack, I think I wrote down the wrong room number on my form. Do you still have it?"

"It's probably in the safe."

That's what I was counting on. This would all be so much easier if Jack walked me back to the towel hut and witnessed my breakup with Michael for himself. "Would you mind pulling it out for me so I can fix it? I wouldn't want you not to get paid because I forgot my room number." Ugh, it sounded even lamer when I said it out loud.

Jack smiled. He knew. He had to know. "Don't worry about it. We'll figure it out."

HONEYMOON FOR ONE

I felt the color rise up in my cheeks but since my face was already sunburned, I figured it didn't show. And since I'd already humiliated myself there was no point in backing down. "I know, but I would just feel better if I could fix it."

"Manny," Jack called to the captain, who was still on the boat. "Would you mind taking Lizzie back to the pool so she can get her form from the safe?"

"Sure, boss," Manuel said. "But wouldn't you rather go yourself?"

They exchanged a look and Manuel laughed before he jumped down onto the dock.

"And don't get lost on the way back," Jack said, tossing Manuel a ring of keys.

"No worries," Manuel said before he turned his attention to me. "So how long you been married?" he asked, as he walked me down the dock.

"Not long," I said, trying to hide both my embarrassment and disappointment, which were present in equal parts.

"And your husband doesn't mind you going off without him?"

"Apparently not."

"Well I'll be free at five if you want some company," which he followed with a gold-toothed grin.

Great. The sleazy boat captain wants to keep me company, but Jack won't even walk me back to the pool. "Thanks, but my husband's a very jealous man."

"I've met jealous husbands before," Manuel said, before looking me over from head to toe.

"I bet you have."

When we arrived at the towel hut, Carmen was working at the desk. "Where's Jack?" she asked.

"Back at the boat," Manuel replied and knelt down in front of the safe.

"Tell him Carmen says hello."

"*Sí, sí*," Manuel said, and then sighed as he shuffled through a stack of papers he pulled from the safe. "Lizzie Mancini?" he asked.

I nodded and Manuel handed me my sign-up sheet. I grabbed a pencil from the cup on the counter, but before I finished writing "Papaya Suite," someone yanked the paper from my hand.

"Michael, what are you doing here?" I hoped that sounded as convincing as it had in the bathroom mirror.

"I thought I'd check in on my wife, but it seems like you have other plans," he said, glaring at Manuel, who was still staring at my padding-enhanced bikini top.

I could smell the beer on Michael's breath. Maybe he thought it would improve his performance. "Actually, I just got back."

"From a tryst with your lover?" he shouted.

I looked around the pool. The six other guests were staring at us, just as we'd planned. "No, I was scuba diving. I told you I was going. Don't you remember?"

"Right. With scuba boy. What's his name again?"

"Jack?" Carmen shouted. "*You're* sleeping with Jack?" She was so incredulous I was almost offended.

"I'm not sleeping with Jack!" And this was not the story we'd rehearsed. Michael was only supposed to accuse me of not loving him, which I was going to deny and point out that he was the one who was always abandoning me. Then he would say I only married him for his money, I would tell him he was crazy, and he would tell me this whole marriage was a mistake and he was leaving. *I* was supposed to be the injured party here, not Michael.

Manuel walked around to the front of the counter. "Hey, mon, I think you need to calm down."

"Who the hell are you?" Michael shouted.

"I'm captain of the scuba boat. I'm telling you, mon, nothing's going on between Jack and your wife."

"Does that mean you want her for yourself?"

"Michael!" He was going too far.

"Hey, mon," was all Manuel managed before Michael took a swing at him. Michael missed, but Manuel's return punch connected. In an instant, the two of them were rolling around on the pool deck.

"Call security," I yelled to Carmen, who was watching like it was a boxing match on TV. Some of the other guests ran over, but no one jumped in to stop them. I couldn't blame them. Anyone who did was likely to get hurt.

Jack and the security guard arrived at the same time. Jack grabbed Manuel from behind while the security guard lifted Michael off the ground. The guard tried to lead Michael away, but not before he tried to hit Jack in the jaw, warning him that he better stay away from his wife. Luckily, the hotel manager arrived a few seconds later and he and the security guard managed to wrestle Michael over to a lounge chair and keep him there.

I wanted to check on Jack, but I walked over to Michael. He had a bloody nose and his shirt was torn, but otherwise he looked OK. "You need to calm down," I said, and I wasn't playacting.

Michael winked at me before he said, "Get away from me, you bitch. I can't stand the sight of you."

"Screw you, Michael. I've had enough of this." I really had.

"So have I," he said. "I want you out of my life. And you're not getting a dime."

In that moment, even though I was looking at Michael, I was seeing Steven. But it was Michael who received my wrath. I won't repeat every word I said, or screamed would be more accurate, but after calling him the most selfish, self-centered bastard I'd ever known, I told him if he ever came near me again I'd make him wish he was dead.

In retrospect, I probably should've chosen my words more carefully.

CHAPTER 16

The pool was silent. Michael stared at me closemouthed, the security guard and the assistant manager stared at me openmouthed, and when I glanced over at Jack, he looked away. I reached down and picked up my Discover Scuba consent form from where it had landed on the deck, wiped Michael's blood off on the wall of the towel hut, and threw it on the counter. Then I hurried out of the pool area through the closest exit I could find.

I hadn't felt this awful since the night Steven walked out on me. Having this fight with Michael was like reliving the entire experience. What was I thinking, planning this charade? In fact, what was I thinking getting involved with Michael in the first place? This whole thing was ludicrous. All I wanted was to go home.

I unlocked the door to my room and went directly to the safe. I'd already pulled out my airline ticket so I could call and change my flight before I remembered the room had no phone. There was no way I was going to the lobby to use the guest phone after the scene I'd just made. In fact, there was no way I was ever leaving this room again. I was going to die in the Blue Bay Resort's Papaya Bridal Suite. I lay down on the bed and cried until I fell asleep.

I awoke a few hours later to knocking on my door and someone calling my name. I ignored it, hoping whoever it was would go away. When it was clear they weren't going to, I got up and answered it.

"Cheryl, what's up?"

"I just came by to see how you're doing."

Could she know about Michael and me already? I didn't remember seeing her at the pool today. "OK."

"That's the spirit. You were too good for him anyway."

She knew. Everyone gave me that same speech after Steven called off the wedding. I opened the door wider and Cheryl walked in. "Who told you?"

"Have you met Michele and Kevin? They're from California too."

I shook my head.

"They were at the pool today when you…" She appeared to be searching for the right word, but finally shrugged and said, "You know."

I collapsed onto a rattan chair and dropped my head in my hands. What was I thinking? This was worse than I imagined. "Does everyone know?"

"I don't know about everyone, but it's a small place."

This was definitely the worst vacation of my life. "Cheryl, can you do me a favor?"

"Anything."

I handed her my airline ticket and my credit card. "Can you go to the lobby and call the airlines for me? Just get me on the next flight that goes anywhere with a connection to LA."

"Are you sure? That's gonna be a lot of money. Besides the change fee, you're going to have to pay the difference in the ticket, and last-minute fares are expensive."

"I don't care." It was worth a few hundred dollars to get home, crawl under the covers, and be anonymous again.

"Sure," she said. "But I don't need to go to the lobby." She opened her purse and pulled out her cell phone.

"Yours works here?" I'd left mine home.

"It's John's. He travels internationally. Don't worry about the charges, his company pays."

Cheryl read my *Vanity Fair* while I called the airlines. When the service rep told me it would cost $2,200 to leave tomorrow instead of next Monday, I decided to stay.

"You were right," I said, handing Cheryl back her phone. "It looks like I'll be here through the weekend."

"Good. You shouldn't let that jerk ruin your trip. In fact, you should stay longer and run up his credit card bill."

If she only knew.

Before Cheryl left she insisted I meet her and John for dinner. Cheryl told me she worked at an animal shelter back in Chicago, so I guessed she viewed me as another lost pet in need of rescue. I didn't have the will to argue with her. I was argued out.

At five o'clock, I forced myself to shower and get dressed, so when John and Cheryl arrived promptly at six I was ready to go. I couldn't work up the energy to apply makeup, but at least I'd blown dry my hair.

John and Cheryl introduced me to the water taxi service that left from the hotel's dock. The wind had picked up from this morning and so had the surf. By the time the taxi dropped us off at the restaurant's dock, my hair was in knots, and Cheryl was puking over the side of the boat. It only took a few minutes on dry land for Cheryl to recover, but my hair was beyond repair. Since I didn't have scissors to chop it off (which was probably a good thing since at that moment I might have used them), I opted for a sloppy bun.

"You should wear your hair up more often," Cheryl said when I returned from the ladies' room. "It's very becoming."

I appreciated the effort, but nothing was going to improve my mood tonight. Cheryl did her best to engage me in conversation, but after a while, she gave up and went back to gossiping about all the other guests at the resort. I learned about the couple from New Jersey who were having trouble conceiving; the husband and wife in the Mango Suite, both criminal lawyers from Boston who fell in love while opposing counsel during their first trial;

and the twentysomething couple I thought were newlyweds who were actually married to other people. I could only imagine what Cheryl would tell everyone else about Michael and me, assuming she hadn't already.

After dinner, Cheryl suggested dancing, but I declined.

"Oh come on," she insisted. "We're not going to let you go back to the hotel alone. It's not like they have TVs in the rooms."

"They have one in the lounge," John said, and Cheryl shot him a look.

"C'mon, Lizzie, it'll be fun," Cheryl said. "Maybe they'll have line dancing."

At that moment, I couldn't think of anything less appealing than line dancing. "I can't, I'm wearing flip-flops."

Cheryl slipped her arm into mine and started walking. "The disco's only a few blocks from here and we're not taking no for an answer."

"Disco?"

"That's just what they call it. I'm sure they don't actually play disco."

Disco wasn't all they played, but I heard more Donna Summer songs that night than I'd heard in my previous twenty-eight years. The DJ also rotated through reggae, funk, hip-hop, and classic rock 'n' roll. But at least no Macarena. I danced one song with John and Cheryl, then planted my butt on a bar stool for what I hoped was the rest of a short night.

I studied the crowd as I sipped my club soda. It was a mix of both locals and tourists, and it was obvious which were which even before they spoke. The locals didn't have sunburns, Belizean men didn't wear Dockers, and the native ladies didn't dance in designer shoes.

A few local men hit on me—apparently in Belize if a woman goes out alone it means she's on the lookout for a man. After the bartender explained this to me, I handed him a twenty-dollar bill to spread the word that I intended to leave on my own. The advances stopped after that. Until Manuel arrived. He slid in behind me at the bar and gave my shoulder a squeeze.

"Lizzie, good to see you. We were worried."

Manuel had fared better than Michael. He didn't have a scrape on him. "We?" I asked.

He turned around and called to Jack, who was at the other end of the bar. Manuel motioned for him to join us and, to the displeasure of the two women who were chatting him up, he did.

"Sorry about that," I said, nodding at the small purple bruise on his lower jaw.

"It's OK," he said, rubbing the spot where Michael's fist had grazed his face. "It was a lucky punch."

After that it was Manuel who kept the conversation going. When I finished the last of my club soda, he offered to buy me another until he found out what I was drinking. "You're on vacation. You need a cocktail."

"I had one already. I don't need any more."

"Do you like rum? Of course you do, everyone likes rum." Manuel called out a drink order in Spanish and the bartender returned with something tall and yellow with a cherry on top.

"What is it?" I asked as I sniffed at the glass, which smelled like pineapple and orange juice.

Manuel told me in Spanish, which Jack translated into English with an embarrassed smile. "It's called a panty-ripper."

Yesterday that would've made me smile too. But my post-jilting depression relapse had managed to cool my ardor for all men, including Jack. Spending the rest of the week alone was now sounding attractive to me. I took a sip of my X-rated cocktail, which tasted cool and sweet. Whatever it was, it went down easy.

"Come," Manuel said, "we're having a party in the back. It's Jesus's eighteenth birthday. I promised him I'd get him drunk and laid, not necessarily in that order."

I didn't know who Jesus was and I didn't care. "Sorry, but I'm not really in a party mood."

He prodded a bit more but soon gave up. When he started to walk toward the back of the room, Jack followed but Manuel stopped him. "Jack, mon, you can't leave the lady alone."

"It's fine," I said. "I'd rather be alone."

"A beautiful lady should never be alone." Manuel gestured toward the rowdy crowd next to us. "Jack will escort you; protect you from the hounds."

Jack looked as uncomfortable as I did.

"I don't need an escort either. I came with some people from the hotel."

"Where are they?" Manuel demanded. "I don't see them."

"They're dancing."

"Then you need an escort. Jack, I'm leaving you in charge. Don't let me down, mon."

They exchanged another one of those looks before Jack raised his hand to his forehead and saluted. "Aye, aye, Captain."

When Manuel had gone, Jack leaned in and I caught his briny scent again, this time mixed with soap instead of sunscreen. "Do you want to find somewhere quieter to talk?"

"Not really."

"Good," he said, visibly relieved. Then he called to the bartender and ordered us another round.

Then another.

And another.

CHAPTER 17

I didn't really notice how drunk I was until I hopped off my bar stool. I was having trouble walking a straight line. After I found the ladies' room, I located John and Cheryl on the dance floor and told them I was ready to leave. I returned to the bar first—I wanted to say goodnight to Jack—but he was already gone.

I managed to walk the few blocks to the water taxi stand without falling down or crashing into anything. Cheryl helped. Then the three of us waited and waited with no boat in sight until a golf cart screeched to a halt in front of us.

"You want a ride?" Jack asked. "The next boat won't be for at least half an hour."

There was no discussion. I immediately climbed into the front seat, and John and Cheryl slid into the back. I introduced them to Jack, and by the end of the ten-minute drive, Cheryl had decided that she and John were taking Jack's scuba class the next morning.

When we reached the resort, Jack parked the golf cart and escorted us out to the bungalows. The path split at the beach, with John and Cheryl's room to the right and mine to the left.

Cheryl leaned in and gave me a hug. I thought she was going to ask me if I was OK. Instead, she said, "Do you need a condom? I think John has one in his bag."

"No!"

She shrugged, and then she and John said, "Goodnight."

When I continued on the path to my room, Jack followed.

"Do you want me to come in?" he asked as I tried to fit the key into the lock. I leaned back against the door and closed my eyes. Did I want Jack to come in? Hmmm.

"Lizzie, wake up." He had me by the shoulder, but I couldn't have been asleep. I'd just closed my eyes for a second.

Jack took the key from my hand and unlocked the door just in time. I reached the bathroom seconds before I started retching. I don't know what Jack did while I was giving back every cocktail I'd drunk, but he was sitting on the couch when I returned to the bedroom. I remember smiling at him right before I fell on the bed.

I woke up to the sound of a fist pounding on the door to the room. It was getting to be a habit, one I didn't like.

Before I could rouse myself, a male voice said, "I'll answer it."

"Jack?"

The door cracked open and sunlight flooded the front of the suite. I could see Jack in his boxers standing inside the room, and the outline of two men behind him in the doorway.

"Is this Mrs. Lizzie Garcia's room?" I heard one of the men ask in a thick Spanish accent.

"Jack, who is it?"

"Lizzie, I think you should get up."

I was still wearing last night's clothes, so I slid out of bed and stumbled to the door with my hair uncombed and the taste of vomit still on my breath. "I'm Lizzie Mancini," I said, trying not to breathe on anyone.

"Are you the wife of Michael Garcia?" the man on the left asked. As my eyes adjusted to the light, I could see they were wearing uniforms, but I still couldn't make out the words on their badges.

"No," I said.

The other man, the younger of the two, held up a Polaroid of Michael's face looking pale and bloated. "This man is not your husband?"

I glanced at Jack. "Ex-husband. Or soon to be ex-husband. We're getting a divorce. Why?"

They looked at each other then back at me. The one with the photo said, "We found your husband on the beach this morning."

"You found Michael on the beach? Is he OK?"

"No," the other man answered. "He's dead."

CHAPTER 18

I dropped my hand and stared at the two men, not caring that I was filling the air with my sour vomit breath. "But I just saw him yesterday."

"Yes," the older man said, "We'd like to talk to you about that."

Jack stepped closer. "Lizzie was with me all night."

Well that answered the *did he or didn't he spend the night* question. I sure wished I could remember it.

"We'd like to ask you a few questions too, sir," the younger man said.

My eyes had finally adjusted to the light and I was able to read their badges. *Camus Caye Police Department.* And I thought this was a bad vacation yesterday. It was turning into a nightmare. My head was pounding, and I was so dehydrated I felt like I was going to faint. "I need to sit down."

"Of course," the older officer said and followed me inside my room.

The couch was warm from Jack's body. I didn't know why he'd spent the night. I was pretty sure nothing had happened between us since I was still wearing yesterday's clothes and he'd obviously slept on the sofa. But whatever his reason, I bet he was regretting it now.

The older officer sat down on the chair across from me and handed me a bottle of water. "Officer Martinez," he commanded, "why don't you give us some privacy."

The younger man nodded and motioned for Jack to follow him outside. I watched him as he grabbed last night's jeans and T-shirt off the floor and slipped into them, but he refused to make eye contact with me.

"Is he your lover?" the older officer asked when the door had shut behind them.

"No!" I said when I'd stopped choking. "Why would you think that?"

He raised his bushy eyebrows and stared at me.

OK, dumb question. He found a man in my room at seven o'clock in the morning wearing nothing but boxer shorts. It was the obvious conclusion. "I swear, nothing happened."

I couldn't tell whether he believed me or not. He nodded and unbuttoned his shirt pocket, pulling out a small pad and pencil. "How long were you and Mr. Garcia married?"

"Excuse me but, who are you?"

He set his pad and pencil on the coffee table. "Forgive me. I'm Sergeant Alejo Ramos of the Camus Caye Police Department. I'm sorry for your loss, Mrs. Garcia."

I thanked him and hoped I looked like a grieving widow, praying for the moment when I'd wake up and realize this had all been a bad dream.

He picked up his pad again and flipped it open to a clean page. "How long did you say you were married?"

"Um, not long." Please understand, under normal circumstances, I would never lie to the police. But when they showed me Michael's picture with Jack standing right next to me, I panicked. What was I supposed to say? "Just kidding, we were only pretending to be married." Then I'd really look like a liar, and that couldn't be good. Better to stay the course until this whole mess was over with.

"What exactly does that mean, Mrs. Garcia? A month? Six months? A year?"

"Oh no, we were on our honeymoon." Best to stick to the story Michael and I had concocted. Surely they'd be questioning the hotel's other guests.

Sergeant Ramos scrunched his forehead, causing his eyebrows to converge into a giant black unibrow. "Didn't you tell me earlier you were getting a divorce?"

"Yes, we are. Or were. We knew right away things weren't working out."

"I see. And who wanted the divorce?"

"I did. We both did." Keeping the lies straight was harder than I'd thought it would be.

He scribbled something on his pad and continued to question me about Michael and our relationship. Of course, he asked me the last time I'd seen Michael and I had to tell him about our fight at the pool.

"Why do you think he reacted that way?" the sergeant asked.

"I don't know. I guess he was jealous."

"Did he have reason to be?"

"Well, Manuel was staring at my chest, but it's not like I was looking back."

"Manuel?"

"The scuba boat captain. He came back to the pool with me to open the safe."

"The safe?"

"In the towel hut. I needed to fix my form."

"What form?"

My head was throbbing, my stomach was gurgling, it was finally starting to sink in that Michael was actually dead, and he wanted to know about a form? You question suspects, not grieving widows, when it occurred to me... "Officer, how did Michael die?"

The sergeant glanced down at his pad. "You were telling me about a form you needed to fix. What was it for?"

"I'm not answering any more questions until you tell me how my husband died. I have a right to know." I was pretty sure a wife would have a right to know. She should.

"He was stabbed," he said in a monotone. "The hotel's groundskeeper found your husband's body this morning washed up on the beach."

Poor Michael. "But why?"

"That's what we're trying to find out. Do you know anyone who would want to harm your husband, Mrs. Garcia? People he owed money to or who might've had a grudge against him?"

"No," I answered honestly.

He nodded again. "You'll need to go to the hospital to identify the body."

Hospital? "Why is Michael at the hospital?"

"Because that's where the morgue is, Mrs. Garcia."

I shivered. I'd never seen a dead body. I'd never even been to a funeral. The only person I knew who'd ever died was my grandfather, when I was five, and my mother wouldn't let me go to the service because she thought it would give me bad dreams.

Sergeant Ramos closed his pad and stood up. "We can talk more later. I'll pick you up at noon."

I nodded and walked him to the door. I was about to shut it behind him when he spun around. "Just one more thing, Mrs. Garcia." He was amazingly agile for a man fifty pounds over-weight. "May we see your husband's things?"

"His things?"

"Yes, his clothes and his luggage. We need to search for something that might give us a clue as to who may have done this to him."

"He doesn't have any things."

"Pardon?"

How could I explain that we not only had separate rooms, but separate hotels? I couldn't. "He took all his stuff with him yesterday."

"After the fight at the pool?"

"No, before. It was gone when I got back here."

"Then he must've been planning on leaving, even before the fight?"

"I guess so." As soon as the words left my mouth, I realized it was the wrong thing to say.

Sergeant Ramos stared at me for a few seconds, and then reminded me again that he'd return for me later and left.

"Sweet Jesus, what have I done?"

CHAPTER 19

I looked at the clock. It was almost 9:00 a.m. Belize time, which meant it was almost 7:00 a.m. in Los Angeles. I grabbed my wallet, ran to the hotel's lobby, punched my credit card number into the pay phone, and dialed.

"Hello?" Jane answered sleepily.

"Wake up, I need your help."

"Who is this?"

"It's Lizzie!" I'd been gone five days and she'd already forgotten my voice?

"Lizzie, what's wrong?"

"I think I'm in trouble," I whimpered. I wasn't sure if the tears were for Michael or for me. Probably both. "Michael's dead."

"Who's Michael?"

"The guy from the bar. Didn't you get my e-mail?"

"Oh my God, Lizzie. What did you do?"

"What do you mean, what did I do? I didn't kill him."

"I know you'd never hurt someone intentionally, but I've seen you when you're angry."

"Yeah, I scream and yell and throw things, but I don't kill people!"

"OK, calm down, I'm only asking."

And this was from my best friend! God only knew what the police were thinking. Of course, they've never seen me throw a vase at someone's head. But Steven really deserved it.

"Start at the beginning," she said. "And don't leave anything out."

Fifteen minutes later, Jane knew the whole story, including a physical description of all the major players. Jane always liked me to describe people in terms of what actor they most resembled so she could picture them in her head. Michael she'd met, Jack was a cuter, unbroken-nosed version of Owen Wilson, and Sergeant Ramos could've passed for a slightly older and overweight version of Miguel Sandoval, the actor who played the DA on *Medium*.

"What do I do?" I asked.

"Are you a suspect?"

"I don't know. They didn't arrest me. But Sergeant Ramos is coming back at noon to take me to ID Michael's body." Just thinking about it made me shiver.

"That's routine," she said dismissively.

"How do you know?" As far as I was aware, she'd never had to ID a dead body.

"*Law & Order*. It's on every night."

"You know I only watch *SVU*."

"They have dead bodies on *SVU* too."

"Occasionally. Most of the time the victims are still alive and they've only been raped."

"Oh please, they kill people off on *SVU* all the time, and they *always* get ID'd by the next of kin."

"Well excuse me for not being up on my police procedure. Would you like to pass along any other useful tips from your extensive television watching?"

"Yes," she said. "The spouse is always a suspect."

That much I knew. "But we're not married."

"Well the police think you are, so you need to come clean with them immediately."

"I wanted to, but after I lied when they showed me Michael's picture I had to follow it through to the end. But you're right. I'm going to tell Sergeant Ramos the whole story as soon as he gets back."

"No! You can't talk to him without a lawyer."

"Why not? I'm innocent."

"Innocent people get convicted all the time, Lizzie. Do you want to spend the rest of your life in a Belizean jail getting raped every day, or worse?"

"What's worse than that?"

"A lethal injection."

My knees started to buckle and I grabbed the side of the phone booth for support. "But I didn't do it. I swear!"

"I know you didn't, Lizzie, and I didn't mean to scare you. Who knows if they even have the death penalty in Belize. And the rape thing only happens in men's prison. Right now you need to calm down and focus on finding yourself a good lawyer."

"How do I do that? Half the country doesn't even speak English. Or not our English anyway."

"I don't know," she said, "but I'll figure something out. Have you eaten breakfast yet?"

"I just told you the police think I murdered a man and you want to know if I've eaten breakfast?" I shouted, and then realized the handful of other people in the lobby were staring at me and lowered my voice. "Are you kidding me?"

"I'll take that as a no. Go eat breakfast and call me back."

"But I'm not hungry," I quietly spat out word by word.

"I don't care. Breakfast is the most important meal of the day and you need to keep your strength up. Order something with lots of protein and go light on the carbs. Carbs make you sleepy."

"And then what?"

"By the time you finish I'll have figured something out."

"What exactly?"

"I don't know yet. Something."

Somehow that didn't bring me much comfort.

I went to the dining room, but just the smell of food made me nauseous, so I ordered dry toast and a can of Coke to go. I ate alone in my room before I finally brushed my teeth, ripped off last night's sweaty clothes, and took a long, hot shower. When I emerged from the steam, I knew exactly what to do. I would find Cheryl and ask her to introduce me to the criminal lawyer couple from Boston. Even if they weren't the world's best lawyers, at least they spoke American English.

I didn't start to panic again until I knocked on Cheryl's door and she didn't answer. I pounded for another five minutes until I remembered that she and John had signed up for Jack's Discover Scuba class this morning. Suddenly last night seemed like another life.

When I arrived at the pool, Jack was passing out masks, snorkels, and fins to his students, which didn't include John or Cheryl. But Jack spotted me. "Lizzie, hold up," he called and left his students in the shallow end while he hurried to my side. "We need to talk," he said quietly.

"I know. Can you come by later this afternoon?" I didn't know how long it would take to ID a body. Luckily, I'd never had to before.

"I can come by after work. Around five?"

We agreed to meet at my room. I sure hoped Sergeant Ramos and his men wouldn't be around for that conversation too.

CHAPTER 20

I found Cheryl sunning herself on a lounge chair at the beach.

"I thought you were taking the scuba diving class."

"I can't," she said. "I'm pregnant. It never occurred to me to ask until I checked the box on the medical form. But Jack said I could still come for the snorkeling tomorrow if I wanted. He's such a sweetheart."

I agreed.

"So what happened last night?" Cheryl asked, lowering her voice.

"You don't want to know."

She closed her paperback and tossed it in her bag. "Of course I do. Tell me everything."

I sat down on the foot of her lounger with my head in my hands.

She nudged my leg with her toe. "C'mon, it can't be *that* bad."

"Wanna bet! He came back to my room, where I promptly puked my guts up, then passed out in bed. But that's not even the bad part."

"That sounds pretty bad to me."

I didn't know how to say it, so I blurted it out. "Michael's dead." And the tears started rolling down my cheeks. Again.

"What!"

The couple on the next set of loungers turned and stared before quickly turning their attention back to their books and magazines.

Cheryl slid down to the bottom of the chair and put her arm around me, shading us both under her extra-wide-brimmed hat. "How did it happen?"

"I don't know. The police told me he was stabbed. That's why I came to find you. Can you introduce me to those two criminal lawyers you mentioned the other night?"

"The police think you had something to do with it?" She was incredulous, which I took as the first good sign. Cheryl had only known me for three days and even she realized I wasn't capable of murder. Surely, the police would too.

"I'm not sure, but they were asking a lot of questions this morning."

"But you were with us last night. We'll vouch for you. And I'm sure Jack will too."

"Thanks, but that's why I need to talk to a lawyer. I have to find out my rights."

She stood up and slipped her feet into flowered flip-flops and tied a matching sarong around her waist. I followed her to the row of bungalows behind the beach along the tree line. "They're two down from us," she said, "in the Banana Suite."

Cheryl knocked on the door of a pale-yellow bungalow, which was promptly opened by a petite dark-haired woman with a killer tan. "Cheryl, what's up?"

"Karen, I'm so glad you're in. This is my friend Lizzie."

"Nice to finally meet you," Karen said and smiled. Clearly Cheryl had gossiped about me too.

"Can we come in?" Cheryl asked.

"Actually, now's not a great time. We're packing and Jeremy's got his crap spread out all over the room."

My stomach clenched. "Packing! Are you leaving?"

"Not until tonight. They told us they'd hold our luggage—what's wrong?"

I couldn't speak. The only thing keeping me from completely breaking down was the thought that I would have someone here with me that would know what to do.

"Lizzie needs a lawyer," Cheryl said. "Her husband, or soon to be ex-husband, was killed yesterday and—"

"Oh my God," Karen said. "Are you OK?"

I nodded and Cheryl said, "She was with us last night, but the police are asking her a lot of questions."

"Of course," Karen said. "The wife, especially soon to be ex-wife, is always a suspect. You better come in."

I didn't see Jeremy, but his stuff was everywhere. Karen grabbed the tennis rackets off the couch and told us to sit down. Then she went into the bathroom and retrieved Jeremy.

"Can't this wait?" he said, as she pulled him into the sitting area. He still had a dab of shaving cream on his cheek and a bloody nick on his chin. "Oh, hi," he said when he noticed Cheryl and me.

"Jeremy, this is Lizzie. Her husband, the one who caused all the ruckus at the pool yesterday, was murdered and the police suspect she was involved."

"Oh my," he said, wiping the stray shaving cream onto the towel draped around his neck.

"I don't know if they think I did it, but they asked me a lot of questions and the sergeant is coming back soon to take me to ID his body."

"And to question you some more, I'm sure," Jeremy said.

"That's why she needs to find a lawyer quick," Karen added.

"I was sort of hoping to hire you two."

Jeremy shook his head. "We're leaving in a couple of hours, but even if we weren't, we can't represent you. We're not licensed here, nor do we know anything about Belizean law."

"But we can give her some general pointers, can't we, honey?" Karen said as she handed her husband a T-shirt, which he pulled over his head.

"Of course," he replied tossing the towel onto the floor and taking a seat across from me. "But you need to find local counsel pronto."

"And how do I do that?"

"I bet the embassy has a list," Karen said.

"Definitely," Jeremy agreed. "You should call them right away and alert them to your situation. They might be able to help."

"Can they get me a lawyer?"

"Probably not," Jeremy said. "But they can help in other ways. First tell me everything you know about what happened to your husband."

Now would probably be a good time to come clean about Michael. As criminal lawyers, he and Karen must be used to people lying to them, so they wouldn't hold it against me. I wasn't so sure about Cheryl. She struck me as more of an honesty is the best policy type.

Jeremy noticed where I was looking. "Cheryl, why don't you go call the consulate while Karen and I talk to Lizzie."

"Oh, I don't need to leave," Cheryl said, pulling her cell phone out of her beach bag. "It's international."

Jeremy looked at me and rolled his eyes. "I know, Cheryl, but you can't be in the room when we talk to Lizzie. It has to be lawyer-client only, otherwise it's not privileged."

I silently thanked him for finding an excuse to get her out of the room.

She jumped up from the couch. "Sorry, I didn't realize. Lizzie, I'll just wait for you out by the pool."

Karen located her purse under a pile of clothes on the bed. "Wait, I'll go with you. I want to see what I can find on the Internet."

When the door shut, Jeremy turned back to me. "Start at the beginning. And we don't have much time, so skip the lies and tell me what really happened."

I told him everything, from meeting Michael at the bar at LAX to Sergeant Ramos finding Jack in my room. I skipped over the part where I was lusting after Jack, but I think he figured that out for himself.

"Boy, you're really in a pickle."

These are not the words you want to hear from your lawyer.

CHAPTER 21

Since it was already a quarter to twelve, Jeremy suggested I go back to my room and wait for Sergeant Ramos while he went to find Karen to see what she had uncovered on the Internet.

"I'm sure all your clients tell you they didn't do it even if they really did, but I swear to you, I really didn't."

"I believe you," Jeremy said. "You had no motive. But I'm not the one you need to convince."

"Do you think I should tell Sergeant Ramos the whole story just like I told you?"

"No! Don't say anything to the police without a lawyer. As soon as you're finished ID'ing the body, call the consulate and ask them to help you find one right away. In the meantime, whatever info Karen dug up we'll leave for you with Cheryl."

I thanked him for everything and he gave me his business card. "We won't get back to Boston until tomorrow morning, but that's got my cell number on there. It should start working again as soon as we reach Miami."

I thanked him again and left. When I arrived back at my room, Sergeant Ramos was already waiting.

"You're early," I said.

"I like to be prompt. Shall we go?"

Sergeant Ramos led me to his police car, a small, white four-door sedan with a single blue light on top. It was the first real car I'd ridden in since I'd arrived.

Sergeant Ramos started chatting even before I'd buckled up. He told me about his family—his wife of twenty-nine years, his two grown sons, and his daughter who was in her last year at Catholic high school.

"Do you have any children?" he asked as he pulled into the parking lot of the Camus Caye Hospital.

"No."

"Do you want children?"

"I guess so." I didn't understand how any of this could be relevant to his investigation.

"Did your husband?"

"I don't know. We never discussed it." At least that was an honest answer.

Sergeant Ramos parked the car and raced around to hold the door for me even though I'd already opened it myself. Very weird. I was starting to feel like we were on a date, except for the part about his wife and kids, of course.

I followed Sergeant Ramos into the squat, gray cinder block building. As we navigated the maze of hallways, he greeted everyone we passed by name. At the end of the last hall, he led me into an empty room with closed doors on both ends. The only furniture was a set of plastic molded chairs. Sergeant Ramos told me to take a seat, then left the room. He returned a few minutes later through a different door, followed by a much younger man in blue hospital scrubs wheeling a metal cart.

"Are you ready?" Sergeant Ramos asked.

I nodded yes even though the answer was no. My heart was pounding and my stomach was doing flip-flops. Please, God, let it not be Michael. Let this all be one huge terrible mistake.

The man in the scrubs pulled back the faded white sheet so all that was visible was a head. I took one look at Michael—puffy face tinged slightly green, pale lips, purple bruise on his cheek where Manuel hit him—and nodded my head. Then I turned around and threw up all over the linoleum floor.

"I'm so sorry," I said, tears streaming down my face.

"It's OK," Sergeant Ramos replied, putting his arm around me and leading me out to the hallway. "Happens all the time." He walked me down another hallway to a ladies' restroom and told me he'd wait outside.

I washed my face, rinsed my mouth, and tried to get the image of Michael's pale and bloated face out of my mind. I still couldn't quite grasp someone being alive and fighting with me one day and gone forever the next. This had to be a nightmare, but no matter how hard I tried, I couldn't wake myself up.

"Better?" Sergeant Ramos asked when I returned to the hallway sucking on a breath mint.

"Yes, thanks," I said and tried to smile.

"Are you hungry?" Sergeant Ramos asked.

"Not really."

"I know a great place nearby," he continued as if he hadn't heard me. "They have the best tortilla soup on the island. I've never tasted better. Shall we give it a try?"

Did I have a choice?

We left the car in the hospital parking lot and walked the three blocks to Tanya's Kitchen, a tiny storefront with a handful of plastic tables and chairs, and walls covered with brightly colored murals. Sergeant Ramos procured us a table under a whirring ceiling fan.

"It's the coolest spot in here," he said.

I believed him, but it was still hot.

He ordered a basket of fish tacos for himself, tortilla soup for me, and two Coke Lights.

"Don't be embarrassed about earlier," he said, pulling two paper napkins out of the dispenser and setting one in front of me. "It's a common reaction. Sometimes even we hardened policemen have a tough time."

I fingered the scratch marks in the table and tried to smile.

"So what made you choose Belize for your honeymoon?"

That was a question I'd been asked many times before and I answered automatically. "Steven wanted someplace tropical, but he didn't want to—"

"Who's Steven?"

Oops. "Did I say Steven?" I forced a smile and said, "Michael likes me to call him that sometimes. Don't ask," I added in response to the question already forming on Sergeant Ramos's lips. "Anyway, he wanted tropical, but not Hawaii because he'd already been, and Jane vetoed Mexico because it's too dirty. My maid of honor," I told him before he could ask. "So I started researching and that's how we ended up in Belize."

Then the food arrived and gave Sergeant Ramos something to focus on besides me. While he enjoyed his fish tacos, I swirled my soup and sipped my Coke Light. When it was clear I wasn't going to eat it, Sergeant Ramos finished my soup, then ordered an espresso and a slice of key lime pie.

"It could take awhile for the autopsy," he said between bites of whipped cream. "Our coroner works on two other islands and he's not scheduled to be back here again until Monday."

I nodded so he would know I was listening.

"But you can start making the arrangements now if you want. I'll contact you as soon as the body's released."

"What kind of arrangements?"

"For the funeral. I assume you want to fly the body back to the States. Will you be having a traditional burial or a cremation?"

Funeral. Body. Cremation. This had to stop. "Sergeant Ramos, there's something I've got to tell you."

He set his fork down mid-bite. "Of course, Mrs. Garcia. You can tell me anything."

"My name's not Mrs. Garcia; it's Elizabeth Mancini. Michael and I weren't married. In fact, I hardly knew the man. I just met him a few days ago at the airport in LA."

His expression remained inscrutable. "This is a very dramatic change of circumstances, Mrs. Garcia, I mean, Ms. Mancini." He pulled his pad and pencil from his breast pocket. "Please tell me exactly how you came to know the late Mr. Garcia."

I spilled my guts to him just as I had to Jeremy. And I know what you're thinking—I was supposed to wait until I had a lawyer. But I just couldn't keep up the charade any longer. Michael's real family had a right to know. His mother had a right to know her son was dead. Assuming he still had a mother. I didn't even know that.

When I finished, he set down his pad and pencil and sipped his coffee, which had to be cold by now. His expression had finally changed. He was clearly angry. "I don't understand. Why didn't you tell me this from the beginning?"

"I wanted to, but I couldn't. Jack was standing right there."

"And when he left the room? Why not then?"

"I was afraid if I told you then, you wouldn't believe me. That you'd think I was lying because I had something to do with Michael's murder and was trying to cover it up."

"And now? Why should I believe you now?"

"Because it's the truth."

He glanced at the check the waitress had left earlier and slammed a handful of bills down on the table. "Ms. Mancini, your false statements have impeded the progress of this investigation, possibly beyond repair. I will take you back to your hotel now, but I expect you to make yourself available for further questions."

"Of course." I felt like a little kid being scolded by my father.

He stood up and I followed him out to the street. We walked the few blocks to the hospital parking lot in silence. I felt bad that he was angry, and I certainly hoped my conduct didn't ruin his chances of finding Michael's killer. But I also felt free. Unfortunately, that emotion was short-lived.

CHAPTER 22

When I returned to the hotel, I immediately began searching for Cheryl. I found her in the dining room, eating lunch with John and another couple I'd seen around the premises but had never been introduced to.

She didn't smile or wave to me, but I knew she spotted me too because the woman she was talking to turned around and eyed me before resuming their conversation. Undeterred, I walked up to their table. "Cheryl, thanks again for this morning. I'm really glad I got to talk to Jeremy. Do you know if Karen found anything?"

"I don't," she replied in an icy tone before stuffing a huge bite of salad into her mouth.

"I'm sorry. I didn't mean to interrupt your lunch. I'm just really anxious to wrap this up. Do you want to stop by my room when you're finished?"

She chewed loudly for several more seconds, then swallowed. "Not really."

She couldn't be this mad because I interrupted her meal, even if she was pregnant. I bent down next to her chair. "Did I do something to offend you?"

John put his hand on my shoulder. "Lizzie, it's probably better if you left now."

"No, John," then Cheryl turned to face me. "I think Lizzie should know we're not as stupid as she thinks."

"I don't think you're stupid. Where did you get that idea?"

"Oh pleeeease. You've been lying from the moment we met you. You and your," she added quote marks with her fingers, "'husband.' You two deserve each other. Too bad he's dead."

"Cheryl!" Even John seemed surprised by her venom.

I was so taken aback I actually fell back onto my butt. "Who told you?"

"That's what you're worried about?" Cheryl sneered.

I'd thought my conversation with Jeremy was confidential. "Cheryl, I'm sorry. We were never trying to fool anyone—"

"Ha!"

"No, really. I just didn't want to spend my honeymoon alone. My fiancé dumped me the day before the wedding and—"

She took another huge bite of her salad and began chewing extra loud. Clue to me—she's not interested.

"Again, I apologize. To all of you."

The other couple at the table looked down at their plates and John said, "I'm sure you had your reasons, but I think it would be better if you left now."

I slunk back to my room, where I found two envelopes sticking out from under my door. The first one had a note from Jeremy:

Lizzie—

Good news! Karen was able to locate some information on Belize police procedure on the Internet. Since it's a former British colony, it's very similar to ours. In other words, you have the right to remain silent. Use it! You also have the right to speak to a lawyer. Call the consulate and ask them to help you find one and tell the police you're not making any statements until your lawyer arrives. Call us when you get back so we know you're OK. Good luck.

Jeremy

The second envelope contained a fax from Jane:

Lizzie,

I called the embassy in Belize and alerted them to your situation. The officer I spoke with faxed me this list of local criminal attorneys. He said they can't call on your behalf or even recommend someone, but off the record, he'd heard that David Barron was pretty good. Start with him and work your way down, then call me so I know you're OK.

Jane

No need for the lawyer now that I'd already fessed up to Sergeant Ramos. And if Cheryl knew the truth, then everyone else at the Blue Bay Beach Resort knew it too (or would by the end of the day). The only person left to tell was Jack.

CHAPTER 23

I'd given up trying to read. I couldn't concentrate on anything. My mind kept returning to the image of Michael's head sticking out from under that white sheet. It just didn't make sense. Why would someone want to murder an anthropology professor?

I was still unsuccessfully trying not to think about Michael when Jack appeared. I've heard people say they craved sex after a funeral. Something about it being life affirming. That must apply to seeing your first dead body too because as soon as I saw Jack—tan legs pushing through the sand, broad shoulders hunched slightly forward, the wind blowing his blond hair into his eyes—I wanted to jump his bones.

He stopped a few feet from my lounge chair and I inhaled the faint odor of salt water and Coppertone. "Hi," he said, and then gave me a half smile.

Don't salivate, Lizzie, it's unbecoming. "Hi, yourself."

"Do you want to go out on the boat? We could watch the sunset and we won't be interrupted."

He must have been reading my mind. "Sure, let me go change."

"You're fine. As you may have noticed, we're pretty informal around here."

I had, although he was wearing what appeared to be a new T-shirt. I could still make out the Harry's Bar slogan on the pocket. Was this a date? I wouldn't have thought being questioned by the police because he crashed on my couch would've made him want to get to know me better. But maybe he's one of those guys that's attracted to dangerous women. Lizzie Mancini, Spider Lady. Ha! Was he in for a surprise. The only crime I'd ever committed was running a red light.

I slipped my shorts and tank top over my bathing suit. "Do you think I need a sweatshirt?"

"I've got a jacket you can borrow if you get cold."

A regular Boy Scout.

Jack piloted the dive boat a few miles out to sea before dropping anchor. For an instant, I thought about Michael, wondering how far out at sea he'd been before he was stabbed and left for dead. I shook my head to banish the thought as Jack appeared with a flannel blanket and two bottles of beer. He spread the blanket across the front deck, and we sat side by side with our backs against the cabin's windows as we watched the sun slowly drop behind the clouds.

"Cheers," he said, clinking his bottle against mine.

"What are we toasting to?"

"I don't know. How about to a better night than last night?"

"Or at least a better morning," I replied and took a swig of my beer. And since he'd brought it up— "Um, nothing happened last night, right?"

"I wouldn't say nothing, seeing as someone murdered your husband. Doesn't that make you a widow instead of a divorcée?"

I knew I needed to come clean with Jack about Michael, but considering Cheryl's reaction, I wasn't eager to. Instead, I said, "No, I meant between us."

He grinned like he was about to say something wicked, then thought better of it. "Nothing much."

Nothing much. That wasn't quite the same as nothing. "If nothing much happened, then why did you spend the night?"

"Can't I just enjoy the pleasure of your company?"

"When you're sleeping alone on a love seat while I'm six feet away half-naked in a king-size bed? No."

"Good point," he said, which he followed with a long swallow of beer but no elaboration. I was still trying to work up the nerve to tell him the truth when he said, "You should be thanking me, you know."

"Why? What did you do?" I knew what I wanted him to do but I didn't think that fell into the category of "nothing much."

"I'm your alibi. If it wasn't for me, you'd probably be in jail right now."

That killed the fantasy. "What are you talking about?"

"Didn't you realize you were a suspect?"

"Not anymore. I told the police everything. They know I had no reason to kill Michael."

Jack gave me a questioning look, then dropped it. "Maybe not, but Officer Martinez sure was interested in your whereabouts last night. Don't worry. I told him you were with me *and* I had proof."

"What proof?" Please let it not involve a videotape destined for YouTube or *Girls Gone Wild*.

"Your snoring." He pulled on his ear with his free hand. "I think you might've punctured an eardrum."

"I do not snore!"

"Are you sure? Because if not, then we weren't alone last night. Someone in your room was sawing down a forest."

I leaned back against the cabin windows and sipped my beer in silence. Steven might've complained about my snoring a few times over the years, but he'd said it had gotten a lot better since my sinus surgery. Maybe it was all the alcohol.

Jack elbowed me in the arm. "C'mon, don't be mad. I might've exaggerated a little for Officer Martinez's benefit."

"I'm not mad," I lied.

"You know what you need, don't you?"

God yes, but I couldn't jump him after he'd just busted me for snoring. "Another beer?"

"That too," he said, checking the level on my almost-empty bottle. "But what you really need is a head massage. It's not only a miracle cure for snoring, but it's guaranteed to make you feel better too."

"You know this from personal experience?"

He smiled and reached for my bottle. "I'll be right back."

When he returned, he allowed me one long sip of my second beer before he set both our bottles aside and told me to lie down.

"Excuse me?"

"I promise you'll want to be lying down for this."

"More personal experience?" I asked before sliding onto the blanket.

Jack sat down behind me and gently positioned my head. He started with his thumbs and slowly circled my temples. Then he added the rest of his fingers and began massaging my scalp. By the time his hands reached the base of my neck, I was hovering between extreme titillation and just wanting to drift off to sleep.

"Good?" he asked as the scales tipped toward slumber.

"Mmmmm. This is better than sex."

He slid his hands down the back of my neck. "Don't be so hasty."

That was enough to tip the scales back. I was flirting with an orgasm and his fingers never even reached below my shoulders.

CHAPTER 24

By the time Jack stopped massaging my shoulders, the sky, which had been shades of pink and orange when he'd started, was blue-black. "We missed the sunset."

Jack slid down next to me and propped his head up on one elbow. "Don't worry," he said and let his free hand rest on my stomach, sending hot sparks shooting in all directions. "There'll be another one tomorrow."

Then he leaned over and our lips had barely touched when a speedboat roared past us, spraying drops of seawater across the bow. I was so startled I bolted upright, smashing my head into Jack's cheek. "Oh my God, are you OK?"

"I will be," he said, rubbing his twice-in-two-days-wounded jaw.

We both watched as the speedboat U-turned and came back for a second pass. But this time, instead of spraying us, it idled alongside.

"Jack, mon, is that you?" the speedboat's captain yelled out.

"Hey, Manny," Jack said, but before he stood up he whispered, "Stay here."

"Whatcha doin' out here? Collecting da turtles again?" It was too dark to see his face, but I could hear the laughter in his voice.

"No, just having a beer," he said and reached down for the one he had left sitting on the deck.

I heard a click and then a bright white light was shining in my eyes.

"That you there, Lizzie?"

"Hi, Manuel," I said, shielding my eyes as I stood up too.

"Yeah," Manny said, "you collecting again, Jack."

I thought of several possible meanings, none of them positive. Jack said, "We were just heading in."

We were?

"Party tonight at the Blue Iguana. You can bring Lizzie."

"Maybe," Jack said.

"OK, mon. See you." Then the light clicked off, the engine revved, and Manny was gone.

I didn't know much about boats, but Manny's was sleek and fast and looked like something beyond the means of a dive boat captain unless there really was still gold left in those old underwater wrecks. "That's his boat?"

"His cousin's," Jack said, pushing one of my wayward curls behind my ear.

"What does his cousin do?" Whatever it was, it must be lucrative.

"You don't want to know."

Before I could answer that I did want to know—I was always on the lookout for a good story—he bent down and kissed me. His lips were rough and chapped, but his tongue felt like velvet as he explored my mouth and teased my own tongue. I was just starting to melt into him when something cold and wet splattered on my face.

"What the—"

"Just a raindrop," Jack said, wiping it away with his thumb. Then he leaned in again, but before our lips touched, another raindrop smacked my forehead.

Jack reached down for the blanket and wrapped it around my shoulders. "Want to go back to your place?"

Oh yes.

By the time we reached my bungalow, our clothes were sopping wet and clinging to us. I could've jumped him right there, but I hadn't showered after my long and sweaty day and I no longer smelled like the hotel's signature papaya-pineapple soap. I left Jack with my collection of airport-purchased magazines and strict instructions not to leave while I showered off the day's sweat and sunscreen. Then I changed into a form-hugging sundress with my black lace bra and panties underneath.

Jack greeted me with a wolf whistle and a bare chest; his T-shirt hung over the back of the desk chair, dripping water onto the purple rug. "Wow," he said. "Maybe I should go home and change."

I pulled the *Time* magazine out of his hands and tossed it on the coffee table, then hiked up my sundress so I could straddle his long, tan legs. "Don't even think about it, Scuba Boy."

"Scuba Boy?"

"You prefer Scuba Man?" Then I leaned in for a kiss, but he placed his hands on my shoulders and held me back.

"Lizzie, I'm not just some dumb beach bum."

"I know. You're a marine biologist." Although how that could possibly be relevant at this point in time when all I wanted to do was have sex with him, and judging from the bulge in his shorts he wanted to have sex with me too, I couldn't fathom.

"Almost," he said. "I'm in the doctoral program at Scripps."

"Scripps? Isn't that in San Diego?"

"Yeah, why?"

"Goddamnit!" I said and slid off his legs and onto the couch. "Couldn't you have waited until after we had sex to tell me?"

"What's wrong with San Diego?"

"Nothing, except it's less than two hours from where I live."

"And that's a problem?"

Of course it was a problem. This was supposed to be a vacation fling. Someone I'd have great sex with then never see again. I couldn't sleep with him if there was a chance I could actually date him. "If you go to school in San Diego, then what are you doing in Belize?"

"Field research. My specialty's loggerhead sea turtles. There's a nesting beach on the other side of the island. I could take you if you're interested."

It was my goddamn honeymoon and I *still* couldn't get laid. This was the worst vacation ever! "You should go."

"What! A minute ago you were all over me and now you want me to leave?"

"Yes," I said and grabbed his wet T-shirt off the desk chair and tossed it at him.

"What the hell is wrong with you?"

"Me? Do you always mention to women you're about to have sex with that you happen to live in San Diego? Was there some reason that little nugget of information couldn't wait?"

"What's wrong with San Diego?"

"Nothing," I said and sat back down on the couch feeling utterly defeated. Why had I even come to Belize?

"Maybe I was being presumptuous," he said as he yanked his wet T-shirt over his head, but his arms couldn't find the sleeves and he pulled it off again, "but I thought you'd be happy to hear we lived near each other."

I knew he wouldn't understand the vacation fling theory, men never do, but he seemed like a nice enough guy and he deserved the truth. "Hold on a sec. There's something I have to tell you."

"What? You really did kill your husband?"

"I don't have a husband. I never did."

"Ha, ha."

"It's not a joke. Michael wasn't my husband. I met him at the bar at LAX while I was waiting for my flight."

Jack's angry smile faded, replaced by a vacant stare somewhere above my head as I told him the story of how Michael became my fake husband and my soon to be fake ex-husband. He already knew the dead husband part of the story. I waited for him to speak, but after a while, I couldn't take the silence. "So what do you think?"

He finally looked at me. "I think you're nuts."

"In a good way?"

"No," he said, heading for the door. "You've been lying from the moment we met. For all I know, this is a lie too. Maybe you're one of those lunatics that can't tell fact from fiction."

"Jack, I swear, this is the truth. I'm sorry I lied but—"

He slammed the door shut behind him. In less than one week I'd managed to get dumped by my fiancé, get another man killed, a third to slam the door in my face, and alienate every other person I'd met on the island. This entire trip had been a mistake. To hell with the $2,200. I was getting out of here tonight.

CHAPTER 25

I went to the lobby to call the airline. The woman on the other end of the phone told me if I could catch the nine o'clock to Belize City, she could get me on the eleven o'clock to Miami, and then I could catch a 7:00 a.m. flight back to LA.

"Book it."

"OK, ma'am. That will be three thousand five hundred and fifty dollars."

"What happened to twenty-two hundred?"

"No, ma'am. The only seats available on the Miami flight are business class." I heard the tapping of her keyboard. "If you want to wait until Saturday—"

"No, just charge it." I'd worry about paying for it after I got home. That's what credit cards were for.

I asked the concierge to call me a taxi and I returned to my room to pack. I didn't even bother to fold the clothes. They were all going straight into the wash anyway. I just wished I could get rid of the memories that easily. An image of Michael on that cold metal table flashed through my head again, but I willed it away.

I didn't bother calling the bellman. My suitcase had wheels so I rolled it back to the lobby myself.

"I hope everything was all right, Mrs. Garcia," the desk clerk said. "May I ask why you're checking out early?"

He must be new if he hadn't heard about me. Even the house-keeper was looking at me funny today.

"Family emergency," I said and signed the bill without reading it. After all the debt I'd incurred for the wedding and now the honeymoon, what was a few thousand dollars more.

I arrived at the airport ten minutes before boarding, which was still plenty of time for my interisland flight to Belize City. I was surprised when I spotted Jeremy and Karen at the snack bar. I thought they'd left hours ago.

"Lizzie," Jeremy called, waving me over. "What are you doing here?"

I collapsed into the chair Karen offered. "Going home. This entire vacation has been a nightmare and I just want it to end."

"I'm so sorry about spilling the beans to Cheryl," Karen said. "It wasn't intentional. She overheard us talking and…"

So that's how Cheryl found out. I told Karen not to worry about it. "She probably wouldn't have taken it any better if I'd told her myself." Jack hadn't. "Now everyone knows."

"Then you told the police?" Jeremy asked.

"After I ID'd Michael's body." I shuddered, thinking about it again. "I know you said to wait for a lawyer but when Sergeant Ramos started asking me about the funeral arrangements, I just had to tell."

Jeremy nodded as he swallowed the last of his hot dog. "The police can be very persuasive. But at least they cleared you."

"What do you mean cleared me?"

"Didn't they tell you it was OK to leave the country?"

"I didn't ask. Was I supposed to?"

Before he could answer, a uniformed man walked up to our table. "Are you Elizabeth Mancini?"

"Yes."

"I need you to come with me, please."

Jeremy jumped up. "I'm her lawyer. What is this about?"

"I received a call from the police chief asking me to detain Ms. Mancini."

"But my flight's leaving—"

As if on cue, the PA cut me off to announce Maya Airlines flight number seventeen to Belize City would begin boarding from gate number three. Jeremy started arguing with the airport security guard, Karen tried to mediate, and I pushed our group toward the gate. I knew this was all just a big misunderstanding, and I didn't want any of us to miss our flight.

I was happy to see Sergeant Ramos walking toward us. He was out of uniform, but still easily recognizable with his badge pinned to his leisure shirt and his gun at his waist. He could explain to the guard that it was OK for me to leave.

He didn't seem as happy to see me. "Ms. Mancini, I thought we agreed you would make yourself available for further questions."

"Is this woman under arrest?" Jeremy demanded.

"Who are you?" Sergeant Ramos asked.

I handled the introductions and Jeremy explained that he and Karen were both lawyers back in Boston and were filling in until I obtained local counsel. "If this woman is not under arrest, you have no right to hold her here against her will."

"Mr. Markowitz, maybe you are not familiar with the laws in this country. I may detain Ms. Mancini if she has information about a crime."

Karen pulled some folded papers from her purse. "According to the Judges' Rules," she read, "if you detain her, you must inform her that she has the right to speak privately with her attorney before she makes any statements."

Sergeant Ramos sighed. "Ms. Mancini, you have the right to speak privately with an attorney. Do you wish to waive this right?"

"No," Jeremy answered. "Don't say a word, Lizzie. I'm calling the consulate. Karen, go find a pay phone."

"But, honey," she said, "we're going to miss our flight."

"I don't want you two to miss your flight." And I didn't want to miss it either. I wanted to answer Sergeant Ramos's questions and go home.

Jeremy shook his finger at me. "No talking, Lizzie."

"Do not intimidate my witness, Mr. Markowitz."

"You mean suspect, don't you, Sergeant Ramos?"

The accusations escalated with Sergeant Ramos threatening to arrest Jeremy for obstruction of justice (which I suspect isn't even a crime and he just picked it up watching American cop shows on TV) when the PA squawked again announcing the final boarding call for flight number seventeen to Belize City.

"Keep them here," Sergeant Ramos said to the security guard before stomping over to the gate. If his hand gestures were any indication, he had a short but heated conversation with the agent before he returned. "Your flight will be delayed ten minutes."

"That's not enough time—"

Sergeant Ramos held up his hand, silencing Jeremy midsentence. "I have a proposal that will allow all of us to get on with our plans for the evening."

"Whatever you want, we'll do it."

"Lizzie," Jeremy chided, "it's best to hear the proposal before agreeing to it."

Sergeant Ramos glared at Jeremy, but spoke to me. "I went to the Tortuga Inn this afternoon. Mr. Garcia did have a room there, and his home address did not match yours. The clerk also told us he had a lady friend with him the night before he died. A woman who did not match your description."

"That bastard!"

"Lizzie!"

"Sorry, Jeremy. But doesn't that prove I'm innocent?"

"Ms. Mancini, did you know Mr. Garcia dealt in stolen antiquities?"

"I knew he was an antiquities dealer, but he never said anything about them being stolen."

Jeremy sighed but didn't yell at me again, so my statement must not have been too incriminating.

Sergeant Ramos nodded. "We recovered some items from his room. But others, including some very valuable pieces, are still missing."

"And you think Michael may have stolen those too?"

"Lizzie, will you *please* stop talking."

"Yes," Sergeant Ramos continued, "we think Mr. Garcia may have been involved."

Jeremy clapped his hand over my mouth before I could answer. "And what does this have to do with my client?"

"We need to make sure Ms. Mancini wasn't involved."

I tried pulling Jeremy's hand away, but he had a firm grip.

"And how do you propose to do that?" Jeremy said.

"By searching Ms. Mancini and her luggage."

Excuse me?

"And if she doesn't have the stolen items in her possession?" Jeremy asked.

"Then of course she's free to go."

"Give me a minute to confer with my client." Jeremy dragged me a few feet away before loosening his grip on me. "I don't think you should agree."

Karen concurred. "If they want to search you, let them get a warrant."

"But can't they just search me at the airport anyway?"

"They can search you here for a weapon," Jeremy said.

"And before your international flight, the customs agents can search your luggage for specific items," Karen added.

"But not this random, 'I'm going to look at everything without probable cause' search," Jeremy continued.

"But they're not going to find anything. Whatever Michael was doing, he was doing it without me."

Jeremy and Karen were still debating the pros and cons of agreeing to a search when Sergeant Ramos interrupted. "I can't hold the flight all night. What's your decision?"

"Search it," I said. "I've got nothing to hide."

We all followed Sergeant Ramos outside to a metal cart piled high with luggage. I pointed to my bag and the security guard pulled it out of the stack and carried it back to the terminal.

I unlocked my suitcase and set my beach bag down next to it. Sergeant Ramos knelt to the floor and immediately began pawing at my clothes, my shoes, even my lingerie. He would shake each piece out, pat it down, then toss it onto a row of molded plastic chairs. When it was clear he wasn't going to stop until he'd pulled every item out of my suitcase, I sat down next to him and began folding.

After he'd finished with the main section of the suitcase, he moved to the zippered compartments on the outside.

"What's this?" he asked, squeezing inside the outermost pocket.

"My suitcase." Seeing all of my belongings, including my thong panties and padded bras, fondled and spread out in the waiting area for every person in the airport to see had not engendered my goodwill. Only a handful of passengers and airline employees were still around at that hour, but I still felt violated. And he hadn't even gotten to the strip search yet.

Sergeant Ramos pulled a Swiss Army knife out of his pocket and flipped open the blade.

"What are you doing?" I yelled as he began to slice a hole in my suitcase from the inside. I heard the lining tear, then…

"And what are these?" he asked.

We all stared at the chunks of jade resting in his hand.

CHAPTER 26

I was momentarily mesmerized by the three angry faces staring back at me. The smallest carving, which was about the size of a quarter, had giant lips and goggle eyes. Its mate had a square jaw, a pointy hat, and a wicked scowl. The largest piece would've been a perfect two-inch square if it didn't have a chunk missing from the upper right-hand corner. This face was the friendliest looking of the three, with squinty eyes, an upturned nose, and giant holes for nostrils.

"I swear to God," I said, still staring, "I've never seen those before in my life."

"What are they?" Karen asked.

"Ornaments." Sergeant Ramos tilted his hand toward Karen so she could have a better look. "They were worn by ancient Mayan kings and noblemen."

"Then why don't they have any gold or jewels?" Karen asked in prosecutor mode.

"This isn't Egypt," Sergeant Ramos replied testily. "In Central America, we used jade and shells."

"How old are they?" I asked, studying the jade faces.

"Pre-Columbian, I think," he said. "More than a thousand years old."

"What are they worth?" Karen asked before I could.

I wondered if she was thinking the same thing I was—if I paid for them, maybe they'd let me go. The large one actually looked

98

very similar to a pendant I'd seen in the hotel's gift shop. That one was brand new and had carvings that were more intricate, and it was only $49.95.

Sergeant Ramos quickly put an end to that fantasy. "They're priceless."

"What now?" Jeremy asked.

Sergeant Ramos nodded to the security guard, who grabbed both of my arms and held them behind my back.

"Hey, what are you doing?" I yelled, followed by Jeremy's, "Let go of her."

"Stand back, Mr. Markowitz," Sergeant Ramos said with his hand on his gun. "Ms. Mancini, you're under arrest."

"For what?"

"Possession of antiquities and intent to export antiquities."

"But I didn't even know they were in my suitcase!"

Sergeant Ramos cuffed my hands and started walking me toward the exit. "You don't have to say anything unless you wish to do so," he said, "but what you say may be taken down in writing and given in evidence. You may also speak privately with an attorney."

I looked back at Jeremy and Karen, too stunned to speak.

"Don't say a word," Jeremy yelled. "I'll call the consulate as soon as we land in Miami." Karen had her hand on his arm and was pulling him toward the gate.

In my mind I was screaming, *Please don't leave me*, but the words wouldn't come.

Sergeant Ramos yakked for the entire five-minute ride to the police station, but I have no idea what he said. My mind was racing: How did that jade get into my suitcase? I had to assume Michael had hidden it there. But why? And when? Sure, he had a key to the room, but as far as I knew, he'd used it only when I was there. He must've snuck in when I wasn't. Otherwise, how did the ornaments end up sewn into my bag? Someone stashed them in my suitcase and I knew it wasn't me.

Sergeant Ramos escorted me up the front steps of a dilapidated wooden structure and held tight to my arm as he unlocked the front door.

"Aren't police stations supposed to be open all night?" I'd always assumed they were a twenty-four/seven operation.

"Not on Camus Caye," he said as he flipped on the lights. I heard barking and turned to follow the sound. In the corner of the room was a six-foot-by-four-foot cell housing two dogs. The barking came from the smaller one, the mutt. Sergeant Ramos told him we had no food and he quieted down. The larger one, the German shepherd, merely opened one eye before falling back to sleep.

"Some guard dogs, eh?" he said and laughed.

The humor escaped me. "Aren't I entitled to a phone call?" People are always entitled to phone calls in the movies. Plus, I was an American. That had to count for something. I didn't want to cry, but I couldn't stop the tears from trickling down my cheeks.

Sergeant Ramos unlocked my handcuffs and handed me the handkerchief from his pocket. "Yes, Ms. Mancini, who would you like to call?"

"I don't know," I blubbered. "Does it have to be local?" The only two local people I could think of were Jack and Cheryl. Besides the fact that I didn't know their numbers, neither of them were speaking to me.

"No, but if it's out of the country you must call collect or charge it to your credit card. We don't have the budget for international calls."

That was obvious. The only furniture in the room was a beat-up desk, a folding table, and two chairs. No computer, no fax machine, not even AC. Just a phone, a fan, and a coffeemaker.

"That's OK," I said, punching in my credit card number and dialing Jane's cell phone. Thankfully, she picked up.

"Jane, it's me."

"Where are you? I called the hotel an hour ago and they told me you checked out."

"I'm at the police station."

I heard her gasp. "Did they arrest you? Do they really think you killed Michael? You better have gotten that list of lawyers I faxed you. The hotel swore—"

"Yes, I got it. But it's not about Michael, or not his murder anyway. They arrested me over stolen antiquities."

"For what?" was all I heard before her voice cut out. After that, I just heard static and the occasional burst of sound, then nothing.

"Jane? Can you hear me? Jane!" When the silence switched to a beeping sound, I handed the phone back to Sergeant Ramos. "We got cut off. Can I call again?"

"Maybe later," he said, settling himself behind his desk and motioning for me to sit too. I eased myself into the only other chair in the room, metal with a ripped vinyl seat.

Sergeant Ramos reached up and pulled the cord hanging from the ceiling fan, causing a flurry among the papers on his desk. He seemed not to notice.

"Ms. Mancini." He leaned back in his desk chair and clasped his hands behind his head, revealing two large sweat rings. "What are we going to do with you?" To be honest, he didn't seem all that concerned.

"You could send me home?"

He smiled. "I'm afraid I can't do that."

"Then I'm all out of ideas."

He picked up the phone and called someone named Paco. They spoke in a mixture of Spanish and English, but I was able to glean the gist of the conversation. Sergeant Ramos wanted to ship me off to Paco's jail, but Paco wasn't obliging. Sergeant Ramos hung up and muttered to himself.

"I still vote for sending me home."

Sergeant Ramos ignored me and focused on the dogs. "Boys, you're going to need to share tonight." The mutt barked, but the shepherd didn't move.

"Please don't put me in there. I'm afraid of dogs." I wasn't. I was just hoping for better accommodations.

"They're very friendly," he said. "Completely useless as guard dogs."

"I'm sure they are, but I'm *really* afraid of dogs."

He sighed. "I guess I could leave them in the bathroom. We don't like to let them have the run of the place because they tend to chew on whatever they can find."

That explained my chair.

Sergeant Ramos unlocked the cell and the mutt, Sundance, began jumping on him. The shepherd, Butch, still didn't move. The irony of two police dogs being named after famous outlaws was not lost on me, but it was lost on Sergeant Ramos. When I asked him about it, he just shrugged and went back to his desk for a box of doggie treats.

"C'mon, boys," he said, shaking the box above his head as he slowly backed out into the hall. Sundance jumped on his hind legs trying to reach them. Butch pushed himself up from his mat with obvious effort and loped after them.

"Satisfied?" he asked when both dogs were locked in the bathroom.

Actually, I had to pee, but I decided now was not the time to mention it. I reluctantly followed Sergeant Ramos back to the cell and was horrified when he lifted Butch's filthy mat from the floor and threw it on the metal cot.

"I'm not sleeping on that."

"Butch won't mind."

"Well I will. It's probably infested with fleas and God knows what else."

Sergeant Ramos ripped the mat off the cot and threw it back on the floor. "Then you can sleep on it without a mattress."

"C'mon," I said, softening my tone, "try to look at it from my perspective. I'm new to the criminal world. Up until a few hours ago, I was on my honeymoon."

He didn't seem amused. "I've got no other place for you. I tried Parrot Caye and their cell's being used. I don't think you want to room with an accused rapist, do you?"

"Definitely not." Even the flea bed would be better than that. "Isn't there somewhere else you could put me?" I pointed to the door next to the bathroom. "What's in that one?"

"Storage."

An hour and a half later, the Camus Caye Police Department had a new cell. We'd pushed the file cabinets into the corner, moved all the boxes to the main room, sent the dogs back to their cell, and transferred the cleaning supplies (which didn't look like they'd received much use) to the bathroom. Then I swept the floor while Sergeant Ramos grabbed a bench from the picnic table outside and a beach towel from the trunk of his car.

"I just need you to help me open these windows," I said, fighting with the rusted louvers, which, judging from the accumulation of dust, looked like they hadn't been opened in years.

He shook his head. "It wouldn't be secure."

"You can't leave me in here all night with no air-conditioning and no windows. I'll suffocate." Surely, even Belize had laws against cruel and unusual punishment.

"Wait here," he said and returned with his small desk fan.

"All that's going to do is blow hot air around."

"Then you can sleep with the dogs in the cell!"

I sighed. "Can't you put something on the outside of the windows?"

"Like what?"

"I don't know. Barbed wire?" Did I have to think of everything? He was the cop, I was just the prisoner, or detainee, as I preferred to think of myself.

"Wait here," he said again and disappeared outside. For a brief moment, I considered running, but before I could figure out where to run to, Sergeant Ramos returned with a hammer and a roll of chicken wire. "Come, I need your help."

I had to secure my own cell? Unbelievable. But if I could make it loose, then maybe... No such luck. Sergeant Ramos had me hold the wire in place while he hammered in the nails.

The phone rang just as we returned. Sergeant Ramos answered it, and then handed it to me with a look that made it clear I'd exhausted his patience.

"Finally!" Jane said when I picked up. "I tried you back as soon as I got out of the canyon, but all I got was a busy signal."

"I guess the Camus Caye Police Department doesn't have call waiting."

"No, but I did get through to my dad, who put me in touch with the ambassador, who promised to have someone out to you first thing in the morning."

Jane's dad was some bigwig in the State Department. I never could figure out exactly what he did, but he always managed to keep his job no matter which party was in the White House. I assumed it was because he made generous contributions to both sides' campaigns, but Jane insisted it was naked pictures. I was pretty sure she was kidding.

"You actually spoke to the US ambassador to Belize?" Mr. Chandler was definitely getting a Christmas card from me for the rest of his life.

"No, he's out of the country, so I had to speak to his deputy chief of something. But I have his home number, so if they don't send someone, there'll be hell to pay."

"You're the best, Jane."

"I know." No one had ever accused her of false modesty. "Do you think you can survive the night? I tried to get them to send someone sooner, but the deputy swore you couldn't get in to see the judge until morning anyway."

"I'll be OK." Now that I knew help was on the way.

"Good," she said. "You're never going to believe what happened to me this week." Then she started filling me in on her latest decorating emergency. Jane, who was rich and demanding herself, designed interiors only for other equally rich and demanding people. They liked her exacting nature and she liked telling them what to do. Running other people's lives is always much easier than fixing your own. Jane had just gotten started when Sergeant Ramos snapped his fingers, then slid his hand across his throat, which I presumed meant my time was up.

"Jane, I've got to go. But I'll call you tomorrow as soon as I'm out."

"Fine," she said, clearly annoyed that I'd interrupted her mid-story. "And I'd just like it noted for the record that I never once said, 'I told you so.'"

"Consider it noted."

"Be safe." Which was Jane's version of goodnight.

"You too," I said, and hung up.

"Anything else you need?" Sergeant Ramos asked. "Curtains for your window perhaps? Or a chocolate for your pillow?"

"I have a pillow?"

"Get inside."

He was gruff, but I think he was starting to like me. He brought me a second towel and even turned on the fan before he locked me in the storage room. I suspected for a warden that was as good as it got.

CHAPTER 27

I woke up with the roosters, literally. They must've lived nearby because they sounded like they were cock-a-doodle-dooing right outside my window. It was only five forty-five in the morning, but I knew I'd never fall back asleep. My back was aching and I could hardly turn my neck. Even with two beach towels, my bench wasn't meant for sleeping. Since I knew it would be hours before my promised lawyer arrived, I decided to make myself useful.

The cleaning supplies were locked in the bathroom, but I still had water and two towels, so I started with the window. I removed each piece of glass, washed it, dried it, and then returned it to the louvered frame. I was about to start on the floor when Sundance began barking. I waited until I heard footsteps and a "down boy" before I yelled for help.

"He wasn't kidding," the officer in the crisp khaki uniform said after he'd opened the storage room door. I guessed he was about my age, with dark hair, dark skin, and a vaguely familiar face.

"Hi, I'm Lizzie Mancini." I held out my hand, but it took him a few beats before he shook it. "I'm going to use the restroom, if you don't mind."

Then I ran across the hall to the bathroom before he could object. After I'd washed my face, combed my fingers through my hair, and prayed for a hot shower and a toothbrush (neither of which materialized), I emerged from the bathroom and found the officer still standing where I'd left him in the doorway to my storage room/cell.

"This place looks really good," he said.

"Thanks. You should see what I can do when I'm not a prisoner."

He didn't even crack a smile. That's when I finally remembered where I'd seen him before—he was the other policeman who'd appeared with Sergeant Ramos at my hotel room yesterday morning. It was hard to believe that was only twenty-four hours ago.

"So what's for breakfast?" I asked. I couldn't remember the last time I'd eaten and I was starving.

"I don't know," he said.

"Well what do you usually feed your prisoners?"

"We don't normally have prisoners," he finally smiled, "unless you count Butch and Sundance."

At the mention of his name, Sundance started barking again.

"I should go walk them." The officer motioned for me to return to the storage room.

"I could walk them with you." I was dying to leave the building, even if it was just for a few minutes.

"I don't think that's allowed."

"Why not? Even prisoners on death row get to exercise."

He shook his head. "I'd better not."

The more he said no, the more determined I became. "But I'll be with you the whole time. You can even handcuff me if you want to." Sundance moved on to whimpering and jumping back and forth, and even Butch barked twice. "I don't think they're gonna last much longer. And I'm not cleaning up that mess."

I don't know if it was my haranguing or the dogs' incessant barking, but the officer agreed. "You better not try anything," he warned as he reached for his handcuffs.

"I promise," I said as I held my hands out in front of me.

No leashes required on Camus Caye. No pooper-scooper laws either. Michael had been right—the beach by my hotel was much nicer than on this side of the island. But the view was just as good. The same clear turquoise waters, the same swaying palm trees, and another small island off in the distance. Maybe that was Parrot Caye. If you didn't notice the handcuffs or Officer Martinez's badge and gun, you'd think we were just a nice young couple taking their dogs for a walk on the beach.

When we returned to the station, I sat on the ripped chair, trying to ignore the shards of vinyl digging into the backs of my legs, while Officer Martinez fed the dogs and started a pot of coffee.

"Mmmm, food," I said, sniffing the air and inhaling the scent of bacon.

"Next door," Officer Martinez, or Juan as I was now calling him, said. "I eat breakfast there most mornings."

"But not today?" I asked as my stomach rumbled.

He shook his head. "Today I was more anxious to see what kind of joke Large Sarge was pulling on me."

"Large Sarge?"

"We used to have a third guy here, a skinny little guy named Marcos Cantalleros. That's what he called the Sergeant."

"What happened to him?"

"He transferred out. He and the Sarge didn't get on so well."

If he was calling him Large Sarge behind his back, I could understand why. "And now it's just the two of you?"

"Until Belize City sends us a replacement."

After Juan's stomach started rumbling too, I convinced him to go next door and buy us both breakfast. I even offered to pay, but he refused, which was a good thing since I had no idea where my wallet was. The last time I'd seen it, it was in the trunk of Sergeant Ramos's police car, along with my suitcase.

After the best bacon and eggs I'd eaten in years, which probably had more to do with my hunger than the quality of the food, Juan helped me move the bench/bed out into the hallway so I could wash the storage room floor. Then we sat at Sergeant Ramos's desk playing gin rummy while we waited for the floor to dry. I'd just won the third round when Sergeant Ramos walked in. Standing behind him were a man and a woman, both in business suits.

Juan immediately jumped up. "I was just keeping her out here until the floor dried," he said. "Lizzie cleaned the whole storage room."

Sergeant Ramos inhaled the bleach fumes. "So it seems. Ms. Mancini, your lawyer's here."

The woman standing behind him could've been a shampoo model. Her silky blonde hair shone in the sunlight and shimmied every time she turned her head. It was her gray pencil skirt and pearls that screamed *I take myself seriously.* "Hi, Lizzie," she said, extending her hand. "I'm Donna Kramer, consul with the US Embassy in Belize City." She turned to the man standing next to her. "This is your attorney, David Barron."

"Pleasure to meet you, Ms. Mancini," he said and offered his hand. "I wish it was under better circumstances."

The British accent startled me. I knew Belize had once been a crown colony, but David's was the first English accent I'd encountered since I'd arrived. Otherwise, he seemed like any other lawyer—expensive suit, leather briefcase, and receding hairline.

"I want you to know that the embassy normally doesn't bring attorneys when our citizens find themselves in trouble," Ms. Kramer said, "but your friend Jane was quite insistent."

"Yes," I said. "She can be." Thank God.

"I'd like to speak with my client," my new lawyer told Sergeant Ramos. "Is there somewhere we can talk privately?"

"Her cell," he replied.

"Right," David Barron said, "then perhaps you can excuse us."

Juan moved the bench back into the storage room so David would have somewhere to sit, and I stretched my legs out in front of me on the newly clean floor.

"This isn't bad, really," David said as he glanced around the storage room.

"It's not?"

"Be thankful you weren't arrested in Belize City," he said as he popped open his briefcase and removed a long yellow pad and an expensive-looking pen. "You'd have two or three people in here with you."

"Forgive me for not feeling lucky, Mr. Barron."

"Please, call me David. And start at the beginning."

CHAPTER 28

I didn't start at the beginning, but I managed to tell him the whole story anyway. All I wanted to know was, "When can I get out of here?"

"First we have to get you in front of a magistrate," David said. "If I can't get the case dismissed, which to be honest at this point I probably can't, I'll at least get you out on bail. How much cash can you access?"

"I don't know. I'm not sure of the limits on my credit cards."

"Lizzie, I don't mean a few thousand dollars. Bail will likely be somewhere in the neighborhood of fifty to one hundred thousand dollars."

"I don't have that kind of money."

"Do you own a house you can stake as collateral? We have bail bondsmen here in Belize. It's more complicated with an international transaction, but it can be accomplished for a fee."

"No, I still rent." And I could barely afford that. He obviously had no idea how little freelance journalists were paid.

"Parents?" he asked.

"Yes, but they think I'm still on vacation. My dad's sick and I don't want them worrying about this too."

"Is there anyone else you can ask for help? A sibling or a friend?"

"Maybe," I said. I never wanted to borrow money from Jane, although she'd offered many times. But she did have a trust fund and this was an emergency. "You get the money back, right?"

"Yes, at the end of your trial, or sooner if we can get a favorable plea deal."

"What would a favorable plea deal be?"

"If all they ultimately charge you with is possession and intent to export antiquities, I could likely get it down to a small fine. It's hardly a crime in most of Central America. I'm more concerned that they're using this as a ruse to keep you here until they gather enough evidence to charge you with Michael's murder."

"Can they do that?"

He nodded sympathetically. "I'm afraid so."

"But I didn't kill him, I swear. I didn't even have a motive."

"Lizzie, you need to understand that the Belizean police aren't known for their diligence. If not the obvious suspect, at the moment, you're the only suspect. In the meantime," he pulled two sheets of paper from his briefcase and handed them to me, "my retainer agreement. And I'll need an initial deposit of five thousand dollars, preferably by the end of the day."

At least my lawyer accepted credit cards.

David arranged for a hearing in front of a magistrate judge that afternoon. He told me the smaller cayes like Camus all shared a traveling magistrate, but he wasn't scheduled to arrive here until next week. The only way to speed up the process was to travel to an island with its own magistrate, and the closest was Parrot Caye.

"The remaining hurdle," David said, "is transportation. Sergeant Ramos, might I impose upon you to point me in the direction of the nearest boat charter?"

"Why don't we just take your boat, Sarge?" Juan piped in.

Sergeant Ramos glared at him. "I don't think Mr. Barron would want to use my boat. It's barely seaworthy."

"Sarge, your boat is dope."

Someone had been watching American TV.

"We would, of course, pay you," David said, "assuming it's not a departmental vehicle."

"No," Sergeant Ramos replied. "It's not."

"Then I'd be happy to write you a check for whatever's the going rate."

Sergeant Ramos nodded and picked up the phone.

Whatever I was paying David, he was worth every penny. He'd convinced Sergeant Ramos that I shouldn't be forced to appear before the magistrate in my unwashed state. Since the police station didn't have a shower, Sergeant Ramos grudgingly agreed to let David rent me a room in a nearby hotel, so long as Juan came along to guard me. We were all happy with that arrangement. I got a hot shower and a real bed to nap in, and Juan got to feel like a hotshot cop for half a day.

David even retrieved my clothes from my luggage (Sergeant Ramos insisted on keeping the suitcase as evidence) so I could change into something more appropriate for court. He chose my black linen dress and high-heeled sandals, and Consul Donna Kramer let me borrow her strand of pearls so I'd look like I was going to the office instead of out on a date.

David, Donna, Juan, and I met Sergeant Ramos at the dock at one o'clock. And for the record, his boat was dope.

CHAPTER 29

"Nice ride," I said, climbing aboard the speedboat.

Sergeant Ramos merely grunted. It wasn't new, and it wasn't large, but there was enough room to comfortably seat four passengers, and we were only three. Sergeant Ramos had ordered Juan back to the station to "keep an eye on things." Juan looked disappointed, but he didn't voice his complaint.

I almost forgot I was a prisoner during the half-hour ride to Parrot Caye. The sun was shining, the wind was blowing, and since Sergeant Ramos was within earshot, Donna, David and I kept our conversation to the two of them and how they came to live in Belize.

Donna told me she'd graduated from Georgetown with a degree in international relations and was working her way up the diplomatic ranks. David was third-generation British Belizean. His parents had shipped him off to boarding school in England when he was only nine, but he moved back to Belize permanently a few years after he'd graduated law school. I got the impression the pair might be more than just friends.

Parrot Caye looked a lot like Camus Caye, only larger. Same brightly painted wooden buildings, same palm trees, a few more cars on the street, but plenty of golf carts and bicycles too. We walked the five blocks from the dock to the town hall, where the magistrate judge resided. The two-story white building with the columns out front was the stateliest building on the island, according to Sergeant Ramos. But it still didn't have central air-conditioning.

After Donna and I visited the town hall's ladies' room to wash the sweat off our faces and detangle our hair, we joined David on a bench outside the magistrate's office and waited for my name to be called. Sergeant Ramos sat across from us, chatting with another officer whose prisoner was stuck in coveralls and handcuffs.

I glanced over at David, thankful that I had the best representation Visa could buy. "Do they have much crime on the islands?"

"Not compared to Belize City," David said. "Why?"

Before I could reply a pretty, dark-haired woman holding a clipboard called out my name. She ushered us into the office of the Honorable Walter Wallace, according to the plaque on his door. The man behind the desk had freckled skin, thinning white hair, and a tan shirt whose buttons looked like they were about to give up the fight trying to hold back his ample belly.

"Come in, come in," he said, in the same clipped British accent as David, but without the charm. "We haven't got all day."

David motioned for me to sit in one of the two straight-backed armchairs in front of Judge Wallace's massive desk. He and Donna stood behind me, and Sergeant Ramos stood at attention behind the other chair.

The judge donned his wire-framed glasses and scanned the thin manila file his secretary had handed him. "I'm missing your statement, Sergeant...?"

"Ramos," he said. "I apologize, Your Honor. Due to the speed of these proceedings, I didn't have time to file it. But I have it with me." He unbuttoned his shirt pocket and pulled out a sheet of paper folded into a neat square.

"Fine, fine," the judge said. "Hand it over."

"Your Honor, I must object. The defense was not provided with a copy of this document."

The judge waved his hand at David. "Settle down, Mister...?"

"David Barron." He stepped forward. "I'm Ms. Mancini's counsel, and this is Ms. Donna Kramer, consular officer for the US Embassy. Pursuant to Article six point two of—"

"I'm familiar with Article six point two, Mr. Barron. Please dispense with the recitation."

"Yes, Your Honor," David said and returned to his post behind my chair.

The judge read Sergeant Ramos's statement but stopped halfway through. "What's this word here?" he asked, pointing to the handwritten sheet of paper.

Sergeant Ramos leaned over and squinted. "Pre-Columbian."

The judge nodded and continued reading. When he finished, he set his glasses on the desk and handed the sheet of paper to David.

"What do you have to say, young lady?" the judge asked, directing his attention to me. "Did you steal these pieces?"

All I managed was a no before David squeezed my shoulder. At least he was subtler than Jeremy. "Your Honor, let me—"

"Not now, Mr. Barron. Just tell me how your client pleads."

"Not guilty, Your Honor."

Judge Wallace nodded and returned his glasses to his nose. "Sergeant Ramos," the judge asked, without looking up from the form he'd begun to fill in, "do you intend to offer Ms. Mancini a plea?"

"No, Your Honor."

Judge Wallace stopped writing and peered up at him. "Why not?"

"We believe this case warrants a trial," Sergeant Ramos answered, still standing at attention and staring straight ahead. He must've been a soldier at some point in his life.

"Who's we?" the judge asked.

"The people of Camus Caye," Sergeant Ramos replied.

I hoped he wasn't going to be my jury too.

The judge set his glasses on his desk and began rubbing the bridge of his nose.

"Your Honor, I must object."

He opened his eyes and looked up. "You're objecting to a trial, Mr. Barron?"

"Yes, Your Honor. I believe the police are only prosecuting this ridiculous case to give them more time to charge my client with another crime."

"Is that true, Sergeant Ramos?"

"What's true is that Ms. Mancini is the key witness in another crime. A murder, Your Honor."

I wanted to yell out that I didn't witness any murder and I'd already told the police everything I knew, but David spoke for me, and more eloquently than I could've myself. The judge allowed David and Sergeant Ramos to argue back and forth while he consulted his calendar. He ended their debate with, "The trial is set for the twenty-seventh."

"Bail, Your Honor?" David asked.

The judge turned to Sergeant Ramos.

"We oppose bail, your honor. Ms. Mancini is a flight risk."

"Then I'll keep her passport until the trial," the judge said.

"But that won't stop her from leaving the country illegally," Sergeant Ramos replied.

"What would you have me do, Sergeant? Send her to a holding cell in Belize City for the next three weeks?"

"R-O-R, Your Honor?"

I didn't know what R-O-R was, but if David was asking for it, I knew it had to be good.

The judge considered it for a moment, and then said, "No, Sergeant Ramos has a point. Bail is set at one hundred thousand dollars. We're done here."

There was no climactic gavel rapping like there always was on TV. I stood up and the judge's secretary ushered us out into the hallway and called the next name on her list.

"What now?" I asked David.

"Now you call everyone you know and ask them to lend you fifty thousand dollars."

"I thought bail was a hundred thousand?"

"Belizean dollars," David said. "The exchange rate is two to one."

Somehow, I couldn't imagine that making much of a difference.

CHAPTER 30

But I was wrong. Jane said if it had been six figures, she would've needed the trustee's cosignature on the withdrawal. But since it was only five figures, she could authorize the wire transfer from her trust fund herself. Once the money arrived, David would take care of everything.

"And I added an extra ten thousand for your legal fees," Jane said.

"Why?" I'd already thanked her a million times for lending me the bail money, which she'd get back after my trial. I didn't want to accept any more charity. "I told you I already paid him."

"Five thousand dollars? That'll last you about a day and a half."

"But Jane, I can't pay back all this money." The credit card people could hate me, but Jane was my best friend.

"Don't worry. I won't send anyone to break your legs if you're late with a payment, and I guarantee my interest rate is lower than Visa's."

"What's your rate?"

"Somewhere between zero and we'll discuss it over drinks when I get there."

"You're coming to Camus Caye?"

"You're going to be there for the next three weeks, aren't you?"

And possibly longer if David couldn't get me off. But I was trying not to think about that. "Yes, but I'm going to have to get a job. I've got a lawyer to pay, and now that I'm out of jail I'm going to need a place to sleep."

I could hear her tapping on her keyboard. "Which do you think would be nicer, a suite at the Hotel Del Sol or a private villa at the Tradewinds?"

"Jane, please. You've already done enough."

"You can't get a job in a foreign country without a work permit, and they're not going to give one to a possible felon. Besides, what would you do?"

"I don't know." I didn't think there'd be many employment opportunities for a freelance writer on Camus Caye. "Maybe I'll get a job as a cocktail waitress."

"Need I remind you that you were fired from your one and only waitressing job?"

She was referring to my short-lived career at Cheeks, a bar near USC that specialized in selling pitchers of cheap beer and baskets of hot wings to underage students. It was a lot like Hooters, except we highlighted different assets. I lasted only a week. "That's because I wouldn't let the manager pinch my ass."

"And you think the men in Belize will be more respectful?"

She had a point, but I needed money. I also needed something to occupy my time for the next three weeks. Otherwise, I'd go nuts obsessing over the state of my life, and no good could come of that. "What part of my vacation has made this sound appealing to you?"

"You said the diving was fabulous."

"But you don't dive. You barely swim."

"That is so unfair. You know I take a water aerobics class every Wednesday morning."

"In a four-foot-deep indoor pool." I'd accompanied Jane to her health club a few times on guest passes. "It was you who refused to take the ferry to Ellis Island because the Hudson River was too wide."

"I just didn't want to wait in line with all the tourists."

"Jane, I applaud the adventurous spirit you seem to have developed in the last five days. But Belize is hot, humid, there's no good shopping, and I've yet to see Dom Pérignon on any restaurant's wine list."

"That just means you're not eating at the right restaurants."

"I'm serious, Jane."

"Well if you don't want my company, you can just say so. You don't have to trash the whole country."

"I'm not trashing the country. I'm just pointing out some of the characteristics I know you find less than appealing in a vacation destination. Of course I would love for you to come. That's—"

"Good, because I'm arriving at ten thirty-five tomorrow morning. Meet me at the airport and don't be late. You know I hate to wait."

I hung up the phone and breathed deeply. I loved Jane like the sister I never had. And if I was stuck in Paris or London or Abu Dhabi, there'd be no one I'd rather have meet me. But Jane thought the Four Seasons in Budapest was lacking in amenities because her bedroom wasn't equipped with its own DVD player. Jane wasn't going to be happy on Camus Caye, and I'd never known her to be shy about expressing her displeasure.

CHAPTER 31

After a night spent waking up from nightmares about bandits and cab drivers and angry men with jade heads, I stuffed my belongings into a giant trash bag and checked out of the Gables Guesthouse. I didn't know where Jane and I would be staying, but I knew it wouldn't be this place. Not that the Gables Guesthouse was a fleabag—it wasn't. My room was small, clean, and had an old window air conditioner, which placed it in the three-star category by Camus Caye standards. But Jane was a five-star kind of girl. Luckily for her, she could afford to be.

I watched all the passengers depart Maya Air's 10:35 a.m. from Belize City, but Jane wasn't among them. Nor did she arrive on the 11:05, or Tropic Air's 10:50 or 11:20. By the time Maya Air's 11:35 arrived sans Jane, I was seriously worried. I asked the girl at the counter to check the passenger manifest, but she told me she had access only to outbound flights, not inbound flights. After much begging on my part (which was useless) and a twenty-dollar bill (which was quite persuasive), the clerk called her counterpart in Belize City, who confirmed that Jane was scheduled for the 10:05 flight, but she never boarded the plane.

I called her cell phone for the third time and left yet another message. Since I didn't know what else to do, I went back to the Gables Guesthouse to check back in.

"Ms. Mancini," Gloria, the desk clerk, said, "I'm so glad you're back."

"Why?" They weren't hard up for business. I'd snagged the last room.

"Some woman's been calling for you. I told her you checked out this morning but she's very persistent. She offered me three hundred dollars to go to the airport to look for you."

I was surprised she didn't take it. It was probably more than she made in a week.

As if reading my mind, she said, "No one could cover for me."

"Did she leave a number?"

Gloria handed me a piece of paper with a seven-digit extension I didn't recognize. "It's local," she said. "No country code."

I thanked her and went to the pay phone.

"Finally," Jane yelled. "I've been trying to reach you for hours. I still can't believe you didn't bring your cell phone with you."

"I told you, it's not international."

"You could've gotten the card changed for thirty bucks."

"If I knew my honeymoon was going to turn out this way, trust me, I would have."

"Well it doesn't matter now because I rented us both local cell phones. They're good anywhere in the country."

I'd ask why later. Now all I wanted to know was, "Where the hell are you?"

"Still at the airport in Belize City. I need you to meet me."

"Why?"

"I can't get on the plane."

"Why not? What's wrong?"

"Do you know how small it is?"

"Yes, Jane, I took it, remember?"

"Why didn't you warn me?"

"I did warn you. I told you it was a commuter flight."

"I thought that meant forty seats, not eight."

I let her rant while I tried to think of alternative transportation. "How about a boat?"

"I checked. The boat ride's over an hour. The plane's only fifteen minutes."

"Yes, except you won't get on the plane."

"I can if you meet me. Then I can take a Xanax and not have to worry if it zonks me out."

"You want me to fly to Belize City so I can stand guard while you take a tranquilizer, then get back on the same plane so I can hold your hand for the fifteen-minute flight back to Camus Caye?"

"You don't have to hold my hand," she said. "Just be there to make sure no weirdos try to hit on me or steal my bag."

I knew I was wasting my breath, but I said it anyway. "You do realize how ridiculous you're being?"

"I don't think it's ridiculous to want to travel with another person when you're medicated and your judgment's impaired. I'd call that prudent."

"I'd call it insane."

"I can't believe how selfish you're being. I put my own life on hold to come down here and help you and this—"

"Help me? Jane, how're you going help me when you won't even get on the fucking plane?"

"Have you got something better to do with your day?"

She had me there. "OK, when's the next flight?" Sure it was crazy and I'd actually have preferred if she hadn't come, but if it wasn't for Jane, I'd still be stuck in a broom closet at the Camus Caye police station. I owed her one. I owed her lots of ones.

Hours later when we'd both finally arrived at the Camus Caye Airport, I called the Tradewinds Hotel on my new rented cell phone while I tried to keep Jane from falling asleep. I'd had to practically drag her onto the plane, and that was after she'd taken half a Xanax. She swallowed the other half dry when we hit our first patch of turbulence.

Where the Blue Bay aimed for quirky comfort, the Tradewinds went straight for luxury. Our villa had two bedroom suites, each with its own Jacuzzi tub and separate stall shower, and a shared living room, dining room, and kitchenette. The forty-two-inch plasma TV was bolted to the wall, but it came with a state-of-the-art home theater system, including DVD player and satellite TV.

I occupied myself with the premium channels while Jane slept. She awoke three hours later, hungry and ready to go.

"Go where?" I asked.

"I don't know," she said. "Where do you want to go?"

"Home." Lying on the couch watching American television had left me melancholy. I knew doing nothing would be bad for me. Too much time to think. And watching the last half of *Midnight Express* probably hadn't helped either.

"Let's go out to dinner. What's the best place to eat?"

"I have no idea."

Jane knew that wasn't true. She knew I had a file filled with reviews for every restaurant on the island, but she chose to ignore me and called the concierge instead.

"We have a reservation for seven at Gemini," she said, hanging up the phone. "Go shower and get dressed."

I did as I was told and came out of my bedroom wearing a rumpled sundress.

"Don't you have anything that isn't wrinkled?"

"No."

Since I disliked ironing and Jane didn't know how, she lent me one of hers. It was too tight in the hips, too loose in the bust, and three inches too short, but Jane swore I could pull it off and I didn't have the energy to fight with her.

We were the only female-female couple at the restaurant, but Jane didn't seem to notice. She ordered champagne with dinner (the restaurant didn't stock Dom Pérignon, so she settled for Veuve Clicquot) and insisted we toast.

"To what?" I asked.

"How about 'facing your fears' or 'just doing it'?"

"You sound like a Nike ad."

"Will you cheer up already? God, you're such a downer."

"Sorry," I said. "But the thought of life in prison isn't really lifting my spirits."

"Stop exaggerating. Your lawyer told me the maximum sentence for antiquities smuggling is five years and a ten-thousand-dollar fine, and nobody gets the max."

"Thanks, that's very comforting. Did he also tell you that he thinks the whole antiquities thing is bullshit and that they're really just trying to keep me here longer so they can pin Michael's murder on me? I'm pretty sure the maximum penalty for that one's life in prison."

"Actually, it's the death penalty, but let's not focus on that right now."

"Sure, Jane, wouldn't want to ruin your great vacation."

She set down her glass of champagne and waved away our hovering waiter. "If we're going to get you out of this, you're going to have to start thinking positive."

"I'm positive. I just don't understand how *we're* going to get me out of this. I thought you came for fun and sun."

"Geez, you're so gullible. That's how come you're in this mess in the first place. I didn't come here to work on my tan, I came to save your ass."

CHAPTER 32

She told me the whole story over dinner. Jane and her therapist, Dr. Tobler, had been discussing the idea of Jane facing her fears for the last few weeks. When Jane told him about my situation, he thought it was the perfect opportunity for her to act since there was a real need, not an artificial circumstance, and I'd be there to bolster her if things turned ugly. Assuming, of course, I wasn't in jail at the time.

"Don't you think it's a great idea?"

"No, I think you need a new therapist."

"Dr. Tobler warned me you might react this way. He said people are used to their prescribed roles, and whenever one person in the relationship tries to change, it upsets the status quo."

There was no point in arguing. I couldn't possibly win. "OK, Jane, I'll go hide out in the hotel room for the next three weeks and you can explore the country and figure out how to get me out of this."

"No, we have to do it together."

"But that's just it. What are we going to *do*?" Besides hiring a good lawyer, which apparently I'd already done, I was out of ideas.

"We're going to figure out who planted the jade in your suitcase, which is going to lead us to Michael's killer."

"And then what? Bring the killer to the police so he can confess?"

"Sure. We'll make a citizen's arrest. Then we'll be heroes for solving the case."

When I stopped laughing I said, "OK, Columbo, where do you propose we begin?"

Jane actually pulled a package of index cards from her purse. "I thought we should start by writing down everyone's name and what we know about them. Then tomorrow we can go and take everyone's picture. And don't worry, I bought one of those portable picture printers before I left because I thought it might be hard to get them printed here."

"Good thinking," I said and took another bite of my shrimp Creole. Jane had hardly touched her broiled salmon, no oil, no butter, no sauce. Facing her fears apparently didn't include trying new foods.

"Do you think there's a Staples or something where we could get one of those giant dry erase boards? No matter," she said before I could answer. "We can just tape everything to the wall in the living room. I think I remembered to pack the Scotch tape."

"You're serious about this?"

"Of course. I'm not going to let them put you in prison for the rest of your life."

I'd watched *The Fugitive* enough times to know that the only way we could ensure that I wasn't wrongfully convicted of Michael's murder was to find the real killer ourselves. "Don't you think we should hire a private detective? Someone who lives down here and knows the landscape?"

She shook her head. "We can't risk it. Detectives are bribable. We could hire one and he could still be working for the police, or more likely the bad guys, or even more likely, they're one and the same."

"I don't believe that."

"Trust me, Lizzie, it happens."

Jane's mother used to be a researcher for Oliver Stone. God only knew what sort of bedtime stories she told her kid to turn her into the conspiracy theorist she was today.

"If that's true, then why do you think finding the real killer will help? Won't the police just cover it up and still pin the murder on me?"

"It's not in their best interests. Even down here, not every cop is corrupt. You're just the easy solution to their problem. But if we give them an even easier solution, then they'll let you go."

I wasn't quite following.

"Lizzie, they don't actually want you to be guilty. Imagine the bad publicity if they put an American woman to death. It'll kill the tourist trade."

"Well I wouldn't want that kind of guilt on my shoulders."

"I'm serious. If we hand them a viable alternative they'll jump at it."

"And by viable alternative you mean the real killer?"

"Of course," she said. "You don't think I'd frame an innocent person, do you?"

"No, but that means we have to find the real killer ourselves, and we don't have a clue how to do that. Nor do we have any of those nifty gadgets the police have like guns and warrants and bulletproof vests. Not that we'd know how to use them if we did."

"Aah, that's where you're wrong," she said and paused for a dramatic sip of champagne. "I stopped at the spy shop in Hollywood before I left. We'll be receiving a large FedEx delivery tomorrow morning."

Sometimes I really wished I had a trust fund.

The next morning the bellman brought the FedEx box to our hotel room door. Jane ripped it open and pulled out a lock pick set, night vision binoculars, two stun guns, and my favorite, a set of fake badges encased in their own wallets.

"And what are we supposed to do with these?" I said, holding up the gold badge embossed with *Special Investigator* in black lettering. "Pretend we're cops?"

"I think they're cute," Jane said. "Don't you?"

I just shook my head and went to the kitchenette to pour myself another cup of coffee.

"Will you get me one while you're up?" Jane yelled.

When I returned to the living room, Jane was sitting on the floor inserting a nine-volt battery into the stun gun. "Come here, I want to try this out on you."

"Hell no," I said, jumping back and spilling coffee all over the rug.

"Never mind," she said, rummaging through the box while I cleaned the stain. "It came with an instructional video."

Unfortunately the lock pick set didn't. After half an hour unsuccessfully attempting to pick the lock on the bathroom door, we both gave up. But with the curtains drawn and the lights turned off, the night vision binoculars worked just fine.

"Now what?" I asked after we'd played with all our new toys.

"Now we start the investigation."

"And did you order a *Murder Investigation for Dummies* book with the rest of this junk?"

"No," she said, reaching for her coffee mug. "I think we've both watched enough *Law & Order* to do this on our own."

"I don't think it works the same in real life as it does on TV. And besides, we're not cops."

"Maybe not. But I'm channeling Mariska Hargitay and you're better looking than Christopher Meloni."

"Gee, thanks. And why do I have to be the bad cop?"

"Because if one of us is going to lose control and throw a punch at somebody, it's going to be you."

We both dressed in shorts and T-shirts, although Jane's came from Barneys and mine were purchased at the Gap, and took the hotel's shuttle into town. We could've walked, it was only half a mile, but Jane was breaking in a new pair of very cute Marc Jacobs sandals and didn't want to risk the blisters.

As we walked the main street of Camus Caye, I pointed out all the buildings I knew—the police station, the Gables Guesthouse, a couple of restaurants, and the disco.

"We should go dancing tonight," Jane said. "I haven't been to a disco in ages."

"I thought you came down here to help me."

"That doesn't mean we can't have fun too. But that's for later," she added, looking at the expression on my face. "Now we work. Where's the morgue?"

"Why do you want to go there?"

"So the coroner can tell us how and when Michael died. Isn't that what Detectives Benson and Stabler always do?"

"He died Wednesday night from being stabbed to death."

"Maybe that's just what it looks like on the surface, but that's not what really killed him. Or maybe Sergeant Ramos just wants you to think that."

"Or maybe Michael faked his own death and he's really alive somewhere and the writers are planning on bringing him back next season."

Jane stopped with her hands on her size two hips. "I came down here to help you. A little appreciation would be nice."

"I do appreciate you. I really, really do. But this isn't an episode of *Law & Order* or *CSI* or even *Monk*. Maybe there's some corruption down here, I don't know, but I do know that there's no high-tech crime lab analyzing DNA samples and no coroner working for the police department who's going to help us solve this case."

"Did you actually see Michael's body?"

"Yes," I said, shuddering from the memory. "I threw up all over the floor."

"But did you see the stab wounds?"

"Jane, have you listened to a fucking word I've said?"

A couple with two small children taking pictures of a statue frowned at us disapprovingly.

"That's why you're the bad cop," she said when the family had moved on.

"I'm sorry, but I'm just trying to insert a dose of reality here."

"The reason I asked if you saw the wounds was because I wanted to know if he was stabbed in the front or the back."

"I don't know. Sergeant Ramos never told me and I saw Michael only from the neck up. Why?"

"Because if he was stabbed from the front, especially if he had cuts on his hands or arms, then he was fighting with his attacker, but if he was stabbed in the back, then he was running away."

She at least sounded like she knew what she was talking about.

"Impressed?" she said.

"Maybe."

"Then maybe now you'll start listening to me for a change."

I walked Jane the three blocks to the hospital, but I refused to go in. One viewing of a dead body was enough for me. Not that I believed that they'd allow Jane to see Michael's body anyway. I thought her scheme to pretend that she was a private investigator from the US looking into Michael's murder for his family back home was doomed to failure despite her fake badge, but she insisted.

I'd barely gotten through the first article in the free tourist newsletter I'd found on a bench outside the hospital when Jane reappeared with a triumphant smile.

"They actually let you in to see him?"

"Better," she said. "They told me where to find his sister."

CHAPTER 33

She filled me in on the walk back to Front Street. Jane had used her private investigator line on one of the nurses, but the nurse had told her she'd have to call Sergeant Ramos for authorization.

"So what did you do?"

"I asked her which way to the ladies' room and I left. But on the way, I ran into a very friendly orderly who was more than happy to point me in the direction of the morgue. When I told him I was investigating Michael's death, he told me the dead guy was getting more action than he was, which I took to mean Michael had had other female visitors."

"How astute of you."

"Thank you," she said, choosing to ignore my sarcasm. "I probed a little more and found out Michael's other visitor was named Mona Garcia."

"How do you know it's Michael's sister?"

"Because that's what she wrote down on the form when she signed for Michael's body."

"She took Michael's body?"

"No, not yet. She's flying home with him tomorrow night."

We walked a little way in silence while I digested this information, when it occurred to me to ask, "How did you get this guy to tell you all this?"

"I just happened to mention that I'd be at the disco tonight and I'd be extremely grateful for the information."

"What did you do that for? Now he'll be waiting for you."

"Which is why we'll be going tomorrow night instead."

Jane and I had to return to the hotel for lunch because we couldn't find a restaurant in town that served a grilled chicken breast salad with fat-free dressing on the side. While Jane ate her six grams of protein, no-fat lunch at the Tradewinds poolside patio, I devoured a cheeseburger and fries.

"Ooo la la," Jane said, pushing down her sunglasses for a better view.

I turned and followed her gaze. "Oh my God, that's Jack."

We both stared openly as he climbed out of the shallow end of the pool. With the sun reflecting off the water, his chest literally glistened.

"I thought you said he looked like Owen Wilson."

"I said he was cuter than Owen Wilson and without the broken nose."

"He's way cuter than Owen Wilson. He's practically Brad Pitt."

"He doesn't look anything like Brad Pitt."

"Maybe not Brad Pitt now, but remember him in *Thelma & Louise*?"

I did remember. I was fourteen years old and on my first real date with Craig Heins. He spent the whole movie trying to feel me up and I spent the whole movie trying to figure out exactly what Brad Pitt had done to Geena Davis to make her so happy. I didn't find out from Craig.

"He's bigger than Brad Pitt."

"I know," Jane said. "He's Matthew McConaughey."

We watched three teenage girls giggle and swoon as Jack demonstrated the proper way to clear a mask. "Yeah, I'll give you Matthew McConaughey."

We finished our lunch and returned to the villa without talking to Jack. Jane wanted to meet him, but I refused. He'd made it pretty clear the last time I'd seen him that he didn't want to have anything to do with me, and I'd had enough rejection for one week. Besides, we had work to do.

I pulled out one of my guidebooks and made a list of all the hotels on Camus Caye. I took A through L, handed Jane M through Z, and we both started calling front desks, asking for Ms. Mona Garcia. I found her on my third try—the Coconuts Hotel. The clerk told me there was no phone in her room, but he could take a message.

"Do you know if she's in?" I asked.

"I doubt it," he said. "It gets pretty hot in the rooms this time of day."

"Do you think she might be out by the pool?"

"We don't have a pool. The beach is only two blocks away."

I asked for directions, thanked him for his help, and hung up. "If the place has no air-conditioning and no pool, she's probably not going to be hanging around in the daytime, but she has to come back eventually. I think we should go over there around five and wait for her."

"Good plan," Jane said. "It's two thirty now. What do you want to do until then?"

I didn't want to sit by the pool and ogle Jack, which is what Jane wanted to do, so I sent her by herself while I snuggled up on the couch to take a nap. Of course, I couldn't sleep. I couldn't stop thinking about this case.

Maybe we were going about this the wrong way. After all, I hadn't been charged with Michael's murder, only smuggling antiquities. Maybe we should be spending our time trying to figure out who planted the jade in my suitcase and why. I assumed it was Michael since, besides me, he was the only one with a key. But if Jane could buy a lock pick set then a criminal certainly could. And a criminal could probably figure out how to use it.

I bounded out to the pool to share my new theory with Jane, but stopped short when I caught her flirting with Jack. He was staring at her chest, which wasn't unusual, most men did. I turned back as soon as I saw them, but Jane had already spotted me.

"Lizzie, wait," she called out.

I didn't.

A few minutes later, she was standing in the living room in her bikini top and a beach towel wrapped around her waist. "That wasn't what it looked like."

"Oh no? It looked a lot like flirting to me."

"I was just scoping out a suspect."

"Since when is Jack a suspect?"

"Since now," she said.

CHAPTER 34

"Jack couldn't have killed Michael. He was with me the whole night."

"You don't know that," Jane said, plopping down on the chair across from me. "You were passed out. In fact, maybe you weren't drunk. Maybe he drugged you."

"He didn't drug me."

"How do you know?"

"I woke up with a hangover. I know what that feels like." Especially on this trip.

"Just because you drank doesn't mean he didn't drug you."

"Jane, Jack didn't kill Michael." Thinking that was the end of the discussion, I went into the kitchenette for a bottle of water, but Jane followed.

"How do you know?"

"I think I'd know if I'd spent the night with a murderer."

"You see what you want to see, Lizzie."

I slammed the fridge door shut. "What's that supposed to mean?"

"The handwriting was on the wall with Steven for a long time. You chose to ignore it."

"I was supposed to know he was going to dump me at the altar?"

"No, I thought you'd get married and then divorced a few years later when you realized your mistake."

"Screw you!" I said and stomped back into the living room, where I flung myself onto the couch.

After a few seconds, Jane followed. "I'm sorry, Lizzie, but it's the truth."

"I can't believe this. You were supposed to be my maid of honor."

"And I would have. I had the dress, the shoes, I even wrote the toast."

"Even though you knew Steven didn't love me?" I said, trying to hold back the tears.

"Even though I knew you weren't in love with him."

"Yeah, I was faking it for five years."

"You were comfortable. So you took the next logical step, you got engaged. I know on some level you loved him, just like you love those sweatpants with the holes in them that you refuse to throw away, but you weren't *in love* with him."

"Oh don't give me that bullshit. Maybe your life's a fairy tale with your fabulous vacations and your trust fund, but the rest of us live in the real world."

"And people don't fall in love in the 'real world,'" she said, using her fingers for quotes.

"Obviously not the way you do," I yelled before I ran out. Our villa faced the ocean, so that's where I headed. But I didn't get far. Our stretch of beach was deserted, so I collapsed on the sand in front of our room and let the tears roll. The worst part about it was that I knew Jane was right, at least a little bit. I loved Steven, but I wasn't head over heels. But honestly, after five years together, was I still supposed to light up every time he walked in the room? Every married person I knew said the passion always faded. But I supposed it should still be there when you're walking down the aisle.

This whole episode was giving me a headache. I was debating whether to go back to the villa to hibernate or take a stroll on the beach when Jane appeared. She sat down next to me in the sand and we both stared out at the ocean in silence. For ten seconds.

"Are we speaking yet?" she asked. "Because you know I hate it when we're not speaking."

"You really think I didn't love Steven?"

"I think you didn't love him enough to commit to him for the rest of your life. And I was right, wasn't I?"

"No, he left me."

"He just did what you wanted to do but were too afraid to do because you didn't want to disappoint everyone."

"You really think so?" I didn't actually believe her, but I wanted to.

"Absolutely. Once that wedding train pulls out of the station, it's pretty hard to stop."

That much was true.

"Friends?" she asked.

"Friends," I said, and we had one of those awful Hallmark moments with the hugging and the crying. All that was missing was the sappy music.

Then Jane looked at her watch. "We gotta go. I don't want to miss Michael's sister."

CHAPTER 35

We needn't have hurried. Jane and I loitered in the Coconuts Hotel's small lobby for almost an hour before the desk clerk finally got so annoyed with us that he told us Mona's room number just so we'd leave him alone. She was in room number eight—one flight up at the end of the catwalk.

Unfortunately, he wouldn't give us her room key too, so we had to sit outside her door waiting for her to return. As we neared the end of the second hour, Jane wanted to call it a night, but I refused. Mona was our only lead for more information about Michael, and I didn't want to take the chance of missing her before she returned to the States.

Fifteen minutes into hour number three, I sent Jane on a mission for food and entertainment. She came back with bananas, bottled water, one copy of *Vogue*, and a deck of cards.

"Jane, this *Vogue*'s in Spanish."

"I know; it was that or *People*. At least with this one we can look at all the pretty ads."

"And what's with the fruit? They didn't have any Cheetos?"

"You know I don't eat that crap."

"But I do."

"Well I'd be happy to come back in the morning if you'd like to go out for a real meal."

I peeled myself a banana and started shuffling the cards. After I'd won fifty-four dollars off her playing blackjack, she read *Vogue* and I switched to solitaire.

By nine o'clock, I was ready to strangle her. The light was too low, the air was too muggy, the concrete floor was too hard on her butt. I was bored and hungry too, but you didn't hear me complaining. I begged her to go back to the hotel without me, but she refused. She insisted it wasn't safe for me to wait alone. I finally promised her if Mona didn't show by ten we would leave her a note and try again in the morning. Forty-five minutes later, she arrived with a man on each arm.

Mona was short and plump, but her tight minidress revealed both shapely legs and a lot of cleavage, and wavy black hair framed her pretty face. As she moved closer, I could see the resemblance to Michael, especially around the eyes, which were big and brown and surrounded by a thick fringe of lashes that I could never duplicate no matter how much mascara I used.

Mona and her buddies were talking so loudly we knew they'd been drinking even before we saw the bottle. Unfortunately, they were speaking in Spanish, so we still had no clue what they were saying.

"Are you Mona Garcia?" I asked as the threesome approached.

"Sí," the woman answered.

"Michael Garcia's sister?"

"Yes, who are you?"

"I'm Lizzie Mancini and this is Jane Chandler. We were friends of your brother."

"Wait a minute," the man with the beer said. "Is one of you the girl he pretended to marry? The one who came down for a honeymoon *sin un marido*?"

"Without a husband," Mona translated.

"Yes," I said, bristling at the description despite its accuracy.

The three of them looked from me to each other, then burst out laughing.

"That's it," I said to Jane. "We're leaving."

"Oh no we're not. You made me sit here all night waiting to talk to Mona. We're not going anywhere."

I stood and fumed until the three calmed down.

"I'm sorry," Mona said through her giggles. "But we were just talking about Michael and how we couldn't believe he went along with it."

"What do you mean went along with it? It was his idea."

"That's true," Jane said. "I was there when they met and it was definitely your brother who hit on Lizzie."

"Of course he did," the taller man said. "She's a beautiful woman, as are you, señorita. May I buy you a drink?"

And that's how the five of us ended up at the Iguana Bar. I had one beer with the group just to be friendly, then switched to club soda. Jane started with club soda and never switched, which didn't improve her mood any.

The shorter man, the one who had been holding the beer bottle, was Michael's cousin Ernesto. The taller one, Rodrigo, described himself as a "friend of the family." Both men lived on neighboring Parrot Caye. When I asked them what they did for a living, they shifted the conversation back to Michael.

Mona beamed as she talked about her brother. He was the first person in her family to go to college, the first one to buy a house, and he'd been helping her and her parents out financially too.

"Yes, Michael's a saint, blah, blah, blah," Jane said, flapping her hand like a sock puppet. "But what we want to know about is his antiquities business."

That was a conversation killer.

"What business?" Rodrigo finally said.

I nudged Jane under the table, which I hoped she understood meant let me do the talking, and said, "Michael told me he was an antiquities dealer. He even showed me some of his pieces. They were very nice. Jade, I think."

"Oh yes," Mona said. "He used to buy jewelry from the Mayans and sell it in the States. It helps sustain their culture. They're very poor."

She was clearly out of the loop, but likely to be the most cooperative. Ernesto wouldn't look up from the table, where he was carving his initials with his fingernail, and Rodrigo stared straight at me with his arms folded and his jaw clenched.

"Did you meet Sergeant Ramos?" I asked Mona.

"No," she said. "Ernesto told me the police haven't found Michael's killer yet."

"Do they have any suspects?" Jane asked.

Mona shook her head and started to tear up. After wiping her nose on her cocktail napkin, she excused herself to use the ladies' room.

I waited until she was gone before I asked Ernesto, "Did Sergeant Ramos ever mention finding stolen antiquities in Michael's hotel room?"

He looked up at me and then at Rodrigo.

"You shouldn't believe everything the police tell you," Rodrigo replied.

This time Jane nudged me under the table, which I assumed meant "I told you so" until she said, "Did you know Lizzie was arrested for attempting to smuggle stolen antiquities out of the country?"

"No," Rodrigo said, sporting the same inscrutable expression. "That's a very dangerous business."

"I would've thought in a town this small it would've made the local paper," Jane continued.

"I don't read the paper, señorita."

"I didn't do it. Someone else put that jade in my suitcase."

No response.

"Do you have any idea who might've done such a thing?"

More silence. I didn't expect an honest answer, but I thought it would provoke some type of reaction. Instead, Ernesto continued to carve up the table and Rodrigo swigged the rest of his beer.

When Mona returned, Rodrigo suggested they leave, and Mona wished us goodnight. The three of them filed out of the bar, but Rodrigo turned back. "A word of advice, señorita. Be careful who you do business with. Many sellers try to pass off fakes as the real thing." Then he nodded at us and left.

We sat in silence, sipping our club sodas, until Jane said, "Do you think he was trying to threaten you?"

I didn't. "I think he might've been trying to help me, or at least get rid of me."

"How do you figure?"

"If the pieces they found in my suitcase are fakes, then there's no crime."

"And the police would have to drop the charges and let you leave."

"Yes, but how do we prove it?"

CHAPTER 36

It was too late to call David, so we went back to the Tradewinds and booted up Jane's laptop. Within minutes of logging on to the Internet, Jane had found a newspaper article about an art detective—an anthropologist who worked at a museum in New York whose job was authenticating pre-Columbian art.

"Do you think she would look at my pieces?"

Jane scanned the article. "It says she just came back from Mexico, so why not Belize? Or maybe we could send them to her."

We resolved to call David in the morning. And I had the best night's sleep I'd had since I'd arrived on Camus Caye.

"Lizzie, I'm so glad you called," David said, even though it was eight o'clock on a Monday morning. "It looks like I'll be able to move your trial up to a week from Friday, assuming I can't convince Sergeant Ramos to settle before then. He is being a bit of a hard arse about this."

"I've got some good news too." I told David about my conversation with Mona and Rodrigo, and my suspicion that the antiquities Sergeant Ramos found in my suitcase were fakes.

"It's possible," he said. "Probably half the antiquities on the market these days are fakes. Although to be honest, even most of the originals aren't terribly valuable. The smaller pieces usually fetch only a few hundred dollars at auction."

"Sergeant Ramos told me they were priceless!"

"Technically that's true. In archaeology, anything more than three or four hundred years old is considered priceless. But on the open market, everything has a price."

"I don't understand. If they're not even that valuable, then why won't he let me just pay a fine and leave?"

"I think you had the bad luck to run into a policeman who actually cares about his country's heritage and doesn't want it sold off piece by piece."

"Maybe." Perhaps all of Jane's conspiracy theories were starting to rub off on me, but I wasn't ready to let him off that easily.

I gave David all the information I had about Mary Alice Conte, the New York art detective, and he promised to call her as soon as we hung up.

David called me later that afternoon with even more good news. Although the police had refused to ship the pieces out of the country (allegedly their own expert was looking at them), David researched Mary Alice Conte and found out she was currently attending a conference in Mexico City. He was able to track her down at her hotel and convince her to fly to Belize before returning to New York.

I didn't even want to know what that was costing me. But as Jane reminded me, when your life's hanging in the balance, it's no time to be cheap.

By the time David and I connected again, I was frantic. I'd already left him five voice mails and had text messaged him twice.

"You were right," he said. "The pieces they found in your suitcase were forgeries. Very high quality, according to Ms. Conte, and possibly antiques themselves, but definitely not pre-Columbian artifacts."

I let out the breath I'd been holding since I'd picked up the phone. "So when do I get to go home?"

"That's a little more complicated."

"Why? If they're fakes, then I haven't committed a crime."

"Not exactly. Ms. Conte couldn't pinpoint the exact age of the pieces. Anything more than one hundred fifty years old is still considered an antiquity under the law. But that's not really the issue anymore."

"It's not?"

"No."

I heard the knock at the door, but Jane went to answer it. I looked up from the sofa and caught a glimpse of Sergeant Ramos in the doorway before Jane closed the door behind her and joined him outside.

"David, why is Sergeant Ramos standing outside my hotel room?"

"Lizzie, the only way the police would allow us to have our own expert examine the evidence was if we agreed to one of their investigators being present for the tests."

"But you just said the tests proved they were fakes."

"As you know, Belize is not a rich country. Our crime labs don't have the most modern equipment."

"So?"

"Ms. Conte had to bring her own equipment with her. She works for one of the largest museums in the world, so naturally she has access to the best resources available."

"David, will you get to the point!"

"Lizzie, she found trace evidence on two of the pieces, evidence the police missed."

"What kind of evidence?"

"Blood. Michael's blood."

CHAPTER 37

Michael's blood? The words were still ringing in my ears. How did Michael's blood get on fake antiquities that someone hid in my suitcase? And what did it mean?

My own thoughts blocked out all other sound, but I could still see. Sergeant Ramos was standing before me, Officer Juan at his side. I think Jane was yelling at them—her lips were moving and her face was flushed—but I couldn't make out the words. And I thought I heard David calling my name, but it sounded like it was coming from a long way away.

Then suddenly my ears popped. Jane was screaming that they had no right to do this, Officer Juan was telling her to calm down, and David's tinny voice was yelling for me to pick up the phone. But the only one I was listening to was Sergeant Ramos.

"You're under arrest for the murder of Michael Garcia. You're entitled to speak privately with a lawyer. You do not have to speak unless you wish to do so, but if you do, what you say can be taken down in writing and offered in evidence. Now please stand up."

When I didn't, he reached down and grabbed my arm and pulled me to my feet.

"Don't worry," Jane said. "I'm calling David right now. He's going to take care of this."

I wanted to tell her to just pick up the phone, that he was still on the line, but I couldn't form the words. Instead, I allowed Sergeant Ramos to steer me outside. He walked me down the beach to the Tradewinds' private dock, where his boat was tied up next to another that I recognized. The passengers were debarking and I heard someone calling my name, but Sergeant Ramos was pushing me forward, and I couldn't see.

He sat me in the back of his boat and told Officer Juan to guard me, while he cast off and steered us out to sea. I remember shouting to Officer Juan over the sound of the wind and the engine. I asked where we were going and he told me Parrot Caye. I had a flashback of the prisoner in handcuffs outside the magistrate's office. The one who was going to get convicted because he couldn't afford a good lawyer. And now that was going to be me.

I was fingerprinted, photographed, searched for weapons, and handcuffed to a bench while Sergeant Ramos and another officer I didn't recognize fought over where I should be housed. Sergeant Ramos lost. He had to bring me back to the one-room police station on Camus Caye.

It was almost dark when we arrived, but I could make out Jane's form sitting on the police station's steps. As soon as she saw us approach, she jumped up. "Are you OK? You're not hurt, are you?"

"No." I was still in a daze, but the fog was beginning to lift.

"Do you need anything?"

A new lawyer. A new life. A reset button so I could go back and start this whole week over.

"Are you hungry?" she asked.

I shook my head.

"I brought you some fruit anyway," she said, pulling a banana and two oranges out of her purse.

I couldn't grab them because my hands were still cuffed behind my back, so Officer Juan took them for me while Sergeant Ramos unlocked the front door.

Sundance started barking even before he opened it.

"We don't have any food, Sundance," Sergeant Ramos and Officer Juan called out simultaneously. Even I cracked a smile.

"But we do have food," Jane said, pointing to the fruit still in Officer Juan's hand.

"Only to you, Jane."

Sergeant Ramos heaved himself behind his wooden desk and told Officer Juan to unlock me. I sat down on the ripped vinyl chair, comforted by the familiar vinyl shards digging into the backs of my thighs, while Officer Juan retrieved the bench from the storeroom for Jane.

"Here we are again, Ms. Mancini. I've missed another dinner over you, and my wife is a very good cook."

That I believed.

"I don't know what I'm going to do with you," he said, then sighed.

I offered my now standard response: "You could let me go."

Jane snickered, which didn't endear either of us to Sergeant Ramos.

"You can put her back in the storage room," Officer Juan said, stating the obvious.

I turned to Jane. "Be careful, you're sitting on my bed."

"You're kidding," she said.

I wished I were.

After the bench, the desk fan, and I were all back in the storage room, Sergeant Ramos did accede to my one request. He allowed Jane to leave me her Xanax. There's no way I would've survived the night without it.

I woke up achy, but at least I'd slept. After the rooster had quieted down, I stood up and stretched, then stared out the window through the chicken wire at the ocean and beyond.

Officer Juan arrived at eight and unlocked me. After I used the bathroom, I followed him outside uncuffed (I promised not to run away) and we walked Butch and Sundance on the beach. When we arrived back at the station, he fed the dogs while I made coffee and called our breakfast order in to the restaurant next door. We were eating at Sergeant Ramos's desk when David and Jane arrived.

"This doesn't look like cruel and unusual punishment to me," David said, inhaling the scent of bacon.

"You haven't seen her bed yet," Jane said.

"Actually, he has, the last time he was here." It felt like déjà vu. "Are we going back to the hotel so I can shower and change before the next hearing?"

"Right," David said, "we should talk about that. Officer, will excuse us?"

Juan nodded with a mouthful of fried plantains.

I divided the rest of my breakfast up in my Styrofoam container and pushed the food into Butch and Sundance's unlocked cell. Sundance moved faster, so he got the larger half, but Butch was bigger and swallowed his portion in one gulp. I knew at least I'd have two friends on the inside.

"I can't believe you slept in here," Jane said, following David and me into the storage room.

"You should've seen it before I cleaned it," I replied, rubbing away a spot of dirt on the floor. "So about my bail?"

David stared down at his briefcase. "I'm really sorry, Lizzie."

These were not the words I expected to hear. I figured it would be like the last time. I'd spend the night in the storage room, today we'd go to court, Jane would write another check, and I'd be back at the hotel by dinner.

"I know it's routine in the States," David continued, "but in Belize, judges don't normally grant bail in murder cases."

"Can't they make an exception?" Jane asked.

"The magistrate has some discretion," David acknowledged, "but I rang him this morning and he refused. He believes you're a flight risk."

"But he's already got my passport."

"There are other ways of leaving the country."

I looked up at Jane. I could see her wheels turning too.

"But I wouldn't," David added, acknowledging the unspoken thought that had passed between us. "The US has an extradition treaty with Belize."

"But not every country does," Jane said. "And we're not without means."

"Stop right there," David said, and held up his hands. "I'm an officer of the court. I cannot advise you to flee the jurisdiction and fight extradition. And if, in fact, I thought you were serious, I'd be under a legal obligation to notify the court. As it stands, this discussion is irrelevant, as Lizzie has not been granted bail."

We stopped discussing it, but as far as I was concerned, it was still an option.

"You mustn't lose hope," David continued. "Their case is completely circumstantial and they have no motive."

"But they must have some theory," Jane said.

"They think Lizzie and Michael were in business together and had a falling out." He turned to me. "The indictment mentioned a fight you two had the day before his death."

"That was a fake fight. We planned the whole thing so Michael could disappear."

"Then it worked." He smiled, quite pleased with his joke. Neither Jane nor I was amused.

"Sorry," he said. "But I need you to stay positive and ingratiate yourself to Sergeant Ramos as much as possible. Officer Martinez already seems quite taken with you, so just keep it up."

"Why? If they like me, will they let me go?"

"No, the point is to keep you here as long as possible."

"Excuse me," Jane said, "but isn't the point to leave here as soon as possible? Isn't that why we're paying you?"

David ignored Jane and spoke directly to me. "You may not like it here, but it's a lot better than Hattieville Prison, which is where murder defendants are normally housed when awaiting trial. The conditions are somewhat better for women than for men, but it's still not a place you want to be. The longer we can keep you on Camus Caye, the better."

"And how long is that?"

"I don't know yet. Murder cases aren't heard by the magistrates, they're referred to the district supreme courts. The next session doesn't begin until the third Tuesday in June."

"You want Lizzie to stay here for another two months!"

"I can try to move the case to another district, but I'm afraid it would jeopardize her situation here, and two months is not very long to prepare for a complex trial. I'd prefer longer."

"This is completely unacceptable," Jane said. "I want you to contact the embassy right now. And I'm calling my father," she added, pulling her cell phone out of her purse.

"There's nothing they can do," David said. "The best we can hope for is detention here at the police station and a speedy trial."

I agreed with Jane. Two months locked in a storage closet was completely unacceptable. There had to be another way.

CHAPTER 38

The first hurdle was coming up with a plan. Sergeant Ramos had to let me speak privately with David because he was my lawyer. There was no similar rule in place for best friends, although both Jane and I took David's advice and attempted to ingratiate ourselves with Sergeant Ramos as much as possible.

Jane convinced him that it would be easier and cheaper for him if he allowed her to bring me my meals. Three times a day she arrived with food from the best restaurants on the island. And she always brought extra for him and Officer Juan.

She also brought supplies to make everyone's lives easier. A folding beach chair with a real pillow and blanket for me, bones and chew toys for Butch and Sundance so they'd stop gnawing on the furniture, and a portable outdoor shower. She even offered to send faxes for Sergeant Ramos from the hotel so they didn't have to pay the dollar per page rate at the pharmacy.

Unfortunately, this didn't leave much time for investigating Michael's murder—for Jane or the police, and the latter seemed perfectly content to let me take the rap. David told us he'd hired a private investigator in Belize City, but so far he hadn't turned up anything. The good news was that the prosecutor assigned to my case was inundated and didn't have the time or the resources to pursue his own investigation. David thought we had at least a 50 percent chance of winning just by poking holes in the prosecution's case.

"But that means there's a fifty percent chance of losing too."

"Yes," David admitted in one of our twice-weekly meetings. "But even if we lose at trial, we can always appeal. The prosecution has a very flimsy case."

"But wouldn't that take years?" It did in the US.

"Well, yes, but sometimes that can be the basis for reopening a bail application."

"David, I can't spend the next five years on this island. I have a life back home." And a career too, assuming anyone would hire me again after I'd indefinitely postponed all of my assignments. Jane had been sending e-mails and making phone calls on my behalf, but editors wouldn't wait forever. And I needed the income to pay my mounting legal bills. Jane was lending me the money, but I still had to pay her back.

"I know it's hard, Lizzie, but you don't have a choice."

I disagreed.

My best shot at speaking with Jane privately was in the mornings. I was alone with Officer Juan from eight until ten when Sergeant Ramos arrived. After Officer Juan and I walked Butch and Sundance, we'd wait for Jane to show up with breakfast and her hotel copy of *USA Today*, which she'd bring for Juan, who was enamored with all things American. He was happy to eat breakfast alone and read the paper while Jane and I chatted in the storage room.

"I found something interesting yesterday," I said, handing her a police file. "Ernesto, Michael's cousin, was arrested three years ago for money laundering. He was caught swimming to shore with a plastic bag filled with half a million dollars in twenties strapped to his back."

"He swam all the way from the US?"

"No," I said between bites of spinach and Gruyère omelet. "They found his boat a mile off shore. The genius ran out of gas."

She scanned the arrest report while she ate her granola-yogurt parfait. "Where did you find this?"

"In the file cabinet. I finished my book last night and there was nothing left to clean, so I started reading the arrest reports."

"What do you think it means?"

"I don't know. Maybe he and Michael were in business together."

"But Michael wasn't smuggling money."

"I know. Yet I can't help but feel there's a connection somehow. Can you do some searching on the Internet?"

"Of course," she said. "I'll do it tonight."

The next morning, Jane brought Officer Juan her old *Entertainment Weekly* along with the newspaper to ensure we'd have lots of private time.

"I couldn't find any stories linking Ernesto and Michael."

Sigh. "It was just a hunch."

"But I did find mention of his release. Ernesto was never convicted. The story said the charges were dropped for lack of evidence."

"That can't be right. According to the arrest report, they caught him with the money *and* he confessed."

She shrugged. "I don't know. Greased palms, maybe?"

"Ernesto didn't strike me as someone with a lot of influence."

"Maybe the person he works for is."

We both agreed that one of us needed to talk to Ernesto again. Since I was in jail, Jane was the obvious choice.

"But I don't think you should go alone."

"Who do you want me to take, Officer Juan?"

"If I thought he'd go, yes. But I don't think he or Sergeant Ramos have any interest in following up on new leads. Maybe you should call David."

"I tried already, just to see if he knew anything about Ernesto. His secretary told me he's in trial this week."

"What about the investigator?"

"All I could get out of her was that he was unavailable."

I could only think of one other person. "How do you feel about asking Jack for help?"

"Your Jack?"

"He's hardly 'my Jack.' And he seemed pretty interested in you that day at the pool."

"Oh please," she said, "he's so not my type."

"I'm not telling you to sleep with him. But he can help you find Ernesto and I bet he would if you asked."

"Why would he?"

"Chivalry is not dead in Belize." And Jane was a cute blonde with big tits.

Jane slipped me a note that night with dinner: *I spoke to J. We're on for tonight.*

I was so worried about Jane I hardly slept all night. I was a wreck the next morning, and Jane didn't look much better.

"Three words," she said, settling onto my beach chair/bed. "Boat at night. It was horrible. I needed to take a Xanax just to leave the shore, and I was still seasick the entire time. Good thing Jack was there, because I was really out of it."

"So you don't think he's a murderer anymore?" OK, I was a little jealous.

"Not last night, he wasn't. And don't worry; we spent the whole time talking about you."

"Yeah, right."

"It's true. It's not like Ernesto told us anything."

"Nothing?"

"It was a complete waste. He denied everything."

"Even the arrest?"

She laughed. "He said it was a case of mistaken identity."

"And the confession?"

"Coerced. He said the police are much nicer to you than they were to him."

That I believed. "Did you tell him I was arrested for Michael's murder?"

She stopped smiling and turned serious. "No, but he already knew."

"It's a small place. Maybe my arrest made the news."

Jane began twirling the ends of her hair around her fingers, which meant she was either nervous or plotting.

"What?" I asked.

"Maybe the reason he knew you were in jail was because he, or the person he works for, has an in with the police. Maybe they even planted Michael's blood on the jade pieces knowing our expert would find it. Or maybe," she said, standing up and pacing my cell, "he killed Michael with the jade and then planted those pieces in your suitcase."

She had me right up until the end. "Michael was stabbed. And Ernesto never even met me until after Michael was dead."

"But he'd heard of you."

That was true. "But he didn't even know my name. All he knew was I was the woman who went on her honeymoon without a husband."

"That doesn't mean he, or someone he works for, couldn't have found you. Michael probably told him what hotel you were in. Didn't you tell me you gave Michael a key?"

"Yes, and he lost it, but he had a copy made."

"How do you know he lost it?"

"He told me. But why would he lie about it?"

"I don't know," she said. "Did you ever get the copy back?"

I had to think about that. "No, when I checked out I gave them only my key. The weird part is they never asked me for the other one. And Michael had made such a big deal about them charging me for it."

"Maybe that's because they already had it."

Now I was confused. "You think someone at the hotel killed Michael?"

"No, I think Ernesto killed Michael, then used his key to plant the jade in your suitcase."

"And he returned it at the front desk on his way out? That makes no sense."

"Maybe. But there's a connection here. I can feel it."

I couldn't deny that the coincidences were starting to pile up.

"Good news," Sergeant Ramos announced later that afternoon. "The police on Parrot Caye arrested a woman for attempted murder last night."

"How is that good news? Did she confess to killing Michael too?"

"No, she went after her husband with a meat cleaver. But they're holding her on Parrot Caye overnight, then transferring her to Hattieville in the morning and you're going with her."

I could actually feel my heart skip a beat. "You're sending me to Hattieville? Why? I'm a model prisoner."

"You're better than most," he said, patting his stomach with both hands. He'd probably gained five pounds just since I'd been rearrested. "But it's too hard getting Juan out of the station with you and your friend around."

"So you're punishing me because Officer Juan has a crush?"

"You're not being punished. You're being treated like everyone else."

"I'm being treated like a criminal and I'm not one. Does David know about this?"

"My very next call," he said as he picked up the phone.

Sergeant Ramos couldn't reach David either, but his secretary assured him she would deliver the message. I delivered my own message to Jane that night. I slipped her a note after dinner: *You need to get me out of here* TONIGHT!

CHAPTER 39

As the stars came out, I waited for Jane and tried to figure out the next step. The police would discover me missing in the morning and I was sure the first place they'd look would be Jane's hotel room. And after that, every other hotel on the island. I'd have to find another place to hide. But where?

I still hadn't come up with a solution when Jane knocked on my window at eleven o'clock. She clicked on her keychain flashlight and I could see she was wearing black pants, a black sleeveless shirt, and her blonde hair was pulled up into a black beret.

"Who are you supposed to be, a cat burglar?"

"I didn't know what to wear. It's not like I've ever broken someone out of jail before."

"So what's the plan?"

She reached into her purse and pulled out a nail file. Not wire cutters, or a sledgehammer, or even the lock picks that neither one of us could master. She brought a paper nail file to break me out of jail.

That's when we started arguing and the guy with the machete showed up.

"Jack, what are you doing here?"

I turned to Jane, but she said, "Don't look at me. I only brought the file."

"I heard they were sending you to Hattieville in the morning. What's that for?" he asked, pointing to the emery board.

"Don't you start too," Jane yelled, and we both shushed her.

"So what's your plan?" Jack whispered.

"We don't have one," I said, glaring at Jane. "But there's no way I'm going to Hattieville."

"Then you need to get out of here."

Jack picked up his machete, and Jane jumped off the over-turned garbage can she'd been standing on so she could reach my window, which caused it to tip over and immediately start rolling toward the shore. It probably would've hit the water and floated out into the Caribbean if it hadn't run into a palm tree with a loud clank, which set off Sundance's barking.

"There's no food, Sundance," Jane and I called out to him, while Jack ran down the beach to retrieve the can. He set it upright far away from Jane, then picked up his machete again, and went to work. He slipped the tip of the knife under the head of one of the nails holding the chicken wire in place outside my window and jiggled it until it loosened. When he could pull it out with his finger, he moved on to the next nail.

"Wouldn't that be easier with a hammer?" Jane asked.

Jane didn't even own a hammer, let alone use one to pull nails out of a wall. She must've seen a workman do it. Probably a very cute workman.

Jack lowered the machete. "Do you want my help or not?"

"Of course we do," I said and shot Jane a look, even though I doubted she could see me.

"Then tell your friend not to micromanage," he said, jiggling the machete again.

"I tell her all the time, not that it does any good."

"Hey, don't talk about me like I'm not here," Jane said, jumping up into my field of view. "And micromanaging *is* my job, in case you've forgotten."

Jack and I exchanged a smile.

For a few minutes, the only sounds we heard were the waves on the beach and Jack's machete scraping against the wood, when Jane said, "Lizzie, where are you going to stay? I'm sure the hotel's the first place Sergeant Ramos will look."

"I know, I thought that too. Any suggestions?"

"There are lots of deserted islands around here," Jack said. "I could drop you off somewhere until you figure out your next move."

"A deserted island?" Jane said. "You mean the kind with snakes and bugs and no bathroom?"

Jack smiled in at me while he continued to work the nails. "That's generally who inhabits deserted islands, and no, they don't come with flush toilets and hot showers."

"Lizzie, you know I can't do that."

I knew. To be honest, I was surprised she'd made it this far. Flying in a small plane was major progress for her, and going out on a boat at night, even with a tranquilizer, was off the charts. Snakes and bugs and peeing in the woods were not even in the realm of possibility.

"Don't worry, I wasn't going to ask you to. And I want you to know that I'm really proud of you. You've accomplished a lot this week. Dr. Tobler's going to be thrilled."

"Thanks," she said. "If not for you, I never would've gotten on that. It's been—"

"I don't mean to interrupt," Jack said before we could slip into another Hallmark moment, "but I think I know a place you can both hide."

"Where?" I asked.

"You could stay at the turtle camp. The rest of the volunteers have gone home. I'm the only one left."

"What's a turtle camp?" Jane asked.

I was envisioning doggie day care, but for turtles, which sounded sort of fun.

"It's a turtle nesting beach on the other side of the island," Jack said. "The eggs have already hatched, so everyone's left, but the building's still standing. It's not the Tradewinds, but there's a bed and a roof and indoor plumbing."

It sounded good to me.

Jack jimmied out the last of the nails and tossed the chicken wire into the bushes that separated the police station's grounds from the café next door.

I didn't want to be accused of micromanaging too, but I also didn't want Jack to get in trouble. "Do you think it's safe to leave that stuff here with your fingerprints all over it?"

Jack tried to suppress a smile. "This isn't LA, Lizzie. I don't think the police even know how to dust for prints. But if you've got a blanket or a towel, I'll take it."

I slipped him Sergeant Ramos's beach towel through the slats in the window, and he wrapped it around the bottom pane.

"You think the glass might break?"

"Not really," he said, "but no sense leaving obvious fingerprints."

I smiled but didn't say a word.

With half the panes removed, I was able to squeeze out the bottom of the window. Jack caught me on the way down, and for a moment all those fantasies I'd had of him came rushing back to me. But there was no time for that now.

Jane and I followed him through the bushes (that's where the machete really came in handy) and down to the rocky section of the beach where he'd left his motorboat.

"There's no way I'm getting in that thing," Jane said.

"But you went out in Jack's boat the other night."

"Not that one."

"We took the dive boat," Jack explained. "This one's mine."

"I'm sorry, Lizzie, but I just can't."

"I think it's better if you didn't," Jack said.

I knew Jane could be a pain in the butt sometimes, but I wasn't going to leave her behind.

"She should stay at the hotel so she's there in the morning when the police come," Jack explained, tossing me a sweatshirt from the bottom of his boat. "Sergeant Ramos will already suspect her," he continued. "You shouldn't give him any ammunition."

"He's right," I said to Jane.

She was only too happy to agree.

CHAPTER 40

I stayed with the boat while Jack walked Jane up to Front Street. They both insisted I stay hidden in the trees. Easy for them to say since they weren't the ones being eaten alive by mosquitoes. I ran out in the open as soon as I saw Jack walking up the beach.

"Did you put her in a cab?" I asked.

"No, we decided she should go to the disco for a little while so she'd have an alibi."

I had an alibi and it hadn't kept me out of jail. But in her skin-tight black catsuit, I didn't think she'd have a problem finding men eager to vouch for her.

I helped Jack push the boat into the water, then climbed in while he started the engine. Neither one of us spoke until we reached the other side of the island, where the turtle egg hatchery sat on a deserted stretch of beach.

"The marine reserve's about a mile that way," Jack said, pointing north. "Technically, we're not part of the reserve, but our proximity keeps this place secluded. Although the poachers always manage to find it."

"Poachers?"

"For the turtle eggs. They're considered an aphrodisiac down here. Although sometimes it's just a poor guy trying to feed his family."

We walked past a roped-off area where Jack said the eggs had been buried before they hatched, and I followed him to a cabin on the cusp of the tree line. "This is the hatchery," he said as he unlatched the padlock on the front door.

I was expecting something high-tech and was immediately disappointed. It consisted of a long metal table surrounded by stools, a giant double sink in the corner, and an aquarium with one tiny turtle swimming in circles.

"Who's this?" I asked.

"That's Fred."

"Why is he spinning like that?" I was frustrated just watching him; surely, he must be too.

"Look at his flippers."

They could've fit on my fingertip, but one was definitely smaller than the others. "Can you fix that?"

"Nope," Jack said, turning on the lights in the back room.

"Then what's going to happen to him?"

Jack shrugged. "C'mon, I'll give you the grand tour."

At the back of the hatchery was a dormitory-style room consisting of a narrow bed, a metal desk and chair, a bookshelf made from wood planks and cinder blocks, and a musty couch and coffee table that had probably been rejected by the Salvation Army.

"The bathroom's in there," Jack said, pointing to a closed door next to a cube refrigerator with a coffeemaker and a paint-peeled toaster oven on top. "There are cups under the sink."

"You live here?" I asked, trying not to sound too incredulous.

"No, but when I'm working here it's a good place to crash for the night."

Jack offered me the bed and took the couch for himself. The twin bed really was too narrow for two people, but I still thought he'd try. I supposed after a week in jail I wasn't looking too attractive.

Compared to the beach chair that had been my bed at the police station, the sagging mattress felt like a pillow top, yet I still couldn't sleep. Something was gnawing at me.

"Jack?"

"Hmmm," he said from the couch.

"Why did you come to the police station tonight?"

"I told you," he said through a yawn. "I thought maybe you could use some help."

Actually, he hadn't told me, but it wouldn't have mattered. I didn't believe him anyway. "The last time I saw you, you were pretty angry with me."

"I got over it."

"You got over it?"

"Geez, Lizzie, can't a guy do a good deed without getting the third degree?"

Only if he's got a good reason. But obviously he didn't want to share it with me. "I guess you're right. And Jack?"

"What!"

"I just wanted to say thank you."

"You're welcome. Now can we please go to sleep? I've got to get up for work in four hours."

I woke to the sound of running water. It took me a few seconds to remember where I was. I looked for Jack on the couch, but it was empty. My heart skipped a beat before I realized he must be in the shower, and I fell back asleep. The next time I awoke Jack really was gone. But he'd left me a note promising he'd be back later.

I had no phone, no television, no computer, and no one to talk to, so I decided to go for a walk on the beach. After a lukewarm shower with plenty of soap, I climbed back into my dirty clothes. It was either that or go naked, and they weren't yet grungy enough for me to consider that option.

I walked along the shoreline toward the rocks about a mile away. I climbed the fifteen feet to the top, only slipping once, but decided it wasn't worth the exertion. The other side looked just like my side—beach and ocean, except for a large yellow sign proclaiming it the property of the Camus Caye Marine Reserve. Off

in the distance I spied a dive boat and a group of snorkelers bob-
bing in the water. Not long ago that had been me. It was hard to
believe how quickly my life had changed.

When I could feel my skin burning, I walked back to the
hatchery. After gulping down the last bottle of water in the fridge,
I scanned Jack's bookshelf. All I found were textbooks—turtles,
birds, and marine biology. They'd be great if I was looking for
something to put me to sleep, but I was searching for something to
distract me from my boredom, my hunger, and my sense of doom.
I would've cleaned the hatchery if I could've found cleaning supplies. All I found was Fred.

"Aren't you tired of swimming in circles?"

Fred didn't answer, but he stared at me through his glass
aquarium. He wanted out. I could tell. So I scooped him up with
the net and carried him outside to the beach. I figured we could
race to the ocean. And just to be fair, I was giving him a half-hour
head start.

Fred had barely moved an inch when I heard crunching, then
two sets of beady black eyes popped out of the sand, followed by
two little white bodies. In an instant, the sand crabs had Fred surrounded, and were scratching at his eyes with their pinchers. I
didn't know what else to do, so I kicked sand onto them, grabbed
Fred, and ran.

When I was sure the crabs weren't following us, I slowed down.
"Can you believe that?" I said to Fred. "They would've eaten you alive."

He didn't seem concerned.

I looked around and realized we were on the south side of the
hatchery. Since I hadn't yet explored this beach, I kept walking.
When I spotted a dead palm tree lying across the sand up ahead, I
decided I'd walk that far then head back, but as I approached I heard
raised voices. "Do you think we should go take a look?" I asked Fred.

He had no opinion, but since I doubted Officer Juan and
Sergeant Ramos would be searching for me here, I decided to take
a peek.

Fred and I moved up the beach toward the tree line and crept around the bend. Two men were walking back and forth between a speedboat anchored offshore and something buried in the trees. They were both carrying armloads of plastic bags filled with white powder. It looked like flour but I assumed it wasn't.

Farther away, two other men were standing on the beach shouting at each other in Spanish. The better-dressed one—still in shorts, but paired with a silky looking button-down shirt and loafers—was yelling at the one wearing board shorts and a tank top. Eventually the tank top man stormed off. He had his back to me, but I caught a glimpse of him as he turned and headed out to the boat.

"Fred," I whispered, "that's Manuel."

Fred, as usual, had no response. But he did start nibbling on my finger, and for a little guy he had a surprisingly strong grip. We crept back around the bend and hightailed it back to the hatchery. When we arrived, Jack was waiting for us on the beach.

"Where were you?"

"Fred and I got bored so we went for a walk."

"Fred went for a walk?"

"I walked. He was carried."

Jack took the turtle from my hand and I followed them both into the hatchery. Jack dropped Fred back into his aquarium with a couple of tiny shells, then asked if I was hungry. Ravenous was more like it. I followed Jack into the back room, where he'd laid out two sandwiches and a bag of chips on the coffee table.

"I brought more water," he said. "It's in the fridge."

I grabbed two and joined him on the couch. I thought about what I'd witnessed as I munched my ham and cheese. I couldn't think of a reason not to tell him.

"Jack, I think I saw Manuel today."

He nearly choked on his water. "Where?"

"That end of the beach," I said, pointing in the direction of the dead palm tree.

"What was he doing?"

"Arguing with someone in Spanish."

"Did he see you?"

"I don't think so," I said, reaching for the chips. "I was pretty well hidden in the trees."

"Good," he said, and took another swig of water. "You should stay in the hatchery."

Probably sound advice, but I couldn't just let it go. "It wouldn't have anything to do with the cocaine, would it? Or was it heroin in those little plastic baggies?"

CHAPTER 41

Jack set down his water bottle but didn't answer me.

"Are you in on it?" I finally asked. "Don't worry, I won't turn you in." As a fugitive myself, I was certainly in no position to point the finger at anyone else.

"I can't believe you think I'm a drug dealer!"

"I don't, but you're not answering me. What am I supposed to think?"

"It's complicated," he said. "That stuff's all over down here. Everyone just looks the other way."

"If everyone knows about it, then why is it a problem if Manuel sees me?"

"Because you're supposed to be in hiding, remember?"

Oh, right. I kept forgetting that.

We ate the rest of our lunch in silence.

"Good thing Jane's not here," I said, balling up the empty bag of chips. "She hates it when people aren't speaking to each other."

"Who said we weren't speaking?"

"I just assumed since you're giving me the silent treatment."

"I'm deciding whether or not to tell you something."

"Well you have to tell me now. You can't tease me like that and then not tell me."

He sighed but finally said, "Remember when you asked me last night why I helped you?"

"Yes, and you got mad at me."

"What I told you, well, it wasn't one hundred percent true."

"Oh?" I knew it.

Jack shifted his attention to a string hanging off the hem of his shorts. "The truth is I felt a little bit guilty."

"About what?"

"About your situation."

"Why? It's not your fault. It's not like you killed Michael." When it occurred to me, "Did you?"

He finally looked at me. "Of course not."

"Then I don't understand."

He sighed again and stared up at the ceiling, then blurted out, "It's possible I may have been responsible for that jade ending up in your suitcase."

"What!" I was instantly on my feet. "You planted that jade in my suitcase? Why the hell would you do that?"

He jumped up and grabbed my shoulders. "Lizzie, just calm down."

I pushed him away. "I'm not gonna calm down. This whole thing is your fault. I could spend the rest of my life in prison because of you. And you had the nerve to get mad at me for lying."

"That's why I'm telling you. I believe in being honest with people."

"How about being honest with the police? That could actually do me some good."

"I can't," he said.

"Why not? It's OK for me to go to jail but not you?"

"I'm not the one who planted the jade, and I have no proof who did. All I've got are my suspicions."

"And who do you suspect?"

"Manuel. Or one of his associates."

"Why would Manuel plant jade in my suitcase? Is he an antiquities dealer too?"

"Remember the night we went out on the boat?"

"Yes." Regardless of my feelings for him at that moment, I'd never forget that head massage.

"Remember when Manuel pulled up next to us and how surprised he seemed?"

"Yeah, so?"

"He wasn't. That was for your benefit."

"I don't understand."

"Manuel's the one who suggested I take you out on the boat that night."

"Why?"

He sat back down and ran his fingers through his hair. "I didn't think anything of it at the time. And even when I heard they'd arrested you, it didn't occur to me. But the second time, when Jane told me they'd found Michael's blood on those pieces, I started to suspect."

"Suspect what?"

"Lizzie, how do you think Michael's blood got there?"

"I assumed from the person who killed him. Wait, you think Manuel killed Michael?"

"No, Manuel's not a killer. But some of his associates might be."

"You think one of those drug dealers killed Michael?"

"I don't know," he said. "I've got no proof of anything. But I think you should stay away from Manuel and his friends."

CHAPTER 42

"This better be good," Jane said, splashing through three feet of water to get to the shore. At my insistence, Jack had brought Jane out to see me after he'd finished work for the day. I don't know how he managed to get her on the dive boat without a Xanax, but she obviously wasn't relaxed.

"Nice to see you too." I'd heard Jack's boat coming from miles away and had been waiting for her on the beach.

"And why are you holding a turtle?"

"His name's Fred."

She shrugged and walked into the hatchery. Fred and I followed. "It's not great," she said, "but it's an improvement over last week's accommodations."

"Yeah, there's no chicken wire on the windows and I don't have to use a bucket if I have to pee in the middle of the night."

"Your friend Sergeant Ramos came to see me this morning. He brought Juan too. They looked everywhere for you. Even under the bed."

"Did they find anything?"

"Just the fake badges." Jane smiled, clearly pleased with herself. "I hid the rest of the gear in the rolled-up towels next to the bathtub. They never even thought to look."

Jack walked in with a giant red cooler in his arms. "Does everyone like clams?"

We both nodded.

"Good. Does anyone want to help me start a fire?"

Neither one of us moved.

"OK. I'll be outside if you need me."

Jane peered at the couch in disgust before opting for the bed. "He seems eager to please," she said, leaning back on the pillow.

I pulled two bottles of water out of the fridge and handed her one. "He's trying to make amends for landing me in jail."

"Excuse me?"

Obviously Jack hadn't told her, so I explained.

"That's unbelievable," she said when I'd finished.

"I know. But I've been thinking. It's not just drugs that get smuggled into the US; they smuggle people too. Maybe Manuel can help."

She was shaking her head. "Forget it."

"Why?" I thought it was my best idea yet.

"I called my dad this morning when the police left. He checked the INS site and they already have your name on the watch list. Even if we can get you into the country, the next time you use your credit card or an ATM, they'll pick you up."

"God, is this never going to end? Am I going to be a fugitive for the rest of my life?"

"Of course not. We just have to find the killer ourselves. We already have two new leads."

"Two? Who besides Manuel?"

"Jack." The "of course" was implied. "You're not really buying his whole guilt trip story, are you?"

"I take it you're not?"

"What better way to avoid suspicion than to point the finger at someone else."

"But I didn't suspect him. He's the one who brought it up."

She was twirling her hair again. "I bet he brought you here because he knew you'd see Manuel and start asking questions."

I wasn't very happy with Jack, but I didn't think he was a murderer, or Manuel either. I wasn't so sure about his friends. The one I'd seen him arguing with earlier seemed like he had a short fuse.

"We need to get you out of here," she said.

"Fine by me. What's the plan? Knock Jack out and steal his boat?"

"No, we're bringing Jack with us."

"Why? He already admitted setting me up and you think he's a murderer too."

"Lizzie, when's the last time you watched *The Godfather*?"

"I don't know." Nor did I see the relevance.

"Keep your friends close and your enemies closer. Plus neither one of us knows how to drive a boat."

Jack took Jane back to the Tradewinds and I spent the night alone at the hatchery flinching every time a bird tweeted or a tree branch rustled in the wind. Jane had me completely spooked. I was sure Jack or Manuel or the guy Manuel had been arguing with was going to come and slit my throat in the middle of the night, which was why I was sleeping with a plastic knife under my pillow. It was the best weapon I could find.

"We're leaving," Jack said when he arrived the next morning. "Go pack your stuff."

"I didn't bring anything."

"Then you can help me pack mine."

"Where are we going?" I asked as he tossed notebooks and dirty T-shirts into an overnight bag. I slipped the plastic knife into my shorts pocket.

"Your friend Jane rented a cottage on Parrot Caye."

"A cottage?"

"Her words," he said. "And my scuba class starts at ten."

Jack filled his bag and hurried into the hatchery to grab Fred. When we reached the waterline, Jack set him down in the ocean and gave him a shove.

"You're gonna make him swim to the boat?"

"He's not going to the boat."

"But he'll die in the ocean alone."

"Lizzie, we don't have time for this. He'll adapt to his new environment or he'll become food for something else."

I couldn't believe how heartless he was. "Absolutely not," I said, bending down and scooping Fred up in my hands. He was easy to catch since he was just swimming in circles. "He's coming with us."

"Lizzie, he's a sea turtle. He can't live in your bathtub."

"He can for a little while. At least until we figure something out."

Jack looked at his watch and said, "Fine. You can bring him if you hurry."

The cottage was actually a three-thousand-square-foot house with its own dock, a patio that could hold twenty, and an amazing ocean view.

"Why'd you bring the turtle?" Jane asked as she walked me up the dock.

"I had to. Jack was just going to let him die."

"I told you he was a murderer."

I followed Jane through the back door and she led me to my bedroom. I was hoping she'd remembered to bring my stuff from the hotel, but the room was empty. "I don't suppose my clothes are around anywhere?" Jack had lent me a clean T-shirt, but I'd been wearing the same shorts and underwear for two days.

Jane shook her head. "I gave them to the chambermaid at the hotel."

"You did what? What am I supposed to wear?"

"Calm down. I bought you new ones."

"But there was nothing wrong with the old ones." Or nothing that a little soap and water couldn't fix.

"I couldn't be seen leaving the hotel with all your stuff. What if the police were watching? Besides, they weren't right for the next stage of our investigation."

I didn't want to know, but I had to ask. "Which is?"

"You're no longer Lizzie Mancini, fugitive from justice. You're Gideon Marks, man about town," she said, opening the closet door with a flourish that would've made Vanna White proud. Inside were several pairs of men's pants, two belts, and a handful of button-down shirts.

"You can just wear your tennis shoes," she said. "They're androgynous. I bought extra-long shirts so you can keep the tails out to cover your hips."

Where to begin? "And what am I supposed to do about my chest? Wrap my boobs in an Ace bandage?"

"I don't think that's really necessary, but if it would make you feel better then go right ahead."

"Nice, Jane, really nice."

"You should be glad you're not busty, or no one would ever believe you're a man."

"No one's going to believe it anyway. And where the hell did you come up with Gideon Marks?"

"I went to high school with a Gideon Marks. I always thought he was gay, but it turns out he wasn't. He married Anna Quigley after B-school and now they have three kids. Here," she said, pulling a pair of scissors out of the dresser drawer. "Do you want to cut your hair or should I?"

"You want me to cut my hair?"

"I haven't noticed many men down here with long hair, have you?"

"Jane, I can't cut my hair." I'd been growing it out for over a year so I could have an updo for the wedding.

"Which do you like better, your hair or your freedom?"

An hour later, with short hair and a button-down shirt over safety-pinned strips of T-shirt wrapped around my chest (we were out of Ace bandages), Jane and I ventured out into Cape Town, the business district of Parrot Caye. Jane parked the rented golf cart at the edge of town and we walked from there.

"Where are we going?" I asked.

"Lower your voice or stop talking. You're gonna give us away." She pulled out her map and looked up at the street sign. "It should be on the next block."

"What are we looking for?" I whispered.

"You don't have to whisper, just lower your voice so you sound like a man."

"Like this?" I still sounded like me, but hoarse.

"Forget it," Jane said. "Just don't talk. In fact, why don't you wait outside?"

I grabbed her arm and stopped her in the middle of the dirt path that passed for a sidewalk. "Only if you tell me what we're doing here. I've had enough of this cloak-and-dagger shit."

"I have an appointment at an antiques store that specializes in Mayan jewelry."

"Why?"

"Because if we want to find out who killed Michael we're going to have to meet the players."

Before I could stop her, she pushed open the door to Cape Town Antiques. "There's a park across the street," she said, turning back to me. "I'll meet you there." Then she disappeared inside.

The woman couldn't be in the same room with a spider, but she was seeking out murderers. I wondered what Dr. Tobler would have to say about that.

I had too much nervous energy to sit and wait, so I pulled my baseball cap lower on my forehead and wandered down the main street. I was walking past an open-air restaurant when I almost stopped in my tracks. Sitting at a table sipping fruit smoothies were Cheryl and her husband, John, my former friends from Camus Caye.

CHAPTER 43

What were Cheryl and John doing on Parrot Caye? They were supposed to have flown back to Chicago last week. I wanted to stay and eavesdrop, but I was afraid they'd see through my flimsy disguise, so I crossed to the other side of the street and hurried back to the park to wait for Jane.

"Mission accomplished," she said with a triumphant smile.

"You found Michael's killer?" I asked, sliding over to make room for her on the bench.

"No," she said, brushing it off with the tail end of my shirt before she sat down. "But we have an appointment tomorrow morning with a local antiquities dealer."

"And you think he's going to lead you to Michael's killer?"

"Possibly," she said, pulling a bottle of water out of her purse. "Or maybe he is Michael's killer."

"Well, you could always ask him and find out."

"Ha, ha," she said and made a face at me. "What's got your panties in a twist?"

"Remember that couple I told you about from the Blue Bay—John and Cheryl?"

"The ones that befriended you and then dropped you the minute they found out you lied about Michael?"

She offered me her water, but I declined. "I just saw them."

"Here?"

"Across the street," I said, pointing to Café Lola.

"That's one long honeymoon."

"I know. And it doesn't make any sense. They never mentioned they were coming to Parrot Caye. They told me they were flying home the day after me."

"And this is significant because?"

"I don't know, but it's weird. Don't you think?"

"I'm calling my dad," Jane announced as soon as we reached the front door of our rented "cottage."

"Why?" I didn't object, but Jane rarely spoke to her father more than once a week.

"I was thinking with all the illegal drugs down here, maybe the DEA has agents here too."

"And how is that going to help us? I thought the point of me chopping off all my hair was to keep the police away."

"The local police, yes. But when we find Michael's killer we have to turn him in to someone, and I'd rather it be the US authorities."

"Why?"

She rolled her eyes at me. "Duh. They're less likely to be on the drug dealers' payroll."

Jane went into the living room to place her call and I went in search of food. Our rental house came with a stocked fridge, but the grocery list must've been provided by Jane. The kitchen was filled with fresh fruits and vegetables without a bag of chips or a candy bar in sight. By the time I finished cutting up a melon, Jane was off the phone.

"All he could tell me was that customs and the DEA both have agents down here," she said, joining me in the kitchen.

"He didn't give you any names?" I asked, offering her the bowl of cantaloupe.

She shook her head. "He couldn't. They're undercover. Everything's classified."

"Then I guess we'll have to hope the local police are honest."

"That's not very comforting," she said, peeling herself a banana.

"C'mon, do you really think Sergeant Ramos is on the take? Lazy I'll give you, but corrupt?"

Jane shrugged. "He's got an awfully nice boat for a civil servant."

Jane and I spent the afternoon driving around the island picking up supplies. Batteries for the stun guns, rope, and duct tape so we could tie up the bad guy when we eventually found him, and a camera with an extra-long lens. One more stop at the fish market to buy food for Fred and dinner for us, and we were on our way home.

We were sitting on the patio sipping Pellegrino and waiting for Jack to arrive when Jane suggested we go through the timeline of Michael's murder yet again. I didn't see the point, I'd told her so many times even she had it memorized, but I didn't want to argue with her either.

"That morning I went diving with Jack and the rest of the Discover Scuba class. We got back to the hotel around noon, and I went to the pool so Michael and I could have our big fight."

"The one you planned out the night before?"

"Yes."

"And you tried to get Jack to come with you, so he could watch as you and Michael broke up?"

"Correct," I said. "But he sent Manuel instead."

"And that's who Michael had the fight with?"

"Yes, but that wasn't part of the plan. He was only supposed to have an argument with me and storm off in a huff."

She rolled over on her lounge chair so she was facing me. "And tell me again why you think he fought with Manuel."

"I smelled alcohol on his breath, so at the time I thought he was just drunk and maybe a little jealous." Jane was twirling her hair again. "But you have another idea."

"What if they knew each other, or at least knew of each other, and the fight wasn't about you but about them?" she said.

"You mean like a business dispute? Someone stealing money or encroaching on someone's territory?"

"Maybe. Or it could've been over another woman. Whatever someone would be willing to kill over."

"I'm going with money."

"You would."

"What's that supposed to mean?"

"Nothing," she said. "I just don't want to rule anything out. Didn't Sergeant Ramos tell you that Michael had another woman in his hotel room the night before he died? Someone who didn't fit your description?"

"You think Michael was killed over a one-night stand?"

"You don't know she was a one-night stand. Maybe she was his wife, or his girlfriend, or someone else's wife or girlfriend."

I sat up to face her. "Let's forget for the moment that he was pretending to be my husband. Now you think this whole thing was just an unfortunate chain of events?"

"Not completely," she said. "Don't forget it was Jack who sent Manuel to the pool with you."

"You think Jack set Manuel up?" I didn't want to believe it, but I couldn't completely rule it out either.

She leaned back in her chair. "At this point, I think we have to consider all the alternatives."

Jane missed her calling. She should've been a CIA operative, or a trial attorney, or a mafia boss. She effortlessly elicited information from Jack over dinner that evening without revealing any of her own theories, including that she considered him a suspect. The fact that Jane drank only water and he drank most of the bottle of wine Jane insisted we open probably helped.

Jack confirmed that Manuel wasn't married, but that at any given time he had several girlfriends, all of whom he cheated on regularly. He also told us that Manuel had once flown into a jealous rage when he found out that one of those girlfriends had cheated on him.

"Did he do anything besides get jealous?" Jane asked.

"He didn't kill the guy, if that's what you mean," Jack replied, pushing his plate away. "But I'm sure he took a swing at him."

"That makes no sense," I said. "If he cheated on her first, then he had no right to get mad when she cheated on him. Turnaround's fair play."

"Not in Belize," Jack said.

We all went to bed early that night, but as usual, I couldn't sleep. After two hours of counting sheep, bottles of beer on the wall, and everything else I could think of, I sauntered out to the living room to watch TV. I tried to get Fred to watch with me, but he wasn't interested in channel surfing, so I returned him to his makeshift aquarium in the kitchen sink.

I was half-watching a tennis match and half-asleep when I thought I heard the floor creak behind me. I didn't panic until I felt the hand on the back of my head. Then I screamed.

"What the hell are you screaming for?" Jack asked.

"Why did you sneak up on me?" I yelled.

Jane ran into the living room wearing her pink camisole with matching shorts and her eyeshade pushed up on her head. "What's going on in here?"

"Nothing, I just got spooked."

"Is that what you kids are calling it these days?"

"Jane, we weren't doing anything."

"I don't want to know," she said, heading down the hallway back to her bedroom. "Just use protection," she yelled before she slammed the door shut.

Jack sat down next to me on the couch and placed his hand on my waist, the only crack of skin showing between my pajama top and bottoms.

"Excuse me, but what are you doing?" I said, pushing his hand away. He must've showered right before he went to sleep because he smelled like Ivory soap.

"We've already been busted. We might as well take advantage of it."

"Nice try."

He smiled, but moved to the other end of the couch. "Tell me again why you cut your hair?"

I instinctively reached for the back of my head. Instead of grabbing handfuls of thick curls, all I felt was stubby, uneven ends. *My freedom is more important than my hair,* I reminded myself. "So when I go out in public, people will think I'm a man."

"It's going to take more than a haircut," he said and started massaging my feet.

I closed my eyes and concentrated on his skillful hands as they moved from my heels, to my ankles, to my calves, and then... *crash*.

Jane came flying into the room again. "What was that?"

"I don't know," I said, kicking Jack's hands away and accidentally nailing him in the crotch. Ouch.

"Oh God," was all he said before he doubled over.

"Jack, I'm so sorry. Are you OK?"

"I will be," he croaked, looking up at me from where his head was buried between his knees, his hands shielding himself from another blow.

Jane looked from Jack to me. "I guess that means it's up to us to investigate."

"I'll be OK," he said. "Just give me a minute."

"Are you sure?" I asked, although it's not like we could call the police.

He nodded. "It's probably just an iguana. They're everywhere down here."

"Isn't that a giant lizard?" Jane asked.

"They're more afraid of you than you are of them."

He didn't know Jane.

"Do you think we should get the stun gun?" she asked.

"We don't want to fry him," I said. "We just want him out of the house."

"Here," Jack said, tossing me the rolled-up blanket from the corner of the couch. "Catch him, then release him outside."

Jane looked horrified. "That's a chenille throw."

"C'mon," I said to Jane, handing the blanket back to Jack. "I saw a broom in the pantry. I'll open the back door and sweep him out."

I flipped on the lights in the kitchen and immediately found the culprit. There was no iguana, only Fred, who had climbed out of the sink and had knocked over the wineglass Jack had left on the counter.

We both let out our breath in relief.

"It's your turtle," Jane said. "I'm going back to bed."

She'd already slammed her bedroom door shut again when I found the real culprit—a coconut with a note tied around it with a rubber band. *Gringos Go Home*, it said in a barely legible black scrawl.

CHAPTER 44

The three of us stared at the note as if looking for a hidden message. Jane was the first to lose interest.

"How do you think it got in here?" she asked, moving to the open window above the sink. "It's not even broken."

I joined her at the window. "Someone with good aim could've gotten it through. It probably hit the wineglass on its way down, then fell to the floor." Poor Fred. I'd falsely accused him. I knew how that felt.

"That would have to be someone with amazingly good aim," Jack said. "The opening's not that wide."

"Then how do you think it got in here? I don't see any other broken glass."

He walked to the end of the kitchen and opened the French door to the patio. "How about the back door?"

"That was locked when we went to bed." I'd checked it myself.

Jack and I stared each other down until Jane said, "It doesn't really matter how it got here. What I want to know is who sent it."

"It could've been kids playing a prank," Jack replied. "Or some disgruntled locals. They're not as fond of wealthy Americans on Parrot Caye as they are on Camus."

"You don't think it has anything to do with us looking into Michael's murder, do you?" I asked.

Jack shrugged. "It could be that too."

Jane was the one who jumped into action. "We're not going to figure this out tonight, so we might as well go back to bed. Lizzie, you go shut all the windows, and I'll double-check the locks on the doors. Jack, go turn on the AC. I'd rather have air-conditioning than ocean breezes anyway."

For all her bravado, Jane was shaken up enough not to want to sleep alone. To be honest, so was I. I knew Jack would welcome me, probably both of us, but I opted to spend the night with Jane. I wouldn't be getting any head massages, and definitely no sex, but at least I knew I wouldn't wake up with her trying to smother me with a pillow—not unless I snored really loudly.

The next morning Jane and I rose to the sounds of banging and clanking. We quickly found the source—Jack in the kitchen.

"I made coffee," he said, as if this were a major accomplishment. "How do you like your eggs?"

"I'll cook," Jane said, grabbing the frying pan from his hand.

I poured each of us a cup of coffee, but we waited for Jack to take a sip before Jane and I tried it ourselves. Jane's conspiracy theories had definitely started to rub off on me. I had actually considered the possibility that Jack might try to poison us.

"I don't think this is what Vito Corleone had in mind when he said, 'keep your friends close, but your enemies closer,'" I whispered to Jane when Jack took Fred into the bathroom so we could use both halves of the kitchen sink.

"Maybe not," she whispered back. "But he's here, so make the best of it. And you need to use bleach on that," she added, motioning to the sink. "Who knows what kind of turtle germs are in there."

We were having a relaxing breakfast on the patio when Jane reminded me that we were meeting with the antiquities dealer in an hour.

"I don't know if that's such a good idea. Someone obviously wants us out of here."

"Who's it with?" Jack asked.

"I don't know his name," Jane said. "Philip Gusman at Cape Town Antiques set it up."

"You mean Filipe Guzman?"

"I'm sure it's Philip Gusman," she said, searching her purse for his business card, which she handed to Jack.

"That's the one he gives the tourists," he said, handing it back, "with a twenty percent increase in the price. What are you buying?"

Jane glanced at me before she said, "Just looking. My dad likes antiques and he's got a big birthday coming up."

Jack threw his fork and knife onto his plate and folded his arms across his chest. "Why won't you believe I'm not the bad guy here? I came clean about what I did, and I'm doing everything I can to fix it. So either be straight with me or I'm leaving and you two are on your own."

Jack stared at me, so I turned to Jane. "He did break me out of jail and hide me for two nights."

She shrugged, then said, "I told Gusman or Guzman or whatever his name is that I was looking for one-of-a-kind antique Mayan jewelry. He didn't have any on hand, but he said he knew a local dealer and he'd set it up. I thought the guy might know something."

"You understand that the local antiquities dealer is also the local drug dealer and probably a relative of the looter who stole the jewelry in the first place, right?"

"We understand that might be a possibility," Jane said, glancing at me for confirmation.

"Not *might*," Jack said. "*Is.* And by 'we' does that mean Lizzie's going with you?"

"Of course I'm going with her. I'm not going to let her go alone."

"And you're planning on dressing up as Boy George?"

"No," I said, offended by the suggestion. My look was much more natural. "I'm just going to wear a baseball cap and men's clothes."

"Lizzie, you could shave your head and wear overalls and no one's going to believe you're a guy."

Somehow I found that statement comforting.

"Then what do you suggest?" Jane asked, folding her arms across her chest too. "Lizzie can't live in hiding forever, and the police have no interest in finding the real killer. We have no choice."

"Then I'm going with you," Jack said, uncrossing his arms and pointing at me, "and she's staying here."

"Fine," Jane said.

"Not fine. I have a say in this too."

"Lizzie, don't be stupid," Jack said, followed by Jane's, "He's got a point."

I knew my disguise needed work, but still. It was my life on the line, not theirs. "I won't come to the meeting, but I'm waiting outside. If you two don't come back, someone's got to know where to look for you."

After another ten minutes of arguing, it was agreed. I'd play lookout from the park across the street.

CHAPTER 45

Jane parked the golf cart in the dirt lot two blocks from the antique store. She and Jack left first, and I followed a few minutes later, lugging the camera with the extra-long lens so I'd look like a tourist.

I tried waiting in the park, I really did, but not knowing what was going on inside was driving me crazy. When I couldn't stand it anymore (about forty-five seconds later), I walked around the block to the back of the antique store and crept up to the screen door. I could hear voices, but they sounded like they were coming from upstairs.

I eyed the palm tree only a few feet away. I hadn't climbed a tree since, well, forever actually. I'd never been a tomboy. But if I could just make it up five or six feet, I'd be able to see in the second-story window. I shifted the camera around to my back, wrapped my arms around the tree trunk, and pushed up with my legs. Five minutes later, I was in exactly the same spot. I didn't know how kids did it. The palm had no branches to hang on to, and every time I pulled myself up a few inches, I'd end up sliding right back down.

I was considering my options—none, really, I just kept hoping one would present itself—when I heard the high-pitched whine of a moped and ducked for cover in the bushes. I'd seen a police officer on a moped yesterday. Disguise or no disguise, I wasn't taking any chances getting this close to another.

I peered through the bushes, trying to ignore the insects and wildlife whose home I was invading, and watched as the moped slowed and then coasted to a stop at the antique shop's back door.

I didn't let out my breath again until I saw the Havana shirt and knew that it wasn't a cop. But my relief was short-lived. When the rider climbed off the moped and turned around, I recognized him immediately. It was Michael's cousin, Ernesto.

I felt like I was watching a car accident in slow motion. I wanted to warn Jane, but there was no way I could. All I could do was silently stare as Ernesto slung his knapsack over his shoulder and strode through the back door. Ten seconds later the shouting began, mostly in Spanish. And a minute after that, Ernesto burst through the exit, kick-started his moped, and took off down the alley.

Jack, Jane, and a middle-aged man I didn't recognize but presumed was Guzman followed.

"Ernesto, wait," Jane yelled as he sped away.

"I'm awfully sorry," Filipe/Philip said in a British accent. "I can assure you, Ms. Chandler, I know many dealers in the area. If you can give me a day or two, I'll be able to find you what you're looking for."

"Sure," Jane said, not even bothering to glance back at him. She was following Jack down the alley in the direction of the street. I waited until Filipe/Philip returned to his shop before I abandoned my hiding spot and caught up with them.

"What are you doing here?" Jane said.

Jack stopped and turned around. "I thought you agreed to wait for us in the park."

"Don't worry, no one saw me. What happened?"

"Ernesto came in and ruined everything," Jane said.

"Because he thinks you're a federal agent," Jack opined, leading us back to the golf cart.

"Where'd you get that from?" Jane asked.

"You were standing right there when he said it."

"Jane doesn't speak Spanish either," I explained.

Jane stopped walking. "Maybe we can use this to our advantage."

"How?" I asked.

"Don't federal agents offer rewards for information?"

"They might," I said, trying to remember if I'd seen any reward posters the last time I'd mailed a package from the post office.

"You're going to offer him a reward for information about Michael's killer?" Jack didn't even try to hide his skepticism.

"Why not?" Jane said.

I agreed. "What's wrong with that?"

"For one thing, how are you going to find him? I don't think Guzman will be setting up any more meetings."

"I'm sure *you* could find him," I said, grabbing Jack's arm and making doe eyes at him.

Jane followed suit from the other side. "Yeah, Jack, I bet a big, strong man like you could find anyone."

He shook us both off, but cracked a smile. "Even if I could track him down, what makes you think he'll believe me? And why do you think you can believe him? For all we know, he could be the killer."

"First, you said it was one of Manuel's drug dealer friends."

"I never said that," Jack insisted.

"Now you think it's Ernesto?" I continued.

"Hey, all I said was I thought Manuel might have had something to do with planting the jade in your suitcase," Jack replied. "I never said he was the killer."

"Then how did Michael's blood get on the jade?"

"Maybe Ernesto can tell us," Jane said. "And a bribe's the fastest way to find out."

I was peeling and cleaning shrimp for dinner, leaving the shells for Fred to nibble on, when Jack strode through the kitchen door.

"You owe me big-time," he said.

"For what?" I asked, not even bothering to look up from the sink.

He unfolded a crumpled note and held it in front of my face. "For this."

Cajun Joe's. 10:00 p.m. $10,000.

"Is this supposed to mean something?"

"It means for ten thousand dollars, Ernesto will finger the killer and you go free."

"Will he take a check?" Jane asked, joining us from the patio looking fabulous, as always, in her bikini top with matching sarong around her waist. "A wire transfer will take at least a day."

"No," Jack said, "he's not going to take personal check. This isn't Bloomingdale's."

"Maybe we can pool our resources," I said, drying my hands on a kitchen towel. "I've probably still got a hundred or so in cash."

"I've got two hundred," Jane said, "but I can get another three from an ATM."

Jack pulled his wallet out of his back pocket. "I've got forty bucks."

"What about your dad?" I asked. "Would he have any cash around?"

"Not the kind of money you're talking about. Besides, he thinks I'm in Guatemala visiting a friend for a few days."

"A friend?" I asked.

Jack stared at the floor as he said, "Girlfriend, actually."

"You have a girlfriend?" And he had the nerve to get mad at me for lying. At least my husband was a fake.

"Ex-girlfriend. We broke up a couple of weeks ago."

"I can't believe you never told me."

"There was nothing to tell. Besides, you're the one—"

"You two can finish your lovers' quarrel later," Jane said. "Right now we have to figure out how we're going to get our hands on ten thousand dollars by the end of the day."

CHAPTER 46

It was Jane's idea to call my lawyer.

"But won't he turn us in? He's an officer of the court, remember."

"I'm not going to tell him you're with me," Jane said. "I'll say after you escaped I stayed behind to clear your name."

"I don't know, Jane." It sounded far-fetched even to me.

"You have any better ideas?"

"Maybe Jack could push the meeting a day or two until you can get the money yourself."

"I don't think so," Jack said. "Ernesto was already jumpy. I think if we postpone he'll disappear."

"Then it's agreed," Jane said and walked into the other room to call David.

Jack stayed in the kitchen with me. He peeled the rest of the shrimp while I cleaned them and fed the leftover scraps to Fred.

"Don't get too attached," Jack said, watching Fred nibble on the shell in my hand.

"Why not? Are you planning on feeding him to a shark?"

"If this pans out with Ernesto, you'll be going home soon."

"So? I'll bring Fred with me." My apartment building didn't allow dogs, but I wasn't aware of any prohibition on turtles. "My neighbor's kid has two goldfish and no one's complained."

"Goldfish don't grow to three hundred pounds. Besides, you can't just take him on the plane with you. You have to have a permit to import wildlife."

"Then maybe your friend Manuel can smuggle him in with his cocaine," I said and smiled up at him.

"Cute," Jack said, but he smiled back.

We stared at each other for a few seconds and it took all of my self-control not to reach up and push the hair out of those blue-gray eyes, which were leaning more toward blue today than gray. God he was good-looking. Then Jack leaned in. I closed my eyes and inhaled his suntan scent, expecting any moment to feel his lips on mine. Instead, I heard Jane's voice booming in my ear.

"We've got five thousand," she said, joining us in the kitchen.

I jumped back and tried to refocus my mind on the task at hand. "Is that enough?"

"It'll have to be," Jack said, turning away from me to wash his hands at the sink. "Assuming we can get to Belize City and back before ten. It's going to be tight," he added, glancing at his watch.

Jane shook her head. "David's meeting us, or meeting me, rather, at the bar. He said he wants to be there to record the conversation with Ernesto so he'll have something to bring to the police."

"Ernesto's never going to go for that," Jack said.

"He won't know. David said he'll use a hidden mic."

"Is that legal?" I asked.

"It must be," Jane said. "It was David's idea."

At nine o'clock, the three of us piled into the golf cart and headed out to Cajun Joe's. Jane wanted to make sure she got there early and I used the "I don't feel safe staying home alone" excuse to tag along.

"You can come into town," Jack said, "but not to the restaurant."

"Of course." With David there, I'd have to stay out of sight. But that didn't mean I wasn't going to find some way to listen in.

We parked the golf cart near the dock, three blocks from the restaurant.

"I'll try to get us a table on the patio so you'll be able to see," Jack said, handing me Jane's night-vision binoculars.

"Good idea." I'd forgotten about those.

"But we better not see you," he added.

"Understood."

"Do you have your cell phone?" Jane asked.

"Yes," I said, feeling for it in my pants pocket. I was starting to like wearing men's clothes. They were much roomier than women's.

"Good," she said. "Mine's on vibrate, so you can call if you need us."

"Don't worry, Mom and Dad. I'll be fine. You two have fun."

Jack placed his hand under my chin, forcing me to look up at him. "Be good, young lady, or I'll have to spank you when we get home."

S&M had never been my scene, but I was starting to feel tingly all over just thinking about it. "Being bad is starting to sound good."

"Too much information, people," Jane shouted.

"Hey, I'm on my honeymoon."

"That's true," Jack said, sporting a devilish grin.

"You know what happened to the last guy she brought on her honeymoon," Jane said as she pulled her lipstick out of her purse. "Are you sure you want to go there?"

"She's got a point," he said and let go of me.

"Thanks a lot, Jane."

"It's for your own good," she said as she double-checked her flawless appearance in the golf cart's rearview mirror.

I didn't see how my remaining sex-starved and unsatisfied was for my own good, but I wasn't going to have that conversation in front of Jack. I wished them luck and waited until they had a five-minute head start before I followed them at a safe distance.

The binoculars came in handy. From my current location on the beach, I could see perfectly. Unfortunately, I couldn't hear anything above the general restaurant din. I wished Jane had thought to order a directional mic with the rest of the spy gear. At least the next time one of us gets arrested for a murder we didn't commit and we're forced to find the real killer ourselves, we'll know what equipment to bring.

I waited until I saw David arrive at the restaurant before I made my move. While Jane was busy making the introductions, I sprinted across the dark beach and dived under the deck to Cajun Joe's. The outer edge was at least ten feet above the sand, so there was plenty of room underneath. I crawled around listening to the conversations above me until I heard Jane's voice.

"I can't believe that really works," Jane said.

"Say something," David replied.

"What should I say?"

"Anything."

"Testing one two three."

I heard a click and then Jane's voice sounding very tinny saying, "Testing one two three." I looked up between the slats of the wood deck, but all I could see were David's shoes and Jane's bare feet. I knew those heels weren't as comfortable as she'd pretended.

"That's amazing," Jane said. "I'm going to buy one of those as soon as I get home."

"Where'd you get it?" Jack asked.

"A client of mine gave it to me last Christmas."

"I bet it really comes in handy."

"Actually, this is the first time I've had occasion to use it."

"You should let me wear it. I still don't think you should be here when Ernesto comes."

At first, David protested, but eventually he agreed. Then there was much scraping of chairs and shuffling of feet as David moved to a table several yards away.

I stayed under Jack and Jane's table, listening as they ordered another bottle of water, a beer, and a basket of Cajun chicken wings. I knew Jack didn't like my shrimp fra diavolo. Steven had never liked my cooking either.

"So tell me about Lizzie," Jack said.

"What do you want to know?"

"Is she always this crazy?"

I am not crazy!

"Yes. But she's tame with you. You should see her at home."

That bitch.

"We still have a few minutes before Ernesto gets here," Jack said. "Maybe we should take advantage of it."

I could see Jane's foot inching up Jack's leg. "What did you have in mind?" she asked.

I watched as Jack reached down and placed Jane's foot in his lap and she followed with the other.

I would kill them both when we got out of here.

"That's better," Jack said. "So does Lizzie ever follow directions?"

"Never," Jane said.

"So I shouldn't be surprised if she's hiding under our table instead of staying at the golf cart like she was supposed to?"

"Not in the least."

Jack pushed his napkin off his lap and reached down to pick it up. "Gotcha," he whispered into the slats.

I gave him the finger, but doubted he could see. An instant later, Jane slid her toes back into her heels and Jack was on his feet. I heard a chair above me scrape and Jack said, "Have a seat. You want a beer?"

"Couldn't we sit inside?" Ernesto said.

"It's too stuffy in there," Jane replied. "Out here we have the breeze."

"Relax," Jack said. "It's just the three of us."

"I don't like cops," Ernesto said.

Obviously, Jack hadn't disabused him of his notion that Jane was a federal agent.

"Ernesto, we're not interested in busting you," she said. "We're only interested in finding Michael's killer. I'd think you'd want to find him too since he killed your cousin."

"I do," Ernesto said. "But if anyone finds out I talked, I'm dead."

"No one's going to find out," Jack said. "We'll be very discreet."

"Where's my money?"

Jane reached down to her purse and pulled out an envelope. She tapped Ernesto on the knee with it, but when he tried to grab it, she pulled it back.

"Don't play games with me, Blondie."

The waitress brought Ernesto's beer and asked if they wanted anything else. Jane told her no and she walked away.

"Information first," Jane said. "Money second."

"How do I know it's all there?" Ernesto said.

"You can count it later. Five thousand tonight, and five thousand tomorrow when we find out if your information's any good."

"That wasn't the deal." Ernesto slammed his fist on the table, causing his beer to tip over and rain down on me. I scooted away, but not before it doused me on its way to making a puddle in the sand, which quickly attracted a colony of ants.

From my new vantage point, I had to strain to hear their conversation, plus I was distracted by another couple above David and me talking to someone a few feet away. I leaned toward David's table. I didn't see any other feet and I didn't hear anyone else's voice, so I assumed he was talking on his phone.

"I'm there now," he said, followed by a pause, and then, "no, I'll come to you." Another pause, then, "I don't know where she is, but I'm sure she's not far." Another pause. "Let's worry about him first, then we'll go back for her. They're getting up, I've got to go."

I peered through the slats and saw Ernesto's sneakers moving toward the inside of the restaurant, followed by Jack's Tevas and Jane's strappy sandals. I took the opportunity to make a run for the unlit beach.

CHAPTER 47

I'd been waiting at the golf cart for ten minutes when Jack and Jane finally arrived, and they didn't look happy. Jack took the keys from Jane and slid behind the steering wheel. Then Jane took the front passenger seat, forcing me to ride in the back.

"What did he say?" I asked when it was apparent no one was going to offer up the information on his or her own.

"Didn't you hear?" Jack asked.

I ignored his sarcasm. "Only up until he spilled his beer," I said, holding my shirt out so he could see the stain down the front.

"He won't tell us anything until we get him the rest of the money," Jane replied.

"You didn't give him the five thousand, did you?"

"Of course not," she said. "We're supposed to meet him at the dock tomorrow night with the full ten."

"Does David know?"

"Of course David knows, he's the one who gave us the five."

"Then I think you should cancel."

"Why?" Jack asked, staring at me through the rearview mirror.

"Because I don't trust David."

"Since when?" Jane asked.

Jack screeched the golf cart to a halt at the side of the road and turned around to face me. "What's going on?"

I relayed the conversation I'd overheard and waited for one of them to speak. Finally, I said, "Well, what are we going to do?"

"I think for now we do nothing," Jack said. He cranked the engine and the golf cart lurched forward.

"My lawyer's going to have me killed and you think we should do nothing?"

"You don't know that," Jack said. "You could've misinterpreted the whole thing. They may not have even been talking about you."

"Sure, that's why he said 'they're leaving,' as the three of you walked out. I'm sure it was just a coincidence."

"All I'm saying is you shouldn't jump to any conclusions."

"Easy for you to say since it's not your life on the line." I turned to Jane, who had been uncharacteristically silent. "And you agree with him?"

"I don't know what to think."

I was the first to reach the front door of the house, but I still had to wait for Jack to unlock it with Jane's keys. I stormed directly into my bedroom, grabbed my pillow and my pajamas, and headed for Jane's bed.

Jack followed me inside. "If you want company tonight, I'd be happy to oblige."

"I bet you would."

He sighed, then headed to his own room and slammed the door shut.

Jane appeared in the doorway and motioned for me to follow her into the bathroom, where she turned on the faucet for the tub. I knew I smelled like beer, but she didn't have to be so obvious.

"I was going to take a shower before I went to sleep."

"It's not for you," she said. "Although you might want to wash the beer off. You really reek. This is so Jack can't hear us. I think I've figured out who killed Michael."

"Who?"

"He did."

Not this again. "He couldn't have killed Michael. He was with me the whole night."

"So you keep assuming. The coroner's report said Michael died somewhere between midnight and four a.m."

"When Jack was with me."

"No, when you *think* he was with you. You were passed out, so you have no idea if he was there all night or not. He could've left, killed Michael, stolen the jade, and then, not realizing he still had Michael's blood on his hands, hidden it in your suitcase."

"How do you *not* realize you have blood on your hands? Don't you think he'd be smart enough to wash them?"

"Of course, but you can never get it all off. That's how the cops can always find drops of it with that special UV light."

I did always wonder about that when I saw it on TV. "And his motive?"

"I'm not sure yet. Money, probably. He is a poor student after all."

"But why hide it in my suitcase?"

"He probably planned on coming back for it, but you surprised him by leaving early."

"Only after he blew me off. And besides, Manuel asked him to take me out on the boat that night. Couldn't Manuel have gotten the jade while Jack and I were out on the water?"

Jane reached over and shut the tap before the bathtub overflowed. She put her finger to her lips as she waited for half the tub drain out, before she started the faucet again.

"What if Manuel didn't ask him to take you out? What if he really was surprised to see you out there with Jack?"

This was giving me a headache. I couldn't keep up with who was lying and who was telling the truth. "When we got back to my room that night, I took a shower. If Jack was only after the jade, he had plenty of time to get it back. Why didn't he?"

"Give me a minute," she said, closing her eyes while she twisted the ends of her hair into ringlets. By the time she'd successfully rerouted her conspiracy train, she looked like she'd gotten a bad eighties perm. "I got it," she said, jumping up from the edge of the tub. "Didn't Sergeant Ramos say the pieces they found in Michael's room were part of a collection, and that some of them, the valuable ones, were missing?"

"Yes."

"But the ones they found in your suitcase were fakes, or at least not priceless antiquities?"

"Yes." I still wasn't following. Maybe I didn't want to. I didn't want to believe my judgment about Jack could be so wrong. But I had to admit, my track record with men lately hadn't been too good.

"What if Jack grabbed the originals while you were in the shower, then left the fakes in your suitcase so you could take the fall? Maybe he's even the one who called Sergeant Ramos and tipped him off."

I tried to digest this new theory. It all fit except for one part. "If Jack already has what he wants, then why help me break out of jail? And why is he here with us now?"

"I don't know," she said. "That's what we have to figure out."

"And what about David?"

"Something's definitely going on there, I'm just not sure what. From this point forward, we trust no one but ourselves."

CHAPTER 48

I spent a mostly sleepless night wondering if Jack was going to slip into our room the moment we fell asleep and slit our throats. Finally, around three, I got up and pushed a chair in front of the door. It didn't help. Every time I heard the slightest noise, I was instantly awake.

I finally slept a few hours as the sun was coming up. When I awoke at eight thirty, the door was open and I was alone. I ran into the living room and found Jane on the couch sipping coffee and watching morning TV.

"Jack's gone. He left a note," she added as she handed it to me.

Ladies,
Had some things to take care of. I'll be back before the meeting tonight.
Jack

"That's vague."

Jane shrugged and muted the sound on the television. "I called my dad again. I wanted his take on all this."

"And does Mr. Chandler think Jack's the killer?" I asked, joining her on the couch.

"He has no idea, but he told me I should stay out of it and come home. Don't worry," she said, smiling at the look of devastation on my face, "you know I never take my father's advice. And he knows too, so I was able to convince him to do a little digging. The DEA and customs are running a joint task force down here. Apparently antiquities smuggling has become very popular with drug dealers."

"Don't you find that odd?" I did.

She shook her head. "According to my dad it's an easy way for the dealers to launder their money."

"How?"

"They sell the pieces through legitimate antiquities dealers who don't know they're illegal. Or sometimes they know, but don't care. The antiquities dealer acquires the piece from the drug dealer, then sells the same piece back to someone else on the drug dealer's payroll who just happens to pay in cash. The antiquities dealer gets his vig—"

"Vig?"

"A commission, like a real-estate broker. Then he deposits the rest of the money in the bank as a legitimate transaction and transfers the funds to a dummy corporation set up by the drug dealer's lawyer, who then parcels the money out through shell corporations claiming it's payment for services like cleaning, shipping, preserving, anything really. After that it gets very hard to trace."

"And you think Jack is involved in all this?"

"Maybe. And possibly David too. But I definitely think Michael was. That's probably why he wanted to travel with you in the first place. Newlyweds returning from their honeymoon in Belize are a lot less likely to get stopped by customs than a single Hispanic male traveling alone."

"So wanting me to fly home with him to make the ex-girlfriend jealous was all bullshit?"

"You never really believed that, did you?"

"I guess not." Actually, I had, but I wasn't about to admit it now. "While all this is fascinating, it still doesn't tell us who killed Michael or why."

"No," Jane admitted. "But we're one step closer to finding out."

"And what's the next step?"

"Getting Ernesto his ten thousand dollars so he'll fill in the rest of the blanks."

We both showered and dressed, Jane in a miniskirt and layered tank tops, me in my men's khakis, oversize leisure shirt, and baseball cap, and we headed into town. First Caribbean Bank of Belize was only three blocks from the Parrot Caye police station, but Jane wasn't concerned. I, however, was, so I dropped her off and parked the golf cart at the other end of First Street. I could still keep an eye out for her with the camera, but I'd look like a tourist instead of a getaway driver. Which was how I spotted John and Cheryl riding their bikes.

They stopped in front of the same outdoor café I'd seen them in the last time. I was so busy watching them—they propped their bikes up against the railing of the restaurant, then the hostess seated them at a table just inside the gate—that I hadn't even noticed Jane leaving the bank.

"You could've come and picked me up," she said, slipping into the passenger seat and scaring the hell out of me. "This money is for your benefit."

"Sorry," I said, letting the camera dangle from the cord around my neck. "You'll never believe who I just spotted."

"Leonardo Di Caprio?"

"No, why would you even guess him?"

"I read somewhere that he bought an island down here. Who?"

"John and Cheryl."

"Give me that," she said, pulling on the camera and consequently my neck.

"Ow!"

"Sorry, but I want to check them out before they leave."

"I don't think they're going anytime soon," I said, slipping the strap over my neck and handing her the camera. I pointed in the general direction of the restaurant. "You see the bikes out front?"

"No," she said, and I moved the camera lower. "The two beach cruisers propped up against the railing?"

"They're the couple sitting at the table behind the bikes."

"The two gay guys?"

"No," I said and grabbed the camera out of her hand. She was right, there was a male couple sitting at a table just inside the railing, but behind other bikes. And to my surprise, three tables to the left of them was Rodrigo, the "friend of the family" who had warned me about buying fake antiquities. Of course his warning ultimately got me arrested for murder, so clearly he wasn't a friend to me. And either this was the most popular restaurant on Parrot Caye, or something was going on here.

"What do you think it could be?" Jane asked, ever ready to jump on a new conspiracy theory.

"I don't know," I said, widening the lens so I could see Rodrigo and Cheryl and John in the same shot. "They don't seem to be paying much attention to each other."

"That doesn't mean anything," she said. "If it's covert surveillance you wouldn't be able to tell."

"But who's surveilling who? And why?"

"Let me see," Jane said, grabbing the camera back from me. "Is Cheryl the blonde with her hair in a ponytail?"

"Yes."

"Someone needs to tell her to lay off those fruit smoothies. Either that or she should buy longer shorts."

"She's pregnant," I said in Cheryl's defense.

"She's not carrying the baby in her thighs, is she?"

"Will you stop obsessing over her legs and focus on her face. Do you think she's looking at Rodrigo? Or do you think Rodrigo's looking at her? Or is this all just a coincidence and hanging out with you has made me paranoid?"

"I don't believe in coincidences," Jane said, still peering at our subjects. "And I think you're focusing on the wrong one.

All Cheryl cares about is getting to the bottom of that shake. John's the one who looks antsy."

I grabbed the camera back from her. Jane was right. John was the one whose knee was bouncing nonstop and who kept glancing toward the inside of the restaurant. But Jane didn't even have time to come up with a new theory before the waitress arrived with their check. John barely looked at it before he threw a few bills on the table, and he and Cheryl left. And yes, she did manage to finish that smoothie first.

"Well, aren't you going to follow them?" Jane asked.

Normally she drove, but I was sitting behind the wheel. "Do you think we should?"

"Of course we should. How else are we going to find out how they fit into this mess?"

"You mean *if*, don't you?"

She rolled her eyes at me. "Just drive."

CHAPTER 49

I stayed two blocks behind, and Jane kept John and Cheryl in sight with the camera.

"I don't know what he sees in her," Jane said. "Her ass is huge."

"Everyone's ass is huge when it's on a bike and you're staring at it through a telephoto lens. Even you, Miss Size Two."

"Actually, this skirt is a zero."

"Thanks for sharing." I couldn't fit one leg into a size zero.

"Look for a place to pull over. They just turned into the driveway for that hotel."

I drove past the entrance to the White Sands Beach Resort and pulled the golf cart over to the side of the road. "What now?"

"Now we go inside and find out what they're up to."

"I can't go inside. What if they see me? I'm still a fugitive."

Jane was already out of the golf cart and adjusting her hat.

"They're not going to see you. And even if they do, they're not going to recognize you. You're a man now, remember?"

The good news is that I didn't get rearrested. The bad news is that while I was hiding in the bushes trying to figure out which bungalow John and Cheryl were staying in without them or anyone else seeing me, I stepped on a red ant mound. That put a quick end to my spying as I ran back to the golf cart, slapping at ants and cursing Jane all the way.

Since Jane wasn't a fugitive, she got the job of hanging around the hotel pool waiting for John and Cheryl to show up. Since they'd never met her, she figured she could strike up a casual conversation with them and fish for information. She lasted only forty minutes. Although Jane liked all the theorizing, she just didn't have the patience for detective work.

"Any other bright ideas?" I asked as I scratched my ankles raw. I made Jane drive on the way back so I could give the ant bites my full attention.

"You better stop scratching or you're going to end up with scars."

"If Sergeant Ramos finds me, these scars will be the least of my worries."

"But they didn't even see you."

"Jane, I know you're really enjoying playing girl detective, but I'm not. I want to go home. I want my life back. I don't want to sneak around spying on people, or meeting with drug dealers, or lying awake at night wondering if it's the guy in the next room or my lawyer who's really out to get me. I can't do this anymore!" I didn't want to cry, but the tears didn't ask permission.

Jane pulled the golf cart to a stop at the side of the road, then leaned over and gave me a hug. When my heaving subsided and the tears slowed to a trickle, she let go and handed me a tissue.

"Feel better?" she asked.

Actually, I did. My situation hadn't improved any, but at least I'd released some tension.

"So you want to hear my new plan?"

I couldn't help but smile. "Sure, Jane."

"We know there are DEA and customs agents down here, even if we don't know who they are. I propose we get as much info from Ernesto tonight as we can, then we find a way to contact the agents and offer to turn everything over to them in exchange for your freedom."

"You think they'll do that?"

"Well we're not going to tell them what we know unless they do."

"What if they won't agree?"

"Then we move on to Plan B—we smuggle you out of the country and get you a new identity."

"Is that even possible?" I thought only governments could do that, and characters in movies.

"With enough money, anything's possible."

I had a whole five minutes of feeling better before we walked in on Jack.

CHAPTER 50

"What are you doing?" I screamed as I grabbed Fred from Jack's hands and stared at the cord dangling from the kitchen ceiling fan with a baby-turtle-size noose knotted at its end.

"It's not what it looks like," he said, holding up the steak knife. "I was trying to cut it down."

"What the hell?" Jane asked, joining us in the kitchen.

"It was here when I got back," Jack said, and used the knife to slice off the noose. The rest of the cord, however, was still dangling.

"Why would anyone try to hang Fred?" I don't know if it was my yelling or the brush with death, but the poor turtle was about to shake out of his shell.

"I think it was a warning," Jack said. "To you," he added, and handed me the crumpled note sitting on the floor next to the trash can.

This is your last warning gringas. Go home!

I passed it on to Jane. "Is it time for Plan B yet?"

"Not yet," she said, "but soon. Where did you put the first note?"

"I threw it away."

"Why would you do that?"

Why would I do that? "Why would I keep it? It's not like we could call the police."

"So we can compare the handwriting and see if it's the same."

"You think there's more than one person sending us death threats?"

"It's possible," she said.

This was more than I could handle on three hours of sleep. "Plan B, Jane, Plan B."

I heard Jack ask, "What's Plan B?" as I headed down the hallway to my bedroom. I didn't stop to listen to Jane's answer. I slammed the door shut and lay down on the bed with Fred in my arms. I tried to fall asleep, but of course I couldn't. I was too scared to even keep my eyes closed, not to mention Fred trying to squirm away from me. It wasn't long before Jane was knocking on my door.

"Can I come in?" she asked without waiting for a response. "I called my dad again."

"Twice in one day. He's going to think one of you is dying."

Jane joined me on the bed. "I wanted him to get me the contact info for the agents down here. Of course he wouldn't," she said, rolling her eyes. "It's all classified."

"Plan B then?"

"Not until we talk to Ernesto. But I was thinking in the meantime we should move. Someone obviously doesn't want us here and I think we should oblige them."

"Where to?"

"The last place anyone would think to look for us."

"The police station?"

"No, but we are going back to Camus Caye."

"Jane, you know any hotel we go to is going to ask for your passport. And even if we rent another house, it's a small place. It's only a matter of time before Sergeant Ramos finds us."

"I know," she said. "That's why we're going to the turtle camp."

I sat up. "Jane, you've been to the turtle camp. No three-hundred-thread-count sheets, no Jacuzzi tub, not even air-conditioning. Remember how dirty the couch was?"

"I remember," she said. "I just sent Jack out for supplies."

"I thought you didn't trust Jack."

"I don't, but that doesn't mean I can refuse his help. Neither one of us knows how to drive a boat, remember?"

I didn't want to feed her paranoia, but it had to be said. "And what if he's involved in all this somehow? Do you really think it's safe to go to such a secluded place with him as our only way out?"

"We can always walk up to the marine reserve. You said it wasn't far. They must have security people there or park rangers or something. And if not, we can always hitch a ride with one of the tourist boats."

I didn't like it, but I didn't see any alternative.

"And if we really get into trouble," she continued, "we can always call John and Cheryl. Now we know where they're staying."

"And why would they help us? The last time I saw Cheryl she wasn't speaking to me."

"Because I'm ninety-nine percent sure I've figured out what they're doing here."

"What?"

"They're the undercover agents."

CHAPTER 51

"I thought your dad wouldn't tell you?"

"He didn't," she said with a self-satisfied grin. "It's all elementary, my dear Watson. My dad wouldn't tell me their names, but he did tell me it was a joint agency task force, which means there are more than one of them. And because it's our agencies, we know they're Americans."

"That narrows it down to eighty percent of the population."

"Just think about it. It makes sense. They befriended you and Michael from the moment you arrived. They went to dinner with you, went dancing with you, played pool with you."

"But it all ended the minute they found out that Michael wasn't really my husband."

"Of course, because you were no longer useful. Obviously, they had Michael under surveillance. They probably planned on arresting him, figuring he would cut a deal and testify against some drug kingpin. They must've assumed you were involved, but once you told them the truth, you were useless."

At least this theory made sense. "But how can we know for sure?"

"Well they're undercover, so we can't exactly call up DEA headquarters to verify their identities. But we can contact them directly."

"And say what?"

"After the meeting with Ernesto, I'll call them and tell them I have information useful to their investigation. If they're really just honeymooners from Chicago like they told you, they'll tell me I have the wrong number and hang up. But if they're really DEA, they'll want to hear what I have to say. Pretty good, eh?"

I had to admit, this time she really had worked out all the angles.

When Jack returned with the supplies—food, water, clean sheets, and a radio—we packed up our bags, left the key under the mat, and headed out to Jack's boat for what turned out to be a very bumpy ride back to Camus Caye. The wind had picked up and so had the waves.

"You should have gotten some ginger ale too," I yelled to Jack over the roar of the engine.

"I would've if I'd known," he said. "Do you think she's going to be OK?"

I looked back at Jane, who had her head hanging over the side of the boat. "She'll be fine once we reach dry land."

She wasn't. Not even after a whole bottle of Pellegrino and half a loaf of French bread, which I practically had to force-feed her because of its high carb count. I finally put her to bed on the sagging mattress with its new half-cotton/half-polyester blend sheets.

"I guess I can go alone," Jack said. He and Jane were supposed to meet Ernesto back on Parrot Caye at nine.

Not a chance. Despite all his help, I wasn't letting him abandon the two of us at the turtle camp while he took off with Jane's ten thousand dollars. "I'll go."

"Don't you think Ernesto's going to recognize you?"

"If he saw me, maybe. But he's not going to."

"I don't understand."

"Do you think you could get the dive boat tonight?"

"Did you forget? My father thinks I'm in Guatemala this week."

"Can't you tell him you had a fight with your girlfriend and you came back early? You are broken up, aren't you?"

"What good would the dive boat do us?" He took a step closer. "Or were you thinking of blowing off Ernesto?" he asked with a rakish grin.

As enticing as that offer would've been even a few days ago, I was so stressed now that it barely even registered a tingle. "Your boat's too small for me to hide on, but the dive boat's not. I'll go with you, but I'll stay out of sight."

I was expecting an argument, or at least a warning about the risks. Instead, I received a flash of disappointment, then, "That's a good idea. Maybe he'll open up more if he thinks it's just the two of us."

Hmmm. I couldn't quite decide if his agreeing with me meant I could trust him or not. I'd take a stun gun just in case.

Jack piloted the small skiff to his father's dive shop on the other side of Camus Caye. At his insistence, I lay flat on the bottom of the boat. "Don't move," he said, then threw one of Jane's new blankets over me. "I'll be right back."

It didn't take him long, but he didn't return alone.

"I still don't understand," I heard a gravelly voice say. "How many people—"

"Dad, wait!"

Then something round and heavy landed on my hip.

"Ow," I yelled, rolling both the air tank and the blanket off me. Standing next to Jack was a fiftyish man with a full beard who had Jack's blue-gray eyes, but otherwise could've passed for Ernest Hemingway's brother.

"What do we have here?" the man asked, turning to Jack.

"Dad, this is Lizzie. Lizzie, meet my father."

"John Taylor," he said as he set down the rest of his scuba gear and reached a hand out to me. It was as warm as Jack's and even more calloused.

"It's nice to finally meet you," I said, joining the two of them on the dock.

"Whatever he told you," the senior Taylor said, "it's all lies."

I looked at the air tank perched next to him. "You're going diving at night?"

"Of course," he said. "Do you dive?"

I shook my head. "Not really. But I took Jack's class last week."

He barely glanced at his son. "You haven't really dived until you've tried it at night. It's a whole different world down there. The treasures!" His whole face lit up. "Once when I was diving off the coast of Bimini—"

"Dad, I'm sure Lizzie doesn't care. And we're in kind of a hurry here, so if you'll just give me the keys."

John Taylor clenched his jaw, but he still pulled a set of keys from his shorts pocket and tossed them at his son. "Have it back here by nine. I've got a group leaving at ten."

"Will do," Jack said, leading me away.

"And don't forget to gas it up," John Taylor called out after us.

"I know, Dad," Jack said, as if for the thousandth time.

I waited until we were out of hearing range before I said, "Your dad seems interesting."

"That's one word for him," Jack replied before changing the subject back to our meeting with Ernesto.

The wind was at our back, so the ride to Parrot Caye took less time than we'd expected. When Jack tied us off alongside the dock, it was still only a quarter to nine. We needed something to pass the time before Ernesto arrived.

"So what was it like when you were a kid? Did your dad take you with him on all his adventures?"

After a long pause, Jack finally answered with one word: "No."

Clearly a sore subject. "So tell me about your girlfriend."

"Ex-girlfriend, and there's nothing to tell."

I was too nervous to wait in silence, and I wasn't all that interested in discussing sea turtles. "Your dad or your girlfriend, you choose."

Jack stared at me before he finally said, "Her name's Candace."

Interesting. I would've thought he would've gone with his dad. They must really be broken up. "Did you call her Candy?"

"No."

"How long did you date?'

"I don't know," he said, clearly losing patience with this topic of conversation.

"How can you not know? When did you meet?"

"About a year ago."

"So you were together for a year?"

"I guess."

"You guess? Either you were or you weren't."

"Does it matter? We dated for a while, then she left for Guatemala, I came here, and it ended."

"Was she crushed?"

"I don't think so," he said, followed by a harsh laugh.

"How can you be so sure?"

"Because she's shacked up with my best friend."

Ouch. "How did you find out?"

"She told me. Eventually."

Double ouch. Being dumped is bad enough, but being cheated on by your best friend, that's serious betrayal. No wonder he was so touchy about my lying to him when we first met. "My fiancé dumped me the night before our wedding."

"Is that why you hooked up with Michael?"

"I didn't *hook up* with Michael. I never even kissed him."

"That's not what—" Jack jumped up. "It's Ernesto. Cover up," he said, and threw a pile of life jackets on top of me.

My heart was pounding, but I tried not to breathe, or at least to breathe as quietly as possible. I had made myself a peephole between the arms of the life jackets so I was able to see Ernesto as he climbed aboard our boat.

"Where's the blonde?" Ernesto asked.

"Detained," Jack said. "She sent me instead."

"Did you bring the money?"

"Yes."

"Let's see it."

Jack reached down next to my pile of life jackets for Jane's Prada bag, which she'd filled with ten thousand dollars in twenties. He carried the bag to Ernesto and unzipped the top, giving him a glimpse of the money, but when he reached for it, Jack snatched it back. "You've seen it. Start talking."

"You stupid gringo."

CHAPTER 52

Ernesto pulled something long and silver from his pocket. Jack jumped back so quickly I knew it had to be a knife. Ernesto lunged and Jack swung at him with the purse. The money went flying across the deck and Ernesto followed. Jack tackled him on the way down and the two of them, kicking and punching and grunting at each other, rolled back and forth across the floor. I tried to remain frozen, hiding under the life vests, but my heart was pounding so hard I thought it was going to jump out of my chest. Then I remembered the stun gun.

"You bastard!" I screamed as I burst out from my hiding place and sprinted across the deck. I would've had a clear shot at Ernesto's neck if my foot hadn't caught in the armhole of one of the life jackets. But I still managed to connect the stun gun with Ernesto's ankle on my way down to the ground. I don't know how long I zapped him, but he collapsed on top of Jack.

You'd think with all the commotion some Good Samaritan would've come running down the dock to help us. But all we got were stares from a few curious onlookers out for an evening stroll. When Jack stood up, someone finally called out, "Need any help?"

"We're OK," Jack called back between breaths, and the man kept walking.

Then Jack turned to me. His breathing was still ragged, but he managed a "Thanks for that." Then he reached down, pulled

Ernesto's switchblade from his hand, and shoved it in his back pocket.

"Are you OK?" His T-shirt was torn at the collar and he had a smear of blood on his arm.

"Yeah," he said as he examined his wound. "It's just a scratch. You?"

"I think so." My heart still felt like it was about to burst, but I assumed it was a temporary condition.

"What'd you hit him with?" Jack asked.

"This." I held up the stun gun. "Jane," I said before he could ask where I'd gotten it.

He smiled. "I guess sometimes it pays to be paranoid."

"Or at least to have a paranoid friend."

Ernesto moaned and started to roll over, so I zapped him again. I held the stun gun to his leg for what seemed like an eternity, but was probably no more than a few seconds when Jack pulled my hand away. "You want to disable him, not kill him."

No experience in my life prior to this moment had prepared me for what to do next, so I asked Jack: "Now what?"

"Good question." He seemed as ill prepared as I was, which on some level was a good thing, but at this particular point in time was bad.

We both stood over Ernesto's motionless body and stared at him.

"We could throw him overboard," I suggested.

"We could," Jack said, "but he'd probably drown and I think that would be the same as killing him."

"Yeah, you're probably right."

We stared some more.

"We could tie him up," Jack offered.

"We could," I agreed.

"Let's do that," Jack said.

I guarded Ernesto, stun gun in hand, while Jack unlocked the storage bin next to the engine and pulled out a heavy-gauge rope and a roll of duct tape. I watched as Jack bound Ernesto's arms and legs with a very complicated-looking knot, then sealed his mouth shut.

"Good job," I said when he'd finished.

"Thanks."

"Now what?"

Jack considered my question. "Take him with us?"

"We could."

Jack nodded. "Let's do that."

Jane was waiting for us on the beach. But the dive boat was longer and heavier than the skiff, so Jack had to anchor it twenty yards out. We swam to shore with Ernesto between us. Unfortunately, this agitated Ernesto. Since I couldn't zap him while we were in the water, Jack held his head under, occasionally letting him up to breathe. Ernesto survived the swim and I zapped him again when we reached dry land.

"What the hell happened to you two?" Jane asked. "And what's he doing here?"

"Long story," I said, trying to wring the water out of my clothes while I was still wearing them.

"Then give me the short version."

"Ernesto pulled a knife on Jack, so I hit him with the stun gun. We didn't know what to do with him, so we brought him here."

"OK," Jane said, "now give me the long version."

Jack duct taped Ernesto to the desk chair and the three of us sat on the couch, which was now covered with two nautical-looking blue-and-white-striped bedsheets courtesy of Jane, and stared at him. Every time he started to wake up, I zapped him with the stun gun, which would disable him for another few minutes.

"Lizzie, I think you need to stop doing that," Jane said, after the third or fourth time.

"Why?" I asked. It seemed to be working pretty well.

"Because I think I read somewhere that repeated use of a stun gun can kill a person."

"Probably in the manual," I said.

"Probably," she agreed.

The next time Ernesto woke up and started thrashing, Jack held the knife to his throat. "Ernesto, do you want to be zapped again?"

Ernesto emphatically shook his head.

"Because we don't want to kill you, but we will if we have to. Do you understand?"

Ernesto nodded.

"Good, then I'm going to take the tape off now," Jack said as he ripped it from Ernesto's mouth. The sound alone was painful, so it must've hurt. Ernesto glared at us, then spat on the floor.

We all continued to stare at one another in silence until Jane finally said, "This is boring. Ernesto, did you kill Michael or not?"

"Fuck you, Blondie," he replied.

Jack, who was leaning against the desk next to Ernesto, slapped him hard across the mouth. Ernesto spat again, and this time the puddle on the floor was bright red, but he didn't reply.

"The lady asked you a question," Jack said. "We'd appreciate an answer."

"You think I would kill my own cousin?"

The three of us exchanged a glance. I didn't think any of us was ready to rule out that possibility. "Yes," I finally said.

"I'm not saying nothing without my lawyer."

"Ernesto," Jane said, "we're not the police."

"I want witness protection and a house in Arizona."

Jane rolled her eyes while I said, "We're not FBI, you idiot. Only the FBI can give you witness protection." I wasn't 100 percent sure that was true, but it sounded right.

"Then what did you drag me out here for?"

"To find out who killed Michael," Jane said.

Ernesto spat out a big wad of blood again, then said, "I told you, I'm not saying nothing without my lawyer."

Clearly, we were having a "failure to communicate." Jack returned the duct tape to Ernesto's mouth and moved him into the middle of the room, out of reach of any potential weapons.

"No funny business," Jack said, knife in hand.

Ernesto glared some more and waited until Jack held the knife to his throat before he gave a barely perceptible nod.

The three of us huddled in the doorway, occasionally glancing back at Ernesto to make sure he hadn't moved.

"What now?" I asked.

"Maybe we should call the police," Jack suggested.

"We can't call the police," Jane said. "We'll all be arrested."

"She's right." Besides helping me escape, we were now all guilty of kidnapping. I looked at Jane. "Maybe it's time to test out your theory about John and Cheryl."

"Who are John and Cheryl?" Jack asked.

"Don't you remember? From the Blue Bay. You drove us all back to the hotel the night Michael died."

"They're involved in this too?"

"We're about to find out," Jane replied.

Jack stayed behind with Ernesto while Jane and I walked the beach in search of a cell phone signal. We finally found one when we climbed the rocks separating the rest of the beach from the marine reserve. It was almost eleven, but Jane didn't think it was too late to call. She did the talking, but I listened in.

"Is this John Garecki?" she asked when he picked up the phone.

"Yes," John said. "Who is this?"

"My name's Jane. I'm a friend of Lizzie Mancini's. I called to tell you we know who you are and what you're really doing here."

"What do you want?"

"A trade. Information we're sure you'll find useful in exchange for all charges against Lizzie being dropped."

"We should discuss this in person."

"OK," Jane said. "But no local police. And we want a deal in writing before we give you anything."

"Of course," John said. "But we should meet someplace secluded to ensure we're not being watched."

I nudged Jane and whispered, "I know a place."

CHAPTER 53

"You're meeting them at the drug house?" Jack yelled.

"Is that what it's called?" Jane asked. "I just told them it was a couple miles south of the marine reserve, where the dead palm tree cuts across the beach. It really would be helpful if you people installed some mile markers in this country."

Jack shook his head.

"They wanted a secluded place and it was the only one I could think of," I said. "I didn't want them to know where we're staying."

"It's only a mile away. Don't you think they'll figure it out?"

"Not if we arrive by boat." I came up with that on the walk back to the hatchery. "We could've been coming from anywhere."

Jack considered this. "What about Ernesto?"

"We'll leave him here until we have a deal in writing," Jane said. "He's our ace in the hole."

Jack looked from Jane to me. "I hope you're right about this."

He wasn't the only one.

Jane took the bed, I took the couch, and Jack took the floor, but I don't think any of us slept more than a couple of hours each. Besides the tension of having Ernesto in the same room with us, Jane spent most of the night complaining. The springs in the mattress were poking her, she was suffocating without an air-conditioner, the birds were chirping too loudly. We were all sporting dark circles under our eyes the next morning.

Jack made breakfast—toast and coffee—while we took turns showering and getting dressed. Jack wanted us to get an early start so we could circle the island and arrive at the rendezvous point from the other direction. Since Ernesto had tried to knife him, he was as paranoid as Jane and I.

"Do you really think it's safe to leave Ernesto here alone?" I asked Jack while Jane was still in the shower. "What if he finds some way to escape?"

"You want to bring him with us?"

"No, I was thinking maybe Jane and I should go alone. The only leverage we have is Ernesto and the location of the drug house, assuming John and Cheryl don't already know about it. If they do, then all I've got is Ernesto."

We both looked over at him, head down, napping in his chair. He wasn't much of a bargaining chip. I still didn't know if he killed Michael. And even if he did, I had no way of proving it.

"But if you arrive on foot they'll know you're staying nearby. It wouldn't take them long to find us."

"We could borrow your—"

"Not a chance," Jack said.

"Why not?"

"Have you ever driven a boat before?" he asked.

"No, but—"

"Then you're not going to start today. We'll bring Ernesto and I'll stay with him on the boat while the two of you have your meeting."

Jack used Ernesto's knife to cut the duct tape off him, and the threat of the stun gun was enough to keep him in line on our wade through the four-foot waters to the boat. After Jack tied him up again, I stood guard while he went back for Jane. She'd refused to swim out to the boat after she'd just showered and lathered up with SPF 45, so Jack offered to carry her. Did I mention how cranky Jane gets when she doesn't get her beauty sleep? We needed to get her back to civilization as soon as possible or I really would be guilty of murder.

Luckily, the water was calm today, providing us with a smooth trip around the island. Jack anchored us off the coast in front of the deserted stretch of beach where the drug house was hidden behind the tree line. I guarded Ernesto while Jack carried Jane to shore, then I gave Jack my stun gun (Jane still had hers in her purse), and I joined Jane on the beach.

We waited, huddled together in the shade of a palm tree, until John and Cheryl finally arrived forty-five minutes late in a rented speedboat. (The *Paradise Boat Rentals* in neon-blue letters on the side gave it away.) We'd decided at the half-hour point that we'd give them an hour before we moved on to Plan B.

"Sorry," John said, splashing barefoot onto the beach. "We had a little trouble finding the place." He looked like any American tourist in his cargo shorts, polo shirt, and baseball cap.

"Your directions could've been better," Cheryl added, only slightly friendlier than the last time we'd spoken. She looked like a tourist too, right down to the fanny pack around her waist. "What happened to your hair?"

"Nothing," I said, reflexively running my hand through my shorn locks.

"What was wrong with the directions?" Jane asked.

"For one thing," Cheryl said, "there's more than one downed palm tree on this island."

"And how many of them are between here and the marine reserve?" Jane asked, matching Cheryl's bitchy tone with her own.

"OK, ladies," John said. "Let's take it down a notch."

Cheryl gave him an angry stare, then turned back to me. "Where's the head?"

"Excuse me?" I asked.

"Don't play dumb, Lizzie. If you want us to get the police to drop the charges against you, you're going to have to turn over the head."

My only thought was the jade pieces the police found in my suitcase. "They already have the heads. They took them when they arrested me."

Cheryl looked like she wanted to strangle me, so John stepped in. "Not those little ornaments," he said, waving his hand dismissively. "The one Michael stole."

I glanced at Jane, hoping she had a plan because I sure didn't.

She didn't either, but she recovered first. "I told you," Jane said. "We're not handing anything over until we have a deal in writing."

John pulled a folded piece of paper from his back pocket and handed it to Jane. It had the DEA shield on top, but otherwise it was blank. "Write down what you want and we'll sign it here."

Jane pulled a pen from her purse and wrote:

All charges against Elizabeth Mancini dropped and full immunity for Jane Chandler and any other persons that may have assisted in her escape.

She showed it to me before handing it back to John. I almost added something about us not being charged for kidnapping Ernesto, but thought better of it. John signed the paper and gave it back to Jane.

"Now where's the head?" he asked.

Good question. But a better one would be: What head?

CHAPTER 54

"It's in a safe place," I lied. Or maybe I wasn't lying. To be honest, I had no idea.

"Where?" Cheryl asked.

"Well if we went around telling everyone then it wouldn't be safe, now would it?" Jane replied, hands on hips and attitude to match.

Cheryl took a step closer. "No head, no deal."

"Tomorrow," I said. "We can meet at the police station. We'll bring the head with us." I still had no clue what they were talking about or where to find it, but the only option we had was to buy time and hope we could figure it out.

John shook his head. "No police. We're undercover."

"Even the local police don't know who you are?" I asked, as Jane said, "Then how are you going to get the charges dropped?"

"Back channels," John said. "Half the local cops work for the drug cartels too. We divulge our identity only to officials we know we can trust."

That made sense.

"We'll meet you back here tomorrow morning," John said. "You bring the head and we'll take you to our boss. He'll get you straightened out with the local authorities."

I nodded. "Tomorrow at nine."

Jane waited until John and Cheryl waded back to their boat before she asked, "Now what?"

I had no idea.

Jack had just dropped anchor in front of the turtle camp when a speedboat rushed toward us. "Jack, mon, where you been?" Manuel called out as he pulled up beside us.

"Hey, Manny," Jack said, still struggling with the anchor. "What are you doing out here?"

"Looking for you. Your dad's going crazy because you got his boat."

"Oh shit!" Jack said. "What time is it?"

"A quarter to ten," I said, glancing at my watch.

"It looks like you're pretty busy here," Manuel said, taking in Jane and me. He couldn't see Ernesto because I had him pinned to the floor with my foot on his chest. But the way he was struggling, it was only a matter of time.

"Will you please zap him," I whispered to Jane, who still had the stun gun in her purse.

Jack looked back and saw Jane fighting with the safety catch. "Hey Manny, will you do me a favor and check the anchor. I think it's caught on a rock."

While Manny was busy at the back of the boat, Jack grabbed the stun gun and zapped Ernesto himself.

"No rock," Manny said. "So are you going to introduce me to your new friend?"

"This is Jane," Jack said. "She's a friend of Lizzie's."

I nudged Jane and she waved.

"That's no fair, Jack, keeping two fine-looking women for yourself and none for me."

I thought we were in the clear, a little flirting and he'd be gone. But then he said, "Especially since I know a few policemen who would be very happy to see Lizzie again. Where's your hair, Lizzie?"

"It was my idea," Jane said. "I like my women butch."

We all stared at her.

233

Jane slid her arm around my waist and gave me a squeeze. "C'mon, honey, it's time you stopped pretending." Then she pushed up on her toes and brushed her lips against mine.

I was too stunned to speak.

"Jack, mon, what do you do?"

"He likes to watch," Jane answered for him. "And sometimes we let him join in."

Manuel smiled appreciatively, showing off his gold tooth. "I'd hate to be the one to break up da party."

"What do you mean?" Jack said, taking a step closer to the railing separating our boat from Manuel's.

"Lots of people looking for Lizzie. I really should go back and tell them where she at."

"And what would it take for you not to do that?" Jane asked.

Manuel smiled again, and ran his tongue across his lips. "I don't know, missy. Whatcha offering?"

"How about you don't tell the police about me," I said, "and I won't tell them about your drug house?"

His smile disappeared. "I don't know what you mean."

"Yes you do. It's just down the beach," I said and nodded in that direction.

Manuel glared at Jack, who shook his head. "She found it on her own."

Manuel turned back to me and licked his lips again, this time without the smile. "You drive a hard bargain. Maybe I can watch too?"

I gave him what I hoped was a sultry smile. "I promise next time we're in the mood we'll give you a call."

This time he gave me the full gold-toothed grin. "Jack, mon," he said, but never took his eyes off me, "you better get that boat back to your father or he'll be looking for you with a shotgun. Lizzie, I'll be seeing you real soon."

The definitiveness of that statement sent shivers down my body. When he finally started his engine and took off out to sea I crumpled onto the bench.

"Who was that?" Jane asked, ignoring Ernesto, who was awake and struggling again, but this time he was also trying to speak.

I ripped the duct tape from his mouth and yelled, "What?"

His voice was hoarse, but he croaked out something that sounded a lot like, "That's who killed Michael."

CHAPTER 55

I poured half a bottle of water down Ernesto's throat and asked again.

"He killed Michael," Ernesto said.

Jane was the first to speak. "I thought you weren't going to talk without your lawyer?"

"I want my deal," Ernesto said. "If he sees me, he'll kill me too."

"Then tell us about the head," I said. "The one Michael stole."

"He didn't steal it. He was just holding it for me."

"So you stole it?" Jane asked.

"No, I bought it. That's what we did. Michael and me, we were just middlemen."

"And who did you buy it from?" I asked.

"A supplier," he sneered.

"And you didn't bother asking if it was stolen?" Jane said.

Ernesto looked at her like she was crazy. "I don't ask questions. They bring me pieces, I give them money."

"Then why'd you try to kill me?" Jack asked.

"I wasn't trying to kill you. I just wanted the ten grand."

"We would've given you the money," Jane told him. "All you had to do was answer our questions."

"Good, then give me my money and I'll leave."

"Not until you give us the head," I said.

"I can't. I don't have it."

"Where is it?"

"I don't know," Ernesto replied. "I've been looking for it ever since Michael died."

"You still haven't explained why Manuel would kill Michael," Jack said.

Ernesto managed to shrug even though his arms were still tied behind his back. "I don't know. I heard it was over some woman."

"You heard?" Jack asked.

"I wasn't in the room. If I was, it wouldn't have happened. Now are you going to untie me or not?"

"We'll get back to you," Jack said, and plastered the duct tape over Ernesto's mouth again. Then he motioned for Jane and me to join him at the back of the boat.

"I don't believe him," Jack whispered. "But I've got to get this boat back to my dad. Will you two be OK with him for a couple of hours?"

"Of course," I said and held up the stun gun.

Jack nodded. "Good. And when I get back, I want to hear more about this threesome you're planning."

"We're not planning a threesome!" At least I wasn't. This was definitely a side of Jane I'd never seen before.

"It was the first thing that popped into my head," Jane said.

"Does that mean I don't even get to watch?"

"Jack!" we both yelled in unison.

"OK, OK. A guy can dream, can't he?"

Jack dragged Ernesto back to the turtle camp and tied him up again. But since he was being so cooperative now, Jack took the duct tape off his mouth and I poured another bottle of water down his throat. Jack promised he'd be back in two hours, but programmed his number into Jane's cell phone just in case.

Ernesto stayed silent until Jack left, then we couldn't shut him up. "If you two want to go at it, I can watch. Or if you untie me, I'll even join in."

Was watching two women every guy's fantasy?

"We're not lesbians," Jane said.

"Then I'll sleep with both of you."

Jane and I shared a can-you-believe-this-guy look before Jane said, "Ernesto, if you don't settle down, we'll have to muzzle you again. Is that really what you want?"

He licked his lips. "Ooo chica, you're making me hot. What are you going to do then?"

Jane picked up one of the stun guns and walked over to Ernesto's chair. She leaned over him so his face was only inches from her breasts. "I'm going to zap you in the balls until you beg me to stop," she said in a sultry voice. "Sound like fun?"

Ernesto stopped talking after that, and Jane and I moved into the front room so we could have some privacy.

"Have you ever considered becoming a dominatrix?" I asked as we watched Fred swim circles in his aquarium, indifferent to our presence.

"Not really," Jane replied. "Why? Do you think I'd be good at it?"

"Definitely. With some black leather boots and a bustier, you could make a fortune." Not that she needed it.

"I am getting a little tired of redecorating people's living rooms."

While she mulled it over I asked, "So any ideas how we're going to find that head?"

"Nope," she said. "You?"

I shook my head. "Not a one. Do you believe Ernesto really doesn't know?"

She shrugged, then offered me her stun gun. "You want to torture him and find out?"

"Not really. You?"

She started to shake her head, then stopped and smiled. "But we have other methods."

I followed her into the back room where we found Ernesto struggling to free his hands. He hadn't made much progress, but to be on the safe side Jane wrapped three more strips of duct tape around his wrists and taped his chest to the back of the chair. Then she stood behind him with her hands on his shoulders and leaned his head back so he was looking up at her. It was evident from both the look on his face and the bulge in his pants that he was enjoying the experience.

"Good news, Ernesto. We just talked to our boss and he signed off on your deal. All you've got to do is give us the head and you're home free."

"But I don't know where it is," he whimpered.

"Oh come on, Ernesto," Jane said, "Just because we get off on giving blow jobs doesn't mean we're stupid."

He actually moaned.

She walked around to the front of the chair and put her hands on his knees, affording him the full cleavage view. "You help us and we'll help you."

I wished I had a video camera. She could win an Oscar for this performance.

"I swear." He was practically crying. "I've looked everywhere."

"Where's everywhere, Ernesto?"

"Michael's hotel room, her hotel room," he nodded at me, "Every—"

"You searched my hotel room? When?"

"After Michael died. It wasn't in his room, so I thought maybe he left it with you."

"When specifically?"

"I don't know. The next day, maybe."

"What?" Jane asked, staring at me.

"I know where the head is, or at least where it might be."

CHAPTER 56

"Are you sure leaving Ernesto alone was such a good idea?" I asked Jane as we power-walked down the beach. I wanted her to stay behind to guard him, but she refused.

"Where's he gonna go tied up to a chair?" she said, then steered the conversation back to the head. "What makes you so sure it's in the drug house?"

"I'm not sure. It's just a hunch. If Michael really hid the head in my room, along with those little jade pieces the police found, then someone beat Ernesto to it."

"Manuel?"

"Why not? If he really did ask Jack to keep me occupied that night on the boat, then it all makes sense. We know he's a drug smuggler. Why not antiquities too?"

"But if we steal it back," Jane said, "don't you think Manuel's going to know it was us?"

"Yes, but hopefully by the time he figures it out, he'll be in jail and we'll be back home and far out of his reach."

"Where is this place?" Jane asked after we'd crossed over the dead palm tree and reached the clearing where we'd met John and Cheryl.

"Back there," I said, pointing to the jungle behind the beach.

It had been a lot easier to spot when men were walking in and out with armloads of cocaine. It took me a few minutes, but

I found the path I'd seen the men follow through the trees. We were halfway there when we first heard the music, something with a Latin beat. Damn! It'd never occurred to me that someone else might be there. I thought it was just a warehouse.

We were still fifty feet away when the front door banged open. Jane and I both froze. We watched from the bushes as a skinny, dark-haired teenager emerged. He walked to a nearby tree, unzipped his pants, and took a leak. When he finished, he zipped up and returned to the house, slamming the door shut behind him.

"That's unbelievable," Jane said.

"I know." That kid couldn't have been older than fourteen or fifteen. Where were his parents? Why wasn't he in school?

"How can someone work in a place without a bathroom?" Jane asked, still incredulous. "Where's the kid supposed to wash his hands?"

We stayed crouched in the woods another few minutes. When the boy didn't reemerge, we moved closer and circled the drug house until we found a window.

"I don't suppose you remembered to bring the binoculars?" I asked.

"Sorry," she whispered. "But I've got the stun gun."

I grabbed a giant palm frond off the jungle floor, then left Jane behind while I crept up to the window.

The stun gun wasn't going to help us. The kid had a friend with him, and they both had guns. The kind with bullets. They also had I don't know how many kilos of cocaine, a bunch of pottery, and some jade pieces. I couldn't tell from this distance whether any of them were shaped like a head.

After I'd taken inventory, I crept back to Jane.

"Is it in there?" she whispered.

"It might be. I can't tell."

"Maybe we should come back later with Jack."

"Maybe we should come back later with an army."

Jane raised both brows.

"He looked a lot less scary with his dick in his hand than he does holding a gun."

When the second kid came to the window and flicked his cigarette butt into the trees, we decided it was time to hightail it back to the turtle camp.

My heart skipped a beat when I walked into the back room. "Jane!"

"What's wrong?" she said, running to the doorway.

"Ernesto's gone."

"He can't be gone."

"Do you see him here?" There was no sign of him. No rope, no tape, even the chair we'd tied him to was missing.

"Ernesto," she called and started searching the room.

"He's not a cat," I said. "He's not hiding under the bed."

"People don't just vanish, Lizzie. Do you think someone could've kidnapped him from us?"

"No, Jane. Obviously he escaped." I knew leaving him here alone was a mistake. Why did I listen to her when I knew all of her detective skills come from watching TV?

"With the chair still taped to his back? I don't think so."

We found the chair when we found Jack. They'd both floated up on the beach.

CHAPTER 57

We spotted the chair first. It was sinking into the sand, strips of duct tape still clinging to it, on a stretch of beach just north of the turtle camp. Jack was much farther up the shore.

When we first glimpsed his body lying facedown in the sand, waves rushing in over his feet, we thought it was Ernesto.

"Do you think he's dead?" I asked Jane.

"Let's hope not," she said. "If another man in your life washes up as a corpse, they'll never believe you're not a murderer."

It wasn't until we got closer that I could see the blond hair and realized it was Jack. *Please, please, please, God, let him not be dead* was the only thought in my head as I took off running. Jane and I were both calling out to him, but he didn't so much as twitch.

As soon as we reached him, I dropped down to my knees and flipped him over. His clothes were soaked and he was covered in sand, but he was still breathing. Jane and I each took an arm and dragged Jack a few feet up the beach beyond the reach of the waves. He wasn't conscious, but he was alive.

"Do you have any water?" I asked Jane.

She rummaged through her messenger bag and pulled out a half-full bottle.

I opened Jack's mouth and poured some in. He immediately started choking, which I took as a good sign. Then I remembered my eleventh grade junior lifesaving class and rolled him onto his side.

"What are you doing?" Jane asked when Jack's back was to me and his front was facing her.

"In case he starts to puke."

"I don't want him puking on me." She jumped back. "He's your boyfriend, he can puke on you."

Jack let out a virulent cough, then croaked out, "I'm not puking on anybody," before he spat up in the sand.

"That's disgusting," Jane pronounced. "I think I'm gonna be sick." Then she started gagging and took off running down the beach.

I felt the same, but I stayed. Although I did turn my head away and tried to breathe through my mouth.

When Jack finished retching, he reached for the water bottle and drank it down in one long swallow.

"Do you think you can make it back to the turtle camp?" The sun was beating down on us and we had nowhere to hide.

"Just give me a minute," he said, then lay back in the sand and closed his eyes. Almost instantly, his breathing turned rhythmic.

Jane returned a few minutes later. "What happened?"

"I don't know. He fell asleep again before I could ask."

"You can't let him sleep. He might have a concussion."

"If he has a concussion then he's supposed to sleep."

"No he's not. He could fall into a coma."

"That's just an old wives' tale."

"You willing to bet his life on that?"

I called Jack's name and shook his shoulder, but he didn't wake.

Jane knelt down on Jack's other side, and before I realized what she was up to, she'd slapped him hard across the face.

"What the hell?" Jack said as he opened his eyes.

"What did you do that for?" I shouted.

"He's awake, isn't he?" She stood up and brushed the sand from her knees. "Can you stand up?" she asked a still-groggy Jack.

Jack started to nod, then winced. I gingerly touched the back of his head. There was definitely a lump there that shouldn't have been.

"What happened?" I asked.

"I'm not sure," he said, pushing himself up. "I think I was ambushed."

"You think?" Jane asked.

"I was on my way back when a couple stranded in a sailboat flagged me down. They wanted a ride back to shore."

"You gave strangers a ride on your boat?" Jane asked, her tone incredulous.

Jack shook his head and winced again. "I offered to call the Coast Guard, but when I went for my cell phone something hit me in the back of the head."

"What?"

"I don't know," Jack said. "The next thing I knew, I was in the water."

"And you swam all the way back here?" Now I knew where the great shoulders came from.

"I wasn't that far, plus the tide's coming in."

"You didn't happen to see Ernesto out there, did you?" Jane asked.

Jack stopped rubbing the back of his head. "Why would I have seen Ernesto?"

Jane glanced over at me, and Jack followed her gaze. Apparently, I was the designated explainer. "We think he escaped."

"You think he escaped!" Jack yelled, then grabbed the back of his head again.

"Or someone else might've kidnapped him from us," Jane chimed in. "We're not sure."

"How?" was all Jack said, his voice slightly above a whisper.

"Well, after you left, Ernesto got very chatty. Then Jane did this little dominatrix routine and—"

"Dominatrix?" Jack asked.

"It was Lizzie's idea," Jane said.

"Then Ernesto mentioned that he'd thought Michael hid the head in my room, but when he searched it, it wasn't there, which got me thinking that maybe someone beat him to it."

"Someone?"

"Manuel," Jane said.

Jack closed his eyes again. "Please tell me you didn't."

"It's OK," I said. "Manuel wasn't there. And they definitely had jade, but I couldn't tell if any of it was shaped like a head."

"They?" he asked.

"Two men, boys actually, were guarding the stash."

"Did they see you?"

"I don't think so." If they had, I'd probably be dead.

When we arrived back at the turtle camp, Jack lay down on the bed but told us not to let him fall asleep. I sat down next to him so I could poke him if he started dozing off, and Jane retired to the couch.

"I still don't understand how Ernesto could've escaped," Jane said.

"All he'd have to do is make it to the ocean," Jack replied. "The water would loosen the rope and then he'd be able to maneuver out of the tape."

"Thanks for mentioning that sooner, MacGyver."

"I would've if you'd told me you were planning on leaving him here alone!"

"OK, guys," I said. "This isn't helping."

Jane folded her arms across her chest and Jack buried his head deeper into the pillow. He looked like he might fall asleep again, so I poked him in the chest.

"Ow!"

"Stop being such a baby."

"I've been beaten, robbed, and left for dead. I think I've earned a little TLC."

"You were robbed?" Jane asked.

"Yeah, they took the boat."

"Then how are we going to get out of here?"

A good question that none of us had focused on until now.

"You still have your cell phone, don't you?" Jack asked.

"Yes," I answered for her, "but the person we were going to call was you."

Jane sat up. "We can still call John and Cheryl."

"What good would that do when we don't have the head?" They'd made it pretty clear at our last meeting that my freedom was in exchange for the jade piece.

"We don't know for sure the head's not in the drug house," Jane said. "And even if it's not, the rest of it should be enough to get you off the hook. Besides, they already signed the deal."

"But there are men with guns in the drug house."

"I'm sure John and Cheryl have guns too."

"I didn't notice any when they met us on the beach."

"They probably left them back in the boat," Jane said. "You can't be a cop without a gun."

True. At least on television.

"If we're going to do this," Jack piped in, "we should do it soon."

"Why?" I asked. "Is your head hurting again?"

"He could have a concussion," Jane said. "Maybe we should take him to the hospital."

"I don't have a concussion," Jack said, sitting up. "I just don't think it's safe for us to spend another night here. Too many people know where to find us."

"Do you think Ernesto would come back for us?" Jane asked.

"I don't know," Jack said. "But I'd rather not find out."

I didn't want to send Jane searching for a signal by herself, and I didn't want to leave Jack alone, so the three of us plus Fred traipsed down the beach toward the marine reserve. By the time we reached the rocks, Jack was so worn out he didn't think he could make the climb. So I stayed behind with him and Fred while Jane scrambled to the top herself.

"With any luck," I said, joining Jack and Fred in the sand, "this will all be over in a couple of hours."

"And you'll go back to LA and forget all about Fred and me."

I reached for Jack's hand. "How can you even think that? You know I'd never forget Fred."

"Thanks, Lizzie."

He looked so cute with his hair in his eyes and Fred by his side that I just had to kiss him. It was a long, slow, delicious kiss that probably would've ended in clothes being ripped off each other's bodies if Jane hadn't returned.

"Will you two get a room already!"

I didn't even bother trying to explain. "What did they say?"

"They weren't in," she said. "I had to leave a message."

I groaned. "Now what?"

"I guess we try again later."

I gave Jack a hand up and we all trudged back to the turtle camp (except Fred, whom I carried). The shrimp I'd been feeding him must've been doing some good because he looked like he'd grown. He was now slightly larger than my palm, although he still fit easily in one hand.

We smelled the smoke before we could see where it was coming from. As soon as Jack spotted the flames, he started to run. By the time Jane and I caught up to him, it was obvious there wouldn't be much left. The staked-off area at the front of the turtle camp was still intact, but flames engulfed the two-room cabin behind it.

CHAPTER 58

"What should we do?" I yelled.

"I'll call the fire department," Jane said, but Jack shook his head.

"It's too late."

"But we have to do something. We can't just sit here and watch it burn."

His arms remained at his sides, but he'd balled both hands into fists. "Don't worry. I'll find out who did this, then I'll kill him."

"You don't mean that. You're just angry."

"Yes, I'm angry. Someone just burned down my house."

Technically, it wasn't *his* house, but I decided not to point that out to him.

"Go back to the rocks and call the fire department. Anonymously," Jack added, as if we would've done it any other way. "Then wait for John and Cheryl to call you back."

"What about you?"

"I'll stay here and wait for the firemen. They'll have a lot of questions, and you two shouldn't be here when they arrive."

"Will you call us later?"

"I'll call when I can," he said. "Now go before it gets dark."

Reluctantly, Jane and I left Jack alone at the burning cabin while we hurried back to the rocks with Fred. As soon as she got a signal, Jane called the fire department but they already knew. Other people must've smelled the smoke too.

Jane tried John and Cheryl again, but they still weren't in, so we sat back on the rocks and watched the smoke rise as the sun set.

"I could use a drink," Jane said.

"Yeah, and a place to sleep tonight might be nice."

"And maybe a cell phone charger," she added.

"Please don't tell me the batteries are dead."

"Not yet, but we're down to one bar."

The batteries lasted another hour—long enough for John and Cheryl to call us back. Jane arranged for them to pick us up at the rocks. The moon was a sliver, and the area had no lights, so we had to scream and wave Jane's keychain flashlight in the dark for ten minutes before they found us. John helped us onto the boat and offered us water. Cheryl just wanted to know if we'd brought the head.

"No," Jane said. "But we know where it is."

"Where?" Cheryl asked.

"Somewhere very safe, but it's being guarded by a couple of men with guns, so you're going to need backup."

We couldn't see their expressions in the dark, but their sighs were enough to alert us to their hesitation.

"Don't you have any backup?" Jane asked.

"We told you," Cheryl said, "we're undercover."

"Trust me," I said. "You're not going to want to go in there alone."

"Where is this place?" John asked.

"On the island," I told him, "but in a very secluded spot."

"Who's guarding it?" he asked.

"Bad guys with guns. I didn't catch their names."

"And you know they have it? You've seen it?"

"Yes," I lied.

"What did it look like?" Cheryl asked.

"It looked like a jade head," Jane said. "Do we have a deal or not?"

"Yes," John said. "We have a deal."

"John, we should go back to the hotel and call headquarters," Cheryl said. "Then we can get all the supplies we need and go back in the morning."

"Good idea," John said and started the engine.

"It's more than just the head," I told them. "There's pottery and cocaine too. I really think you're going to want to bring more people with you."

"Understood," John said.

"Lizzie should get a reward out of all this," Jane suggested, "since she's giving you more than just the head."

Cheryl let out a laugh. "We'll see what we can do."

John and Cheryl brought us back to their hotel on Parrot Caye. John told Cheryl to take Jane and me to their room while he tried to find us a place to sleep. The suites at the White Sands were nicer than the Blue Bay, but still not as fancy as Jane's private villa at the Tradewinds. But after the turtle camp, any hotel looked good.

I was surprised to see that the room contained only one bed. "I guess it's easier to go undercover as newlyweds when you really are a couple?"

"Excuse me?" Cheryl said, then realized what I was implying and said, "Yes, much easier."

"What are you going to do when the baby's born?"

"I don't know yet," she said and flopped down on the couch.

The door opened and we all looked up. "The hotel's full," John said, "so they're bringing us a rollaway. You two can flip for it. Loser can sleep on the couch."

"Can I speak to you for a minute?" Cheryl asked, then grabbed John's hand and practically dragged him into the bathroom. We tried to listen in, but Cheryl turned on the fan so we couldn't hear.

BETH ORSOFF

When they emerged a few minutes later John said, "On second thought, we'd like you two to have the bed. Cheryl will sleep on the rollaway and I'll take the couch."

"Are you sure?" I asked.

Jane punched me in the arm. "Of course they're sure. They wouldn't have offered if they weren't."

"Is anyone hungry?" John asked.

"Starving," Jane replied.

John tossed her the room service menu. "No lobster. The federal government can't afford it." Then he told Cheryl he was going to call headquarters and he left the three of us alone in the room.

"Would you mind if I left my turtle in the bathroom sink?"

"Where did you pick him up?" Cheryl asked as I pulled Fred out of Jane's messenger bag.

"He belongs to a friend. I'm just babysitting."

She shrugged her shoulders, which I took as a yes and filled one of the double sinks with water. When I returned to the main room, Jane and Cheryl were both sitting on the couch watching TV.

"It's so good to be back in civilization." Jane smiled and stretched her arms overhead.

"Where have you been staying?" Cheryl asked. "And how did *you* manage to get out of jail?" Cheryl directed at me.

"Where there's a will there's a way," I told her and smiled. I was afraid anything I said could implicate Jack.

That's how we spent the next few hours—watching television and avoiding one another's questions. Every time John or Cheryl asked us where we'd been, how I'd escaped, or how we'd managed to find the head, Jane and I deflected. And every time we asked them about the DEA and their undercover work, they changed the subject.

When Jane asked to see their badges and guns, John decided it was time for us all to go to bed. Despite the new surroundings and my concern for Jack, my exhaustion won out. When I awoke

252

at six the next morning, John was already on the phone with room service ordering breakfast.

After we showered, Jane wanted to go to the gift shop for some clean clothes, but it didn't open for another two hours and John refused to wait. He tossed us each a clean polo shirt and promised he'd buy us both new outfits after we'd recovered the head.

"Meet me at the dock in an hour," he said, then left Cheryl in charge while he went to rent another boat. *The Today Show* droned on in the background while we all flipped through Cheryl's paltry selection of magazines. Except for one *In Style*, which Jane snagged before I could, it was all *Archeologist Digest* and *Antiquities Monthly*.

It was in the spring issue that I finally learned the secret of the jade head.

CHAPTER 59

His name was Kinich Ahau, the Mayan sun god. Back in 1968, a six-inch-tall jade carving of his head was discovered in a Mayan temple at Altun Ha, an excavation site in Belize. To date, he was the largest jade artifact ever recovered from the Mayan civilization.

According to *Antiquities Monthly*, the important phrase was *to date*. Rumors had circulated for years about the existence of a second jade head—a carving of the Mayan rain god known as Chac—as yet undiscovered. But in recent months, the rumors had escalated.

The article's author cited an anonymous source for her claim that a carving of Chac was unearthed by local villagers near the ancient city of Tikal, in Guatemala, just across the border from Belize. Neither the Guatemalan authorities nor the Belize government would confirm the rumor, but a Belizean official from the Ministry of Archaeology was quoted as saying, "The only known jade head is the carving of Kinich Ahau. If a carving of Chac was discovered in this country, it would be in the custody of the ministry."

The author concluded that until Chac appeared in a museum, or more likely in the booming underground market for looted antiquities, the rumors would undoubtedly persist.

"Cheryl, if the head I found really is Chac, how much do you think it's worth?"

"Why? Are you planning on selling it?"

"Of course not. I just thought if it was really valuable the Belize government might give me a reward. I have lawyer's fees to pay, not to mention being out of work for three weeks."

"An archeologist would tell you it's priceless," she said. "But if it went up for auction tomorrow, it would go for millions."

People had killed for a lot less than that.

The phone rang and Cheryl told us to gather our things, which meant two dirty shirts, Jane's purse, and Fred. When we arrived at the dock, John was already waiting.

"Where to, Lizzie?" he asked when we'd all climbed aboard the rented fishing boat.

"Same place as yesterday," I said. "From there we'll have to walk." I still hadn't figured out what I'd do if the jade head wasn't there. I was just praying that it would be, or if not, that the rest of the loot would be enough for them.

John consulted his map, then called someone on his cell. After he read off the coordinates, he said, "In walking distance," before hanging up.

John piloted the boat as close to shore as he could without running aground, and the four of us sloshed up to the beach. When we reached dry land, John unzipped his backpack and pulled out two guns. He tucked one in his waistband and handed the other to Cheryl.

"What about us?" Jane asked.

"Stay close and try not to get shot," he said. "Where to, Lizzie?"

I pointed to the path that led through the jungle. "It's not far. Maybe a quarter mile."

"Lead the way."

"Wouldn't it be better if I stayed behind with Jane? Someone's got to wait for backup and show them where it is."

John smiled. Then he pointed the gun in my direction and said, "Let's go."

"Don't worry," Cheryl said, "I've got your back."

That's what I was afraid of.

I led the four of us to the spot where Jane and I had first heard the music, but there was no music today. John signaled something to Cheryl with his hands, then she headed to the front door while John crept around to the window. Neither of them told me or Jane where to go, so I pulled her with me behind a large tree.

At first, John peered in the window from the left side, then he slid underneath and stared in from the right side. Finally, he led with his gun and stood up. Then he turned back to me.

"What the fuck is this?" he yelled.

"What?" I mouthed. I didn't want the men on the inside to hear us and couldn't understand why he was so unconcerned.

He came over and grabbed my arm and dragged me with him to the window.

I couldn't believe my eyes. The place was empty. No drugs, no pottery, and definitely no jade head. Even the folding table and chairs were gone.

"I swear it was here yesterday."

John put the gun to the side of my head. "Where is it?"

I instinctively raised my hands in the air. "Please, John, I swear I don't know what happened."

Cheryl and Jane both came running toward us, Cheryl calmly saying, "Not this way, John," and Jane screaming, "Let her go!"

"Who else did you tell?" he asked, his hand steady while he pushed the cool metal barrel even harder against my head.

My heart was pounding so hard and so loudly it felt as if it were literally going to burst out of my chest. If John didn't kill me, I'd surely die from a heart attack anyway. I didn't see my life flashing before my eyes, but I did wish for two things: I wanted to call my parents to say goodbye and I wanted to have sex again, preferably with Jack.

As if reading my mind, Jane said, "Lizzie, what about Jack?"

"Who's Jack?" John demanded.

"You met him," I said, trying to turn my head to face him, but I couldn't because of the gun. "He was the scuba instructor at the Blue Bay. He drove us all home from the disco the night Michael was killed."

"He's involved in this too?" Cheryl asked.

"He's been helping us. But he didn't take the head."

"Where is he?" John demanded.

The gun made a clicking sound and my heart nearly jumped out of my chest. "I don't know. His house burned down yesterday and we haven't seen him since."

John finally moved the gun away from my head, but it was still in his hand. "Watch her," he said to Cheryl, then he walked a few feet away and pulled his cell phone out of his pocket. "Motherfucker!" he yelled before throwing the phone at a tree.

"What?" Cheryl said.

"No signal."

Cheryl fished the phone out of the underbrush. "I'll go to the beach and see if I can get one. You wait here with these two."

"No," he said, "we all go."

The four of us walked single file back to the beach with John in front, Jane and me in the middle, and Cheryl in the rear. When we reached the sand, John pulled two sets of handcuffs out of his backpack and cuffed both Jane and me with our arms behind our backs.

"You can't treat us this way," Jane shouted. "We're not criminals."

Actually, we were, or at least I was.

"We have a deal," she said. "In writing."

"We only had a deal if you gave us the head."

"That's not what it says."

"Oh no," John said. "Let me see it."

"Uncuff me," she said. "It's in my purse."

John grabbed Jane's bag, which was still on her shoulder, and pulled it to her wrist before dumping the contents in the sand.

Along with her wallet, water bottle, and cell phone, out came Fred and the stun gun too.

"I'll take this," John said. But as he reached for the stun gun, Fred clamped down on his finger.

"What the fuck!" John yelled. He tried to shake Fred off, but the little guy wouldn't let go.

John lifted his gun and took aim at Fred.

That's when my maternal instinct kicked in (the only explanation since I *knew* it was an incredibly stupid thing to do). "No!" I screamed and lunged for John. But since my hands were still cuffed behind my back all I could do was knock him over, which I did. But that didn't keep the gun from going off.

The bullet whizzed past Fred, who finally let go of John's finger, but grazed me in the shoulder. It was as if someone had sliced me open, then poured rubbing alcohol into the gaping wound. I screamed again, this time from the pain.

"What kind of fucking nut job are you?" John said, pushing me off him.

"Yeah," Jane said. "What the hell were you thinking? It's a turtle, for God's sake."

I couldn't focus on anything except the excruciating burning sensation in my shoulder. Cheryl sat me upright and inspected the wound. "The bullet barely hit you. You'll be fine. Give me the keys," she said to John.

"Why?"

"Someone needs to put pressure on it to stop the bleeding. I'm not going to stand here all day, and she can't do it if she's got her hands cuffed behind her back."

John shook his head, clearly disgusted with all of us, but he pulled a set of keys out of his pocket and tossed them to Cheryl. She unlocked my cuffs, pulled a red bandana out of her fanny pack, and stuffed the handcuffs in. After she washed the wound with Jane's water, she covered it with the bandana and told me to hold it there until the bleeding stopped.

While Cheryl was tending to me, John was sifting through the contents of Jane's bag, which were still strewn across the sand. This time when he grabbed the stun gun, Fred wasn't there to stop him. Fred was ten feet away pushing himself in circles in the sand.

"Give that back," Jane said. "It's mine."

"Did you know it's illegal for private citizens to carry stun guns in Belize?"

"But I'm an American," Jane said.

"It doesn't matter," John replied, checking the safety before stuffing the stun gun into his back pocket. He continued searching until he found the note Jane had written on his DEA letterhead. He read it and laughed before tearing it into little pieces.

"You can't do that," Jane said, aghast. "That's a signed deal."

"I just did," he said and tossed the pieces into the air like confetti. The breeze caught them and blew them toward the water before they rained down onto the sand.

"You are so fired," Jane said.

John shook his head and laughed, then lifted his cell phone in the air and paced the beach until he found a signal. While he talked in hushed tones and indecipherable sentences, Cheryl stuffed the rest of Jane's things back into her bag. She looked like she was about to speak when John turned around. "What are you doing?"

"You mean it was your intention to leave evidence lying all over the sand?"

John said, "Uh-huh," which I presumed was in response to his caller and not to Cheryl, and ended his call. "Backup's on the way," he said.

Thank God. Maybe they could rein in this psycho.

"And I thought he was the nice one," Jane whispered.

Her track record was almost as bad as mine.

CHAPTER 60

We heard the motorboat when it was still a speck in the distance. Watching it approach, my hopes rose. Surely, someone on board could control John. If we were lucky, maybe it'd be his boss and he'd fire him on the spot.

When the boat anchored and only one man debarked, I started to get concerned. But my hopes weren't completely dashed until I recognized the man trudging up the beach.

"Ernesto, my man!" John greeted our former captive. "How's it hanging?"

We kidnapped a DEA agent? Now we were really in trouble. Except he thought we were the agents. Or at least he pretended to. What the hell was going on here?

"Long and hard, my friend," Ernesto said. "And even harder now," he added as he approached Jane and me. We were both huddled in the shade under a palm tree, me holding Cheryl's bandana to my aching shoulder, Jane kneeling next to me with her hands still cuffed behind her back.

"Hello, Ernesto," Jane said in her haughtiest tone.

"You know her?" Cheryl asked.

Ernesto responded by grabbing a handful of Jane's hair and jerking her head back. "Miss me, Blondie?" he asked as he ran a dirty finger down her swanlike neck and into her cleavage.

"Get your paws off me," Jane said, pulling away from him.

Ernesto laughed.

"C'mon," Cheryl said. "This is business." Then she jerked her head toward John and the three of them huddled together farther down the beach.

We couldn't hear what they were saying, so we assumed they couldn't hear us either.

"Why did he just lie about knowing us?" Jane asked.

"I don't know and I don't care." I wasn't particularly proud of kidnapping Ernesto, although I still felt it was the right thing to do under the circumstances. But if he wanted to pretend it never happened, that was fine with me. "What we need to focus on now is getting the hell out of here."

"Where are we going to go?"

"At this point, I'm voting for the Camus Caye Police Department." At least Sergeant Ramos never held a gun to my head.

"We can't quit now," Jane said. "Look how far we've come."

"We're handcuffed on a deserted beach with a bunch of crazy people with guns, one of whom is our former hostage. This seems like the perfect time to quit."

Jane called out to Ernesto and all three turned around. "Will you please tell your friends who really killed Michael so they'll let us go."

Ernesto looked perplexed until John said, "She thinks we're DEA." Then he and Ernesto started laughing.

That's when I realized just how much trouble we were really in.

Unfortunately, Jane needed more convincing. "Excuse me," she said, pushing herself upright and walking over to them.

Of course I followed.

"I don't see what's so funny here," she continued.

"Sit back down," Cheryl warned.

"No," Jane said. "I want an explanation and I want it now."

John pointed his gun at Jane's forehead. "I want that jade head now. How about we trade? You give me the head and I won't blow your brains all over this beach."

"What kind of cop are you?"

"I'm not," he said, still pointing the gun at Jane's forehead. "Any more questions?"

Cheryl stepped between Jane and John and grabbed us both by the arm (thankfully my uninjured one). "If you want to live," she whispered as she pulled us back down the beach, "then keep your mouth shut and do what I tell you." Then she pushed us into the sand and walked back to John and Ernesto.

"I think you're right, Lizzie. I think it's time to quit."

I leaned back against the palm tree and tried to think of a way out. I was shot in the shoulder, Jane's hands were cuffed behind her back, we were miles away from anyone who could potentially help us, our one weapon had been confiscated, our cell phone was dead, and we had no visible means of escape. It didn't look good.

"Got any ideas?" I asked.

"I was hoping you did," she replied.

Apparently, John, Cheryl, and Ernesto were having better luck coming up with a plan than we were. The trio marched back to us and John ordered us to stand.

"Where are we going?" Jane asked as we pushed ourselves upright.

John slapped Jane across the face with his gun. "No more questions, or next time I'll use the bullets."

Jane's cheek was red where he'd hit her, and I could see the tears in her eyes, but to her credit, she didn't let them fall. She stood behind me as we all walked single file through the jungle. This time I was glad Cheryl was behind us. I didn't exactly trust her, but she seemed to be the only one of the three who didn't seem intent on inflicting bodily harm.

CHAPTER 61

John opened the door to the drug house and pushed Jane and me inside. It looked the same as it had from the outside—a big, empty room with a dirt floor and bare walls.

"Is your shoulder still bleeding?" he asked.

"I don't know," I said, easing the bandana away. Both my shirt and shoulder were covered in blood, so it was hard to tell.

"Give me the cuffs," John said to Cheryl.

"What's the point, John? She's not going anywhere."

"I think all those pregnancy hormones are turning you soft."

"You're pregnant?" Ernesto said. "Congratulations."

"Thanks," Cheryl replied.

"I'd like to have a kid someday," Ernesto said, slithering up to Jane. "What do you say, Blondie, you up for it?"

"Drop dead," Jane replied.

Ernesto grabbed Jane by the hair and snapped her head back. "Be nice to me, Blondie. I'm the one with the stun gun now." In case she had any doubt, he unlocked the safety and zapped it in the air next to her cheek.

Jane flinched but kept her mouth shut.

Cheryl grabbed the stun gun from Ernesto's hand. "Do us all a favor, Ernesto. Go find yourself a nice prostitute."

"Let him have his fun," John said. "What's the harm?"

"What's the harm?" I shouted before I could stop myself.

John reached for his gun, probably to give me the same warning across the cheek he'd given Jane, but Cheryl grabbed his arm. "John, we don't have time for this. Let's go."

John followed Cheryl to the door, but Ernesto didn't. "I think I should stay here and keep an eye on these two," Ernesto said. "We wouldn't want them to escape."

"We're in the middle of nowhere," Cheryl said. "Where do you think they're going to go?"

"Let him stay," John said, slamming the door shut behind them. We heard Cheryl arguing with him as he led her away. John assured her that we'd be fine. Of course, he didn't know our history with Ernesto. Not that I think he would've cared.

"It's just us rabbits," Ernesto said, sidling up to Jane.

"How much money is it going to take for you to get us out of here?" Jane asked.

"A lot of money, Blondie. I don't think you have that much."

"Don't be so sure," I said. "She's got more than you think."

"Name your price." Jane managed to sound authoritative even with her hands cuffed behind her back. Maybe it's something you're born with.

Ernesto appeared to consider it, but then said, "Not yet. We still have some unfinished business to take care of."

"Like what?" I asked.

"This," he said, popping the button at his waist and unzipping his pants. "Which one of you wants to go first?"

"Are you nuts?"

"A blow job's fine. I know you girls get off on it."

"She lied, Ernesto." At least where it concerned him.

He pulled a knife from his pants pocket and flicked open the blade. "No matter."

"It's OK, Lizzie," Jane said. "I don't mind."

"You don't mind!" Had he drugged her when I wasn't looking?

"Now there's a girl with a good attitude," Ernesto said, turning to me. "You could learn from her, chica."

Jane winked at me, which I was sure meant something, I just didn't know what.

"You have to at least put on a condom," I said.

He laughed and pushed his pants down to his knees, revealing a pair of faded tighty whiteys.

"Ernesto," Jane said, sitting up, "I know you would really enjoy this more if I could use my hands."

Now I understood.

"I don't have the keys," he said. "You'll figure something out."

When he reached down to pull out his penis, I jumped up. Ernesto dropped his dick and pointed the knife at me.

I raised my one good arm in a sign of surrender. "I just want to help. Jane and I, we like to work as a team."

Ernesto looked warily from me to her.

"Trust me," Jane said, and ran her tongue across her upper lip. "It'll blow your mind."

His lust overtook his judgment. "OK, but no funny business."

I knelt down behind Ernesto while Jane remained in front of him. From this position, maybe we could flip him over my back. It also offered the added advantage that I didn't have to look at him.

I reached around with my good arm and grabbed Ernesto from outside his underwear. He was already rock hard, so at least this would be quick.

"Lizzie, take your shirt off," Jane said.

"What? Why?"

"To make it more pleasurable for Ernesto," she said, and gave him a fake smile. "And so we have something to clean up with."

"You take your shirt off. You're the one with the boobs."

"Yeah," Ernesto said. "You take yours off."

"I can't," Jane said, jangling the handcuffs behind her back. "You don't have the keys."

"That's no problem."

Jane probably thought what I thought—that he'd pick the lock with his knife. Instead, he reached down and slit her shirt up the middle. He was scarily skilled with that blade.

"Oh yeah," he moaned as he gave Jane's shirt a tug and it fell open, revealing a lacy demi-bra hugging C-cup breasts.

When he pulled his penis out himself and shoved it against Jane's clenched lips, I decided this game had gone far enough. I grabbed the bloody bandana from my shoulder, wrapped it around Ernesto's dick, and squeezed as hard as I could. I didn't know if you could actually break a penis, but I was trying.

Ernesto screamed. Jane opened her eyes. And I yelled, "Now!"

Jane pushed herself up and body-slammed Ernesto. He didn't fall backward as I'd hoped, probably because I was still holding onto his penis, but it did cause him to drop the knife. With all of us yelling, Ernesto from pain, and Jane and I trying to tell each other what to do—we both agreed someone needed to stab Ernesto, we just felt that the other should be the one to do it—it's not surprising we didn't hear the ruckus outside.

It wasn't until the gun went off that we all stopped yelling and turned around. Standing in the doorway was Jack. And standing next to him with his gun pointed at the three of us was Rodrigo, the "friend of the family."

"Police," Rodrigo said. "You're all under arrest."

CHAPTER 62

I admit that from where Rodrigo stood, this did look pretty bad. I was kneeling behind Ernesto with my arm wrapped around his leg and my hand still squeezing his dick. Jane was standing in front of him with her boobs on display and her hands cuffed behind her back. And Ernesto, whose pants were around his ankles, was still sporting a major hard-on.

"It's not what it looks like," I said, finally letting go of Ernesto.

Then the three of us all started talking at once—Jane and I in English, and Ernesto in Spanish.

Rodrigo shot his gun into the air again just to get us to quiet down. "Ernesto," he said, pointing the gun at him, "pull your pants up."

Ernesto reached down and very carefully zipped up. He continued ranting at Rodrigo, mostly in Spanish. From the tone and the hand gestures, I gleaned that Rodrigo had set him up. Or at least Ernesto thought he had. I still wasn't sure I had it all figured out.

"You two," Rodrigo said, pointing to Jane and me, "go stand against the wall."

We did as we were told, keeping our eyes on Rodrigo's gun, which he kept pointed at Ernesto even when he bent down to pick up the knife. Once he'd closed the blade and stuck it in his pocket, he reached behind him for a pair of handcuffs.

"Ernesto, turn around and put your hands behind your back."

Ernesto looked like he was following instructions, but when Rodrigo tried to cuff him, Ernesto spun around and took a swing at him.

Another gunshot rang out, and Ernesto fell to his knees, a dark red stain spreading across the front of his yellow shirt.

Rodrigo was easing Ernesto onto his back when Cheryl rushed in, gun first.

"Are you OK?" She was staring at Rodrigo.

"I'm fine, honey. Everything's fine."

Honey?

"Jack, can you help me with him?" Rodrigo asked.

Jack glanced over at Jane and me, then quickly turned his attention back to Rodrigo. "What do you want me to do?"

"Grab his feet," Rodrigo said while he lifted Ernesto by the shoulders. "Lizzie, come with us," Rodrigo added as he and Jack carried Ernesto to the door.

I fell in behind Rodrigo and Jane started to follow when Cheryl said, "No, you stay here with me."

It all starts to run together after that. Rodrigo and Jack carried Ernesto through the jungle and back to the beach, where Sergeant Ramos was waiting with John in handcuffs.

"The Parrot Caye police are on their way," Sergeant Ramos told Rodrigo.

"Good," Rodrigo said. "Let them know we're going to need transport to the hospital."

Sergeant Ramos nodded and reached for his walkie-talkie.

I heard someone calling my name and I looked out to the ocean. Officer Juan was waving to me from Sergeant Ramos's boat.

"You OK, Lizzie?"

I looked down at my bloody shirt. "I will be."

"Good," he said, then went back to doing whatever it was he was doing on the boat. Probably reading a magazine.

Rodrigo and Jack set Ernesto down in the sand and Rodrigo checked his wound. "I didn't hit anything important," Rodrigo told him. "You'll live."

Ernesto replied in Spanish, but I don't think he was thanking him.

Rodrigo turned to me next. "Which one of them did this?" he asked as he pushed up my shirtsleeve and inspected my wound.

"John, but it was an accident. He was aiming for Fred."

"Who's Fred?" he asked.

Jack and I looked around the beach. Jack spotted him first, inching his way through the sand. His circle had widened considerably. At this rate, he might make it to the ocean by nightfall.

"A turtle?" Rodrigo said.

"When Jack brought me to the turtle camp—"

"Later," Rodrigo said. "Right now I need you to give me your statement."

Obviously, he wasn't a turtle person. "Where do you want me to start?"

"How about explaining exactly what the three of you were doing back in that cabin."

"Yeah," Jack said, folding his arms across his chest, "I'd like to hear that one myself."

CHAPTER 63

After Jane told Cheryl everything she knew and I told Rodrigo everything I knew, they compared notes. Our stories matched enough for them to take us back to the Parrot Caye police station without handcuffs. That's when we found out who they really were.

Jane had been half right. Cheryl was a DEA agent. But she wasn't married to John, she was dating Rodrigo, who worked for the US customs agency. Rodrigo explained that they were both part of an interagency task force set up to infiltrate a local drug and antiquities smuggling ring with ties to a much larger Mexican cartel.

"But I thought Ernesto worked for you," I said to Rodrigo. "At least that's the way it seemed that night we met you with Michael's sister."

"He did," he said. "I was undercover too. I tried to warn you. I told you that jade in your suitcase was fake."

"Yeah, but when we got it analyzed they found Michael's blood."

"That was an unfortunate turn of events," he said.

"Yes, especially for me. But since you knew I didn't kill Michael, why didn't you come forward?"

"I couldn't," he said. "Not without blowing my cover and a yearlong operation."

"So you were going to let me just rot in jail forever?"

"No," Rodrigo said, straining to keep his voice even. "I'm the one who arranged for your transfer to Parrot Caye. We planned to extract you during the boat ride, but you disappeared the night before. It didn't take us long to figure out where you were, but—"

"You knew?"

"Of course we knew. You didn't really think that disguise fooled anyone, did you?"

I turned to Jane. "I told you no one would believe I'm a guy. You made me cut my hair for nothing."

"It'll grow," she said without even a hint of remorse.

I turned back to Rodrigo. "Then why didn't you extract me, or whatever you call it, from Parrot Caye?"

"Because there was no need to. You weren't in jail and you weren't in any danger. Not until you contacted Ernesto."

"But what about the notes?" Jane asked.

"What notes?" Rodrigo said.

"The gringo go home notes," I said.

"I don't know about any notes."

We all turned to Jack.

"What are you looking at me for?" Jack said.

"You're the one who found them," I reminded him.

"No," he said, "you found the first one. I found the second."

I continued to stare at him. He looked guilty.

"I told you I thought the first one was local kids playing a prank."

"And the second one?" I asked.

"You were taking too many chances. I just wanted to scare you a little."

"I can't believe it. You almost killed Fred!"

"I didn't almost kill Fred. I was holding him up to the noose, waiting for you to walk in."

We continued to bicker when Jane interrupted. "I for one would like to know who really killed Michael."

271

"We think it was Ernesto," Rodrigo said.

"You *think*?" Jane said.

"He's already confessed to one of the local officers, but we need to make sure it wasn't coerced."

None of us wanted to know any more about that.

"Ernesto told us Manuel did it," I said.

Rodrigo smiled. "It wasn't Manuel."

"How do you know?" I asked.

"I know," he said.

"Is he an undercover agent too?" Jane asked.

Rodrigo closed his pad and put the cap back on his pen. "I think we're done here."

"Wait," I said. "What about the jade head?"

"What about it?" Cheryl asked, walking into the interrogation room.

"Did Ernesto have it after all? Is that why he killed Michael?"

"Ask Jack," she said.

Jane and I turned to face him.

Jack picked up the mesh bag he'd been carrying since we arrived at Parrot Caye and set it on the table. From inside the folds of a life jacket, he pulled out a six-inch-tall jade statue in the shape of a head. It was similar to the picture I'd seen in the magazine, except this one had a long serpent nose.

"You had it all along!"

"No, I found it this morning at my dad's house. After the turtle camp burned down, I had nowhere else to go."

"Your dad stole the head?" This was unbelievable.

"He didn't steal it, he found it. He picked it up diving that night you met him on the dock. He said it was hidden in an underwater cave not far from the Blue Bay. I found it this morning under a pile of fishing nets he wanted me to fix."

"Why didn't you call us?"

"I did," he said. "I left a message on Jane's cell. When you never called back I started to worry. That's when I called Cheryl."

"You're lucky I checked the voice mail," Cheryl said, folding the head back up in the life jacket and tucking it under her arm. "If John had picked up the message, things might've turned out very differently."

"So Michael hid the head in an underwater cave?" I didn't even know he knew how to dive.

"We think he was planning on coming back for it," Rodrigo said. "Probably without Ernesto's knowledge. It's too significant a piece to sell just to launder drug money. Michael knew that. He probably planned on bringing it to a dig site where he could pretend to discover it. A find like that can make a career."

"And Ernesto wouldn't go along with it?" I asked.

"We think Michael made the mistake of telling Ernesto how valuable it was," Cheryl said. "That's when Ernesto contacted John, who offered him half a million for it. John knew he could get five times that much at auction."

"John's an antiquities dealer?" Jane asked.

"And a money launderer," Cheryl said.

"But not the father of your baby?" I asked, although I probably should've waited until Rodrigo left the room.

"That would be me," Rodrigo said.

"John and I were business partners," Cheryl said, "or at least that's what he thought. It was all part of the sting."

"But why did you pretend to be married?" I asked, remembering the story of their elaborate wedding on the lake. I wasn't going to mention the king-size bed.

"That was John's idea," Cheryl said. "He thought we'd have an easier time getting through customs on the way back if we pretended we were down here on our honeymoon. It's a common ruse."

"Is anyone in this country actually married?" Jane asked. "Or are you all just pretending?"

Rodrigo smiled. "Michael always traveled with his girlfriend for the same reason. So when he suddenly showed up with you, we thought you were in on it with him."

"Is that why you were so friendly to me at the hotel?" I asked Cheryl. "You were checking me out."

"That was just dumb luck," she said. "Michael doesn't usually stay at the Blue Bay. But since you two were there, I couldn't pass up the opportunity."

"See," Jane said. "I was right about Michael. If you had listened to me, none of this would've happened."

"And if you hadn't come down here to play girl detective, none of the rest of it would've happened."

"I can't believe you would actually try to pin this on me. You're the one—"

"I still have a question," Jack said, interrupting our argument. "Who planted the jade in Lizzie's suitcase?"

That was a good question.

"It was Michael, wasn't it?" Jane said. "He was using Lizzie as his mule."

"It wasn't Michael," I said. "It was Ernesto, so the police would suspect me of the murder instead of him."

Rodrigo and Cheryl looked at each other, then back at us.

"It was Juan Martinez," Cheryl said.

"Who's Juan Martinez?" Jane and I both asked, practically in unison.

"*Officer* Juan Martinez," Rodrigo said, "formerly of the Camus Caye Police Department."

"You're kidding," I said. "He was always so nice to me."

"You're so gullible," Jane said. "You think anyone who's nice on the surface can't be a bad guy underneath."

"I do not! I just don't look for conspiracies everywhere the way you do."

"Ladies," Cheryl said, "please. We only found out ourselves a few days ago. We asked Sergeant Ramos not to arrest him until after we had Ernesto in custody."

"How did you find out?" Jack asked.

"We always knew someone in that department was working with the drug dealers," Cheryl said.

"We just didn't know who," Rodrigo added.

"There are only two of them," I pointed out. How hard could it be? Jane and I were amateurs, but they were supposed to be professionals.

"There used to be a third," Cheryl said. "We busted him in Belize City last week. He gave Juan up and a few others."

"But why?" I asked. "What was in it for him?"

"Juan was just following orders," Cheryl said. "You met him, so you know he's not a criminal mastermind."

"But where did he get the jade?" Jane asked. "Did Ernesto give it to him?"

"He wouldn't have had to," Rodrigo said. "It's everywhere down here, both real and fake."

"What about my lawyer?" I asked, thinking back to the conversation I'd overheard that night at Cajun Joe's. "Was he really on my side or was he working for the drug dealers too?"

"His only interest was in proving your innocence," Rodrigo said.

"And keeping you safe," Cheryl added. "Which sometimes meant apprising us of your whereabouts."

When ten seconds passed with no one asking a question, Rodrigo stood up.

"Wait!" I shouted. "What about my passport?"

"We should have that for you tomorrow." Rodrigo handed me his pad and pen. "Write down where you're staying and I'll have someone drop it off in the morning."

"I don't think we have a place anymore," I said.

"You can use my room." Cheryl tossed a key card onto the table. "I won't be needing it anymore," she added and gave Rodrigo's hand a squeeze.

"Great," Jane said, grabbing the room key. "We can stop by the gift shop on our way in. I cannot possibly spend one more minute in these disgusting clothes."

CHAPTER 64

After Jane dropped five hundred dollars in the hotel's gift shop for three new outfits even though we were leaving the next day, we went back to the room to shower and change before dinner. I spent one hundred dollars myself, the last money in my checking account, but only because it was the first time in weeks that I could go out without worrying about being spotted by the police. I wanted to celebrate.

When Jack knocked on our hotel room door that night, he was the most dressed up I'd ever seen him. He was actually wearing pants and a button-down shirt with the sleeves rolled up. He'd even slicked his hair back, although I later realized it was just wet. As soon as it dried, it was back in his eyes again.

After dinner at the hotel's restaurant, Jack insisted we take a cab to a local club where we just happened to run into a single male friend of Jack's, who just happened to be immensely attracted to Jane. I had no trouble believing the second part, but the first part was a bit suspicious.

"So you live on Parrot Caye?" I asked Jack's friend, Bill, while we stood at the bar waiting for our drinks.

"No," he said, "I'm just here for the night. I'm working on a research project at the marine reserve on Camus Caye."

"How convenient."

"Not really," Bill said, oblivious to my sarcasm. "It's a half-hour boat ride, then another ten minutes by bike, but Jack convinced me I need to get out more."

"I imagine he can be very convincing when he wants to be," I said, looking directly at Jack, who wouldn't meet my eyes.

"Yes," Jane agreed. "Will you two excuse us for a minute while we run to the ladies' room?" She grabbed my arm before I even had time to set down my drink.

"Watch it," I said as she dragged me down the hallway. "You're going to pull out my stitches."

"All two of them?" she said.

"That's just because I'm a good clotter. Otherwise I would've needed four." At least that's what the ER doctor had told me.

Jane looked at her watch. "It's nine fifteen. I'm giving you two hours. Bill's not bad looking, but he's a total bore."

"Two hours to what?"

Jane stared at me. "Do I really have to spell it out for you?"

"No," I said and shoved my drink at her. Then I ran back to the bar and grabbed Jack.

We managed to keep our clothes on in the cab, but it was only a five-minute ride back to the hotel.

"We should get our own room," I suggested to Jack as we entered the lobby. After all this time, two hours wasn't nearly long enough.

"I tried," he said. "They're booked."

"We could try another."

"The closest is a bed-and-breakfast at the other end of town. It's not very nice and it's ten minutes away."

After jail and the turtle hatchery, not very nice was good enough, but ten minutes was way too long to wait.

We were kissing and grabbing at each other's clothes even before we closed the door to the room. It took all of five seconds for Jack to ease us over to the king-size bed.

"We can't," I said, having already unbuttoned his shirt. He had his hands under my dress.

"Why not?"

"Not in the bed. Jane'll know."

"So?"

"You know what a clean freak she is. She changes the sheets ten minutes after she has sex."

"Then we'll change the sheets," he said, tugging at my panties.

I pulled away from him and looked around the room. "The rollaway." I pointed to the folded-up cot still standing in the corner.

After a little more convincing, Jack finally let go of me and opened the rollaway bed in record time. We immediately picked up where we'd left off, but something wasn't right.

"Do you smell that?" I said.

"Smell what?" He'd gotten my panties off and was unzipping his pants.

I buried my head in the pillow and inhaled. "It's John's cologne. It's freaking me out."

"For God's sake, Lizzie, you're killing me here."

We tried the couch next, but it was just too narrow.

We finally ended up in the shower, which is really more appropriate for a one-night stand anyway. Plus, I'd always wanted to do it standing up. (Steven always insisted it was bad for his back.) Then we moved to the bathroom floor (the hotel had very fluffy towels), and finally the bedroom floor. We were in the shower again when Jane returned.

"I'm home," she yelled. "Time to put your clothes back on."

Jack and I were drying each other off when we realized our clothes were still in a heap on the floor next to the rollaway. I was about to wrap myself in a towel to fetch them when Jane knocked on the door. I pushed Jack back into the shower and cracked the door open. Jane had one hand over her eyes, and the other outstretched holding Jack's clothes.

"Thanks," I said.

"Do you want me to wait outside?" she asked.

"If you wouldn't mind." Jane knew, and even if she didn't, I'd tell her anyway, but it would be less awkward if she wasn't there when Jack left.

"Ten more minutes," she said. "I need my beauty sleep."

"Make it fifteen." Enough time for one more quickie.

CHAPTER 65

Three Months Later

I was really glad I'd had that night with Jack before Jane and I left Belize, because I didn't have much to celebrate when I returned to LA.

If Steven hadn't left me a note informing me that he was taking the furniture, I would've thought we'd been robbed. The living room couch was gone, along with the stereo, computer, and TV. He left me the bed and the dresser, but only because he wanted to buy new ones anyway. Sure, it was all his, but still…

My first call was to my parents to explain that I hadn't actually spent the last three weeks backpacking through Belize as Jane had told them. They were furious at me for lying to them, even though I only did so because I didn't want them to worry. Sometimes you can't win.

The next calls were to every editor I knew. A few were understanding and promised they'd send new assignments my way soon, but most didn't. This presented a major problem since, besides all the money I owed Jane, I was now paying the rent for Steven's and my two-bedroom apartment on my own, plus I'd maxed out my last credit card to pay for my return ticket to LA.

You'd think the government could've kicked in for that one since I was responsible, at least partially, for the arrest of several drug dealers and a major money launderer, not to mention the recovery of a multimillion-dollar antiquity. Unfortunately, the authorities didn't see it that way.

Since I had no furniture and no money to pay the rent, I ended up giving up my apartment, which wasn't that nice but was still only four blocks from the beach, and moving into Jane's second bedroom. It wasn't all bad though. I now lived in a fancy high-rise building on Wilshire Boulevard with a doorman, valet parking, and a pool.

Jane wouldn't let me pay her rent (she owned the place and kept telling me she didn't need my money, which was true, but didn't make me feel any less guilty), so I paid for the groceries she had delivered from the gourmet market once a week, and every time we ordered pizza and Chinese food. It probably ended up about even.

But living with Jane had other advantages. Two well-connected publicists and a magazine editor lived in the building, and Jane mentioned me to them every time she ran into them in the elevator or the mail room. Three months later, I was writing a monthly column for *Westside Living* and pitching celebrity puff pieces to all the major magazines. I wasn't out of debt yet, not even close, but at least I was on my way.

Living with Jane also made the transition from bride-to-be to singleton a lot easier—fewer nights to sit home alone feeling sorry for myself. In fact, this weekend was the first weekend I'd be on my own since we'd returned. It was Jane's father's sixtieth birthday, and they were having a big party for him back in Washington, DC. She wanted me to come, but I begged off. I told her I had too much work to do, which was partly true. I was working as much as I could these days. But I was also looking forward to some time alone.

Or semi-alone. Jack had e-mailed me earlier in the week and asked me if I was free for dinner Friday night. He was going to be in town for the day, attending a seminar at the LA Zoo on the aging patterns of reptiles.

I wasn't really sure what was on his agenda. After that last night in Belize, we'd hardly spoken. I gave him my phone number, but he never called, although he did e-mail regularly for the first few weeks. Then he wrote that he was going out to sea for a month to study loggerhead sea turtles in their natural habitat before returning to classes in San Diego. That was two months ago. This was the first I'd heard from him since he'd been back.

The doorman buzzed me at seven thirty to let me know that Jack was downstairs, and I told him to send him up. I'd been pacing the living room in my best jeans and one of Jane's designer camisole tops for half an hour already.

When I opened the apartment door the first thing he said to me was, "Do you know how bad the traffic is in LA? It took me over an hour to get here from Hollywood."

Not quite, "I've missed you and I want to jump your bones." His tan had faded some, and his hair was darker, but otherwise he looked the same. When he walked past me into the apartment, I noticed his scent had changed. The ocean and sunscreen had been replaced by store-bought cologne.

"You look good," he said, following me into the living room, then, "Wow," when he caught sight of the view. One wall was made entirely of windows, showing off the city lights from downtown to the Santa Monica Pier.

"I'm just a houseguest. It's Jane's."

"If you've got to crash on someone's couch, it's not a bad place to be."

I agreed.

"Where is Jane?" he asked, looking around the room as if she were about to jump out from behind the sofa. "Is she joining us?"

"No, she's out of town. It's just me."

I'd hoped this revelation would provoke a lascivious comment, or at least a wicked grin. I hadn't even had a date since I'd returned from Belize, and Jack and I were very compatible, at least physically. But Jack just nodded and strode to the front door.

"Where are you going?" I called after him.

"Close your eyes," he replied.

"Why?"

"Lizzie!"

"All right, they're closed." I heard the front door open, then shut, and his footsteps along the tile. I opened one eye and glimpsed a huge cardboard box before he caught me.

"No peeking," he said as his footsteps trailed away.

After a couple of minutes more and another peek, I called to him.

"One more minute," he yelled. It sounded like he was in Jane's bedroom.

When he finally allowed me to open my eyes, he was standing before me with his hands in his pockets. "You ready for dinner?" he asked.

"What about the box?" I said.

"What box?"

"The one you just carried into Jane's bedroom."

"Uh-oh, is that Jane's?" he asked, nodding toward the master suite off the living room.

"Yes. Why? What did you do?"

"Maybe you better take a look."

I ran in and didn't see anything unusual except for an empty cardboard box turned on its side, but I heard splashing coming from the adjoining bathroom. I opened the door and found Fred swimming circles in Jane's giant spa tub. He'd doubled in size since the last time I'd seen him.

"I can't believe you brought Fred! How did you get him out of Belize?"

"It wasn't easy," Jack said, joining me. "And you can't keep him. He's just on loan for the weekend."

"Why not?" Fred would be the perfect pet. He didn't bark, he didn't need to be walked, and he wouldn't shed all over Jane's white suede furniture.

"Lizzie, look how big he's gotten in just a couple of months. A year from now he'll be three times that size."

"But he's my Fred," I cried. "I took a bullet for him."

"I know," he said, his finger tracing the half-inch scar on my shoulder. "But I've arranged it so you can visit him whenever you want."

"Where?" Jack's finger had moved from my scar to my bra strap and was sliding down the front of my shirt.

"I tried the LA Zoo but they wouldn't take him. He's going to the San Diego Zoo."

"San Diego. That's a long way to drive just to see Fred."

"True," Jack said, caressing my breast.

"Not that I don't still love Fred." I could hear my voice taking on a dreamy quality, but at least I wasn't moaning. Not yet.

"Of course," Jack said, his other hand reaching inside the back of my jeans.

"But he's not the most demonstrative of pets."

"Uh huh," Jack said, kissing my earlobe before sliding down my neck. He may not have stayed in touch, but he hadn't forgotten any of my erogenous zones either.

"And I'll have to share him with all those other people."

"I suppose I could arrange for a private visit," he said, undoing the tie at the back of my shirt.

"At the zoo?" I asked, holding my arms up so he could slip the camisole over my head. How glad was I that I wore my black lace bra and matching panties, just in case.

"I think my apartment would be better," he said, his kisses moving down my chest. "More privacy," he added, as he closed the bathroom door between us and Fred.

This time I didn't stifle the moan. Fred probably didn't care.

ABOUT THE AUTHOR

Photograph by Steven Bingen

Beth Orsoff is the author of *Romantically Challenged, Disengaged, Girl in the Wild,* and *Vlad All Over.* She was born in New York City and has never lived more than an hour's drive from the ocean—even spending her formative years toiling as a lifeguard where she was "paid to work on her tan." When her parents forced her to get a "real job," she went to law school and forged a career as an entertainment attorney in Los Angeles. Currently, when she's not writing humorous or suspenseful women's fiction, Orsoff can be found at her desk drafting Hollywood contracts. Sadly, she no longer sports a tan.